A TANGLED THREAD

Recent Titles by Anthea Fraser from Severn House

The Rona Parish Mysteries
(in order of appearance)

BROUGHT TO BOOK
JIGSAW
PERSON OR PERSONS UNKNOWN
A FAMILY CONCERN
ROGUE IN PORCELAIN
NEXT DOOR TO MURDER
UNFINISHED PORTRAIT
A QUESTION OF IDENTITY
JUSTICE POSTPONED

Other Titles

BREATH OF BRIMSTONE
PRESENCE OF MIND
THE MACBETH PROPHECY
MOTIVE FOR MURDER
DANGEROUS DECEPTION
PAST SHADOWS
FATHERS AND DAUGHTERS
THICKER THAN WATER
SHIFTING SANDS
THE UNBURIED PAST
A TANGLED THREAD

A TANGLED THREAD

Anthea Fraser

This first world edition published 2015
in Great Britain and the USA by
SEVERN HOUSE PUBLISHERS LTD of
19 Cedar Road, Sutton, Surrey, England, SM2 5DA.
Trade paperback edition first published
in Great Britain and the USA 2016 by
SEVERN HOUSE PUBLISHERS LTD.

British Library Cataloguing in Publication Data

Fraser, Anthea author.
  A tangled thread.
  1. Hit-and-run drivers–Scottish Borders (England and
  Scotland)–Fiction. 2. Detective and mystery stories.
  I. Title
  823.9'14-dc23

ISBN-13: 978-0-7278-8549-4 (cased)
ISBN-13: 978-1-84751-658-9 (trade paper)
ISBN-13: 978-1-78010-712-7 (e-book)

All Severn House titles are printed on acid-free paper.

Severn House Publishers support the Forest Stewardship Council™ [FSC™],
the leading international forest certification organisation. All our titles that
are printed on FSC certified paper carry the FSC logo.

Typeset by Palimpsest Book Production Ltd.,
Falkirk, Stirlingshire, Scotland.
Printed and bound in Great Britain by
TJ International, Padstow, Cornwall.

ONE

A heavy thud from above woke her, followed by the faint sound of her daughter's voice reminding six-year-old Ben that Granny lived beneath them and his jumps and crash-landings endangered her light fittings.

Jill smiled to herself. It was barely a month since they'd moved in but already the house had settled comfortably into its new configuration. After Greg's death last year and with both offspring married, the family home had seemed too big for her. But she was loath to leave it, and for several months had wavered, deciding to sell then changing her mind. Until, miraculously, Georgia and Tim, who had for some time been wanting a larger garden, suggested that both problems could be solved by Jill choosing whichever floor she preferred to make her home while they took over the rest of the house and responsibility for the garden.

It was the perfect solution. She had opted for ground level, thus retaining her sitting room, music room and family-sized kitchen, while the dining room, seldom used, had been converted into a bedroom. And although at the heart of the family she maintained her independence, to which end a door had been erected in the hall, closing off her domain from the staircase by which the family entered their own quarters.

She slipped out of bed and drew back the curtains, letting sunshine flood into the room. Under her window the grass was still heavy with dew and a blackbird busily dug for worms, but beyond the shadow cast by the house, flowers and bushes were already gilded. It was going to be a perfect day. It would also, she remembered with a tug at her heart, have been her thirty-sixth wedding anniversary.

Sadly, her parents had never approved of Greg; they'd thought him unreliable and self-centred, always wanting his own way and usually, since he was handsome and charming, getting it – as was evidenced by Jill being pregnant on her wedding day.

And they'd had a point, she reflected wistfully. It hadn't been an easy marriage; for though on the surface Greg had retained all the traits she'd fallen in love with, he could also be moody if things didn't go his way and was quick to lose his temper. Then there was his gambling – something she'd thankfully managed to keep from her parents but which had given her many sleepless nights, though when she'd tried to broach the subject he'd simply laughed. 'Why are you worrying?' he'd ask. 'I always win!'

Which was undeniably true. He *did* win, eye-wateringly large amounts that were largely responsible for their affluent lifestyle. His great love was poker, though he would bet on anything – horses, dogs, two flies crawling up a window – and his combined winnings had provided the greater part of their income. A mixed blessing, since he'd never felt the need to stick at any job for long. Throughout their marriage his only unswerving commitment had been to the articles he wrote under a pseudonym he jokingly refused to disclose. And it was his final occupation – freelance photography – that had led to his death in a suicide bombing in Egypt.

She picked up his photograph from the dressing table, studying the dancing blue eyes, the dark hair, the smiling mouth. It had been taken soon after their wedding but he'd not changed much over the years, merely acquiring a few lines and a touch of silver at his temples.

She sighed, shaking off reminiscences both painful and pointless. She had made her bed, lain on it and survived, and, on the positive side, since he'd so often worked away from home she was accustomed to long absences, which had prepared her for the final one. She'd a lot to be thankful for, she reminded herself: a loving son and daughter, two healthy grandchildren and her career as a piano teacher, from which she derived intense pleasure and satisfaction.

Which reminded her of Edward French, a prospective new pupil. Though the majority of those she taught were children, she'd also accepted some half-dozen adults who had either dropped music on leaving school or never learned to play. Edward French came into the latter category.

'I took early retirement a few months ago,' he'd told her on the phone, 'and when I mentioned to Giles Austin that I was thinking of taking piano lessons he gave me your name.' Austin was the headmaster of the local grammar school where Jill taught one day a week. 'I haven't an instrument myself,' he'd added apologetically, 'but he tells me you give lessons in your own home?'

'I do, yes.' In fact, the majority of her pupils came to the house, which was why she'd been so anxious to keep the music room; but they all had access to a piano on which to practise between lessons. She could only hope that Mr French had the same facility. It had been arranged that he would sign up for a month of weekly lessons beginning the following Friday, at the end of which he could decide whether or not to continue.

The ringing of the house phone broke into her thoughts.

'Sorry about the thump, Mum,' Georgia apologized. 'Did it wake you?'

'Don't worry, I was just surfacing anyway.'

'We were wondering if you'd like to spend the day with us? Say if you'd rather not, but with it being the first anniversary without Dad, I thought perhaps you could do with some company.'

Though she could count on the fingers of one hand the number of times she and Greg had spent it together, Jill said gratefully, 'That's sweet of you, darling. I'd love to.'

'Good. Then come up for coffee when you're ready and we can plan what to do.'

Abandoning her reflections, both past and more recent, she went to take her shower.

'Isn't today your parents' anniversary?' Victoria Lawrence asked over breakfast.

Richard checked the date on his newspaper. 'Yes, so it is. Or was.'

'Don't you think we should do something?'

'What, exactly? It's not as if there's a grave to visit. Anyway, Georgia will have done the necessary.'

'She's your mother too! At least give her a call to say we're thinking of her.'

He returned to his paper without comment and she resignedly poured herself more coffee, acknowledging not for the first time what a complex man she'd married. Though outwardly controlled as befitted the deputy head of a private school, the occasional flash over the years had revealed hidden depths; for instance, she'd been surprised, early in her marriage, to discover that he was deeply jealous of his sister, an emotion she'd always assumed that in adults had sexual origins but which in this case seemed to have its roots in his relationship with his father.

Who had been another complex character. Victoria had met her father-in-law only a handful of times in the five years of her marriage and at his death felt she knew him no better than on first acquaintance. Yet his complexity was the reverse of his son's; on the surface he'd been outgoing, interested in people and their concerns and able to reduce any company to laughter at his witticisms. But he'd lived what Richard had described as a compartmentalized life: work, family, leisure interests and so on, each in its own airtight container. 'Heaven help anyone who attempts to write his biography!' he'd commented once.

Victoria pushed back her chair. 'I'd better get going; it's my turn to open up.'

She was part-owner of a small art shop that dealt in modern paintings, hand-thrown pottery and locally made crafts. Its opening hours were ten till four on Tuesdays, Thursdays and Saturdays, and though Richard resented her Saturday shift, it was invariably their busiest day and her presence was mandatory.

'I think I'll go to the golf club,' he commented. 'Have we anything on this evening?'

'Dinner at Simon and Tamsin's at eight thirty. See you later, then.'

He watched her over his paper as she hurried from the room, every inch the professional woman in her linen suit, her hair caught up in a chignon. It was a long time since they'd lit any fires in each other, he reflected. He enjoyed her company and she was an undoubted asset in his career, but these days sex was a business-like affair, the satisfying of a need with little emotion in evidence. Not, admittedly, that he was a passionate man; he'd learned early on to keep his feelings in check, and he did wonder occasionally if he'd done right in marrying Victoria so soon after she'd broken off a long-term relationship.

He was aware that his friends envied him, not only his clever and attractive wife but his successful career and comfortable life-style. Only he knew that these achievements resulted from a compulsive desire to prove himself to his father.

His eyes dropped to the date at the top of the newspaper: his parents' wedding anniversary, as Vic had reminded him, and ten months now since Greg's death. He might have known, he thought bitterly, that his father was never going to die peacefully in his bed: he had to go out literally with a bang, blown to smithereens by a suicide bomber. No one had suspected, as Richard held the family together in the aftermath, that in private he'd wept as bitterly as any of them, though for more complicated reasons.

Suddenly impatient, he scrunched the newspaper between his hands and stood up. A game of golf would dispel his introspec-tions, though as he retrieved his clubs from the hall cupboard his thoughts momentarily returned to his mother.

Should he phone her? What could he say? For as long as he could remember he'd loved her with a fierce and protective love, attempting, as he grew up, to compensate as far as he was able for his father's frequent and prolonged absences. Yet now she was virtually living with Georgia, an arrangement that struck him as a kind of betrayal. The family home was as much his as his sister's, but there'd been little consultation before the agreed amalgamation, and any protest he might have made at the outset had been stifled by Victoria's immediate cry of, 'What a brilliant idea!' She didn't see it as he did: Georgia closing the ranks, leaving the two of them on the fringe.

Bloody Georgia! he thought, slamming the cupboard door, and, heaving his golf bag on to his shoulder, he let himself out of the house.

'That bloke's back again,' Nigel Soames commented, coming into the shop as Victoria pulled up the blinds and turned the Closed notice on the door.

She frowned. 'Where?'

He jerked his head towards the café across the road. 'At his usual table – see? It's the third time this week.'

She peered outside. 'You're sure it's the same man?'

'Positive.'

'Perhaps he's hooked on their coffee.'

6 Anthea Fraser

Nigel refused to be diverted. 'I don't like it, Vic; he could be planning a heist.'

She smiled, stooping to lift the post from the floor. 'You've been reading about those art thefts from country houses! Rest assured, we're hardly in that league! Though we've some pretty good paintings, none is worth stealing; added to which, we've an alarm system and he doesn't look the type to descend from the ceiling on a rope.'

'You may mock,' Nigel said darkly, 'but don't say I didn't warn you!'

Despite herself, she glanced outside again. The object of their interest, totally unaware of it, was seated at a window table absorbed in his newspaper. She estimated that he was in his fifties; his hair was receding and he wore glasses. Admittedly, from this distance, he appeared to be the man whom they'd first noticed earlier in the week when he'd spent some time studying their window display before retreating to the café. He'd reappeared on Thursday, this time walking up and down outside The Gallery for about ten minutes. She'd assumed – hoped – he was a potential customer, though on neither occasion had he ventured into the shop. But he looked an unlikely burglar, and, dismissing Nigel's concerns, she turned with a smile to greet their first customer of the day. When she next had a chance to glance outside, the man had gone.

The arrangement at lunchtime was for them to take their break separately, leaving the other in charge, and as Victoria crossed the road she noted that the table where their observer – if that's what he was – had sat was vacant. She seated herself in his place, and, having given her order, gazed with interest at The Gallery's frontage in an attempt to assess how much of its interior could be seen from this vantage point. The answer was very little, since the play of light on the glass acted as a mirror, reflecting passers-by.

On her return, she reported her findings. 'I don't think he's after any future heirlooms,' she ended. 'He was probably just waiting for someone.'

'Who never arrived?'

She shrugged. 'We don't know that, but in any case I doubt he's loitering with intent. Unless, of course, he fancies you!'

Nigel, tall, fair and good looking, was gay, though his manner and appearance gave little indication of it, and it afforded Victoria considerable amusement to watch their female customers trying to flirt with him. They had met through his sister, who'd been at art college with her and who had happened to mention that her brother, a talented portrait painter, was looking for a part-time job. Victoria, who was then considering opening an art shop, had been glad to join forces with him, and their combined finances brought The Gallery within their budget.

That had been three years ago, and within its limits the business was doing well. They made a good partnership, and she felt more relaxed with Nigel than with many of her women friends, occasionally even treating him as a confidant in the certain knowledge that he'd never repeat what she told him.

On her free days she taught at an art class, travelled round the county looking for new stock and artists to promote, and spent one day a week helping out in a charity shop. When Richard was free during the school holidays they visited museums and galleries, went to the theatre and enjoyed long weekends in country hotels. It was a good life, and if her marriage was a trifle humdrum, at least it continued on an even keel and she had no regrets.

They had gone to the coast, and Jill and Georgia were relaxing in deck chairs while Tim and the children explored pools left by the receding tide.

'Has Richard been in touch?' Georgia asked idly.

'Not recently, no.'

'He could at least have sent a card.'

'Be fair, darling; saying what? Hardly "Happy Anniversary".'

'"Thinking of you", perhaps?'

'I'm sure he is,' Jill said quietly.

'He hated Dad, you know.'

Jill swung her head towards her daughter. 'Georgia!'

'Well, he did; you must have known. And to be fair, Dad didn't help. He was always criticizing him and making a fuss of me.'

Jill was silent, acknowledging the truth of the comment but reluctant to face it. 'Not *all* the time,' she protested.

'Yes, *all* the time, which is why Rich has always resented me. I hoped it might be better once Dad had died, but no. And then,' she ended flatly, 'I more or less sealed my fate by moving into Woodlands with you.'

Jill's eyes widened. This was an angle she'd never considered; perhaps she should have done. 'But he said it was a brilliant idea!'

'No, Mum, that's what Victoria said.'

'But he knows the house wasn't a gift and that Tim insisted on paying the full asking price. I even explained that I'd adjusted my will so he wouldn't miss out in the long run. He didn't raise any objections.'

'All the same, it was his childhood home and the way he sees it his spoilt little sister snatched it from under his nose – and you as well, probably.'

'Oh, God,' Jill said numbly.

Georgia leant over and patted her hand. 'Don't worry, Mum, he'll come round. We'll go out of our way to make him feel special.'

There was a yell from down the beach, and one of the little figures came running back towards them, crying lustily.

'Mummy!' Four-year-old Millie flung herself on top of her mother. 'Ben took my shrimp! It was me that found it and he tipped it out of my bucket into his, and he's already got two! It's not fair!'

Georgia stroked the hair from the hot forehead and flicked her daughter's ponytail. 'You know what they say, poppet: there are more shrimps in the sea!'

Millie refused to be comforted. 'But that one was *mine*!'

'What did Daddy say?'

'He wasn't watching so he didn't see.'

Very diplomatic. 'Well, never mind. Would you like a drink of orange juice? And there's one brandy snap left. You can have it, to make up for the shrimp.'

Finally mollified, the child accepted both offers and peace was restored. But Jill continued to ponder on their truncated conversation. The basic trouble, she knew, had been that Greg was so much the alpha male that he resented any others invading his territory, even his own son. She ached to think Richard had been unhappy. She must think of some way to make amends.

Richard himself, blissfully unaware of his family's discussion, had enjoyed his game of golf and the pleasantly long-drawn-out lunch that followed, and was now looking forward to the evening ahead. He decided to take along the special bottle of Burgundy he'd been keeping for a suitable occasion; Simon appreciated good wine.

The golf club was a mile or two out of town and the long country road stretched ahead of him, heat dancing along its surface. A solitary figure was waiting at a bus stop, and as he approached he recognized the red-haired teacher who had started this term. He pulled up alongside her.

'Can I give you a lift somewhere?'

She turned, startled and about to decline an offer from a stranger. Then she recognized him and smiled. 'Mr Lawrence!'

'You could have a long wait ahead of you; this route is notoriously unreliable.'

She hesitated and, looking at her properly for the first time, Richard was struck by her almost ethereal beauty. She looked, he thought in confusion, like a Pre-Raphaelite painting – a cloud of soft auburn hair, alabaster-pale face and delicately arched brows.

'That's kind of you,' she was saying, 'but I don't want to take you out of your way. I live on the far side of town.'

He leant across and opened the passenger door. 'It's no trouble. I can't leave you standing there.'

She glanced back along the road, but as no bus was in sight she slid in beside him and reached for the seat belt. 'This is really very kind of you,' she said again.

'No problem, I assure you, but I'm afraid I can't remember your name?'

'Maria Chiltern.'

He nodded acknowledgement. 'And what, if I may ask, are you doing stranded out here so far from home and without transport?'

'I'd promised to help at a jumble sale. It's being run by the mothers of two children in my class and they were desperate for helpers. Normally, of course, I'd have taken the car but my husband had promised to take our son to the zoo.'

'And was there no one at this jumble sale who could have run you home?'

She pulled a little face. 'Actually it's still going on. It was supposed to end at three, and when it got to half past I made my apologies and left. Toby's friend who's gone to the zoo with them is coming back for tea and I really should be there, though I did leave everything ready.' She paused and said again, 'I do hope I'm not holding you up.'

'Not at all; my wife works on Saturdays and I've been passing my time at the golf club. So, are you new to the area, or only to the school?'

'The area. We moved down here at Easter, much to my parents' distress. They adore Toby and miss him very much; we had to promise to go back at half-term.'

'Is he at the school?'

'Yes, in Reception.'

They were entering the town, and Richard said, 'You'll have to guide me from here.'

For the rest of the drive conversation was directional rather than personal, and he dropped her outside a neat semi-detached house in a quiet avenue. A car was in the drive and children's voices could be heard coming from the back garden.

'It sounds as though you're in time for tea!' he said.

Her face lit up as she smiled. 'Thanks to you! I really am grateful.'

Then she was out of the car and hurrying up the path, searching in her bag for her key. Richard started the car and drove slowly away. An unexpected turn of events, he reflected, but a surprisingly pleasant one.

That evening, while Victoria was changing, he opened his laptop, turned to the school website and clicked on the small photograph labelled *Maria Chiltern, History Teacher.*

I joined Briarfields School in April 2014, she had written, *and am very much looking forward to teaching here. Having graduated with a BA (Hons) in History from Bristol University, I taught at several independent schools in Yorkshire before moving south for family reasons. History has always been my passion and I believe this subject more than any other leads to a better understanding of the world as it is today and the people who live in it. I hope to pass my interest and enthusiasm on to my pupils.*

My leisure activities include swimming, walking, reading and going to concerts.

He stared at the photo for a minute, concluding that it didn't do her justice. It was surprising he'd not really registered her before, but then their paths hadn't crossed and weren't likely to again in the normal course of events. Briefly, he found himself regretting that. Then as Victoria came downstairs he closed his computer, picked up the gift bottle of wine and accompanied her out of the front door.

TWO

Blaircomrie, Scottish borders

'**D**ied?' His voice rose incredulously. 'Martin Petrie's *dead*?'
     'I'm afraid so, yes. This is his son speaking. May I ask who's calling?'
     Johnnie brushed the query aside. 'He can't be!' he said urgently. 'Dammit, I had a drink with him yesterday!'
     A pause, then: 'Would you like to speak to my mother?'
     'No, no.' IIis mind was whirling. 'But I don't understand. What happened?'
     'He was knocked down last night on his way home from work. The car didn't stop.' The young voice wobbled slightly.
     'God!' A ripple of fear snaked down his spine. What the hell had he got himself into? 'Please accept my sincere sympathy,' he said rapidly, and broke the connection.
     The car didn't stop. Which explained why Petrie's mobile was in his family's hands. OK, at a pinch it could have been an accident, but he didn't believe that for a moment. The poor guy had been right to be fearful, and if it was suspected that he'd already spoken out of turn and had been followed to the pub yesterday . . .

     They'd first met a week earlier when Petrie had rung the shop about a problem with his PC. It had been the last appointment of the day and it was after six when Johnnie arrived at the house. As soon as Petrie opened the door his tension was palpable, a tightly coiled spring. It was also clear he'd been drinking.
     Still, his not to reason why. Johnnie got down to work, keeping

up a light-hearted banter in an attempt to put the man more at ease. Petrie had hovered at his side, saying little, but when he'd sorted the problem and was packing away his tools, he said suddenly, 'Would you like a drink? You've finished for the day, haven't you?'

He'd been taken by surprise. 'I have, yes, but—'

The man put a hand on his arm. 'Please. My wife and son are out for the evening and I . . . don't want to be alone.' And to Johnnie's horror, his eyes had filled with tears. 'If I don't speak to someone, I think I'll go out of my mind!' he'd added in a low voice.

Why, he thought now, in God's name hadn't he simply refused and said he had to get back for his dinner? Then life would have continued in its safe if mundane routine and all this angst would have been avoided. But partly out of curiosity and partly because he was sorry for the guy, he'd phoned Beth to let her know he'd be late and followed Petrie into a large, attractive sitting room, where he made straight for the drinks cupboard.

'Whisky?'

'Please.'

Petrie waved him to a seat, came to join him with two brimming glasses and said without preamble, 'I need your advice.'

He'd attempted a light response. 'Not mistaking me for an agony uncle, are you?'

A quick shake of the head, dismissing the humour. 'I don't know you and you don't know me, and that's all to the good. You seem a sound, sensible guy and I think you'd give me an honest answer.' He paused, then flashed him a quick look. 'What do I call you, by the way?'

'Johnnie.'

'Right, Johnnie, and I'm Martin. What I'm going to tell you is highly confidential and—'

Johnnie had moved uncomfortably. 'Look, I'm not sure I want to hear this. I've enough complications in my life without getting involved in any more.'

'I'm not asking you to get involved, just to hear me out, then tell me what to do.'

And before Johnnie could stop him, it had all come pouring out. It appeared his host worked at Parsons Makepeace, the building firm at the heart of an investigation into the collapse of a shopping mall just before Christmas, and Petrie believed the collapse had been caused by the deliberate use of sub-standard materials in an attempt to cut costs and win the contract.

'I can't go to the police because as yet the cause hasn't been established, but if the materials *are* found to be responsible I have proof the firm deliberately took risks.'

'What kind of proof?'

Petrie stirred uncomfortably, not meeting his eyes. 'PM had been having serious problems for some time due to the recession and so on, and things were at a very low ebb when the prospect of a new shopping mall came up. At which fortuitous point – and I was never able to figure out how or why – we were offered building materials at an incredibly low price which enabled us to undercut our competitors and win the contract.'

He paused to take a drink. 'I strongly advised against it at the time, but was overruled. Yet all along I was worried something might go wrong – though God knows I never imagined anything as horrific as what actually happened – so, for my own protection, I suppose, I started to make photocopies of any relevant invoices, receipts and documentation that I could get my hands on. I had to act quickly – they were shredded almost as soon as they came in – and because I was paranoid about them being discovered, I made a verbal recording at the same time, listing it all as I went along. Needless to say, what I have is now dynamite.'

Johnnie stared at him, struck by a sense of déjà vu. He too had known something that was dangerous to know, and the repercussions were an ongoing nightmare. It if hadn't been for . . . But he didn't want to go there.

He moistened his lips. 'If you have proof sub-standard materials were used you should take it to the police. You don't have to wait for the official report.'

Petrie swallowed a mouthful of whisky and when he continued his voice was unsteady. 'The trouble is these people are my colleagues, Johnnie – friends, some of them – and I'd feel like a Judas. Yet – God! – more than a hundred people died!' Tears were now running down his face. 'Can you see how I'm torn in two directions? The investigation's been going on for months and I just can't live with it any longer! But it wouldn't take long for the firm to work out who the whistle-blower was and these are high stakes. If they even suspect what I have, friends or not, they'll try any way they can to silence me.'

There was a pause while Johnnie digested that. Then he asked, 'Have you discussed this with your wife?'

Petrie slapped the arm of the chair with his open palm. 'Of course I haven't, man! It's enough that one of us can't sleep at night.'

'I'm not sure what you want me to do.'

'What would *you* do, in my position?'

Johnnie thought for a moment. 'Print out what you said on your voice recorder, then take the transcript together with all the documents you photocopied and hand them to the police.'

Petrie pulled out a handkerchief and blew his nose. 'I thought you'd say that,' he said dully.

'If it's justice you're after, it's the only way.'

Petrie sat in silence for several minutes, staring into his glass. Then he looked up. 'Thank you,' he said quietly.

And that was how the matter had rested until the previous day, when Fred at the shop had called him to the phone. 'That bloke you saw last week wants a word with you,' he said. 'Thought you'd fixed the problem?'

'I saw lots of blokes last week,' he replied as he took the phone, totally unprepared to find Petrie on the line.

'One last favour, Johnnie,' he said rapidly. 'Meet me at the Rowan Tree on the Hamilton road at twelve thirty.'

'Look, I can't—'

'Please. It's urgent.' And he cut the call.

Fred was looking at him with eyebrows raised. 'Well?'

'It's OK, just a minor point. I'll fix it in my lunch hour.'

Fred shrugged. 'Up to you, mate,' he said.

The pub was a good twelve miles from town, no doubt chosen precisely for that reason, and Petrie had been waiting for him at a corner table, two tankards of beer in front of him.

'Look,' Johnnie began, 'I've given you my advice but—'

He broke off as Petrie pushed a padded envelope across the table. 'And I've been putting it into effect,' he said.

Johnny glanced at it uneasily. 'Good. So what—'

'It's all in there, and I'd like you to read through it and listen to the recording – I jotted the pin number down on the transcript – and check if there's anything I told you the other evening that I've not included or could be put more clearly.'

'Oh, now look,' Johnnie protested, pushing the envelope back, 'this is really nothing to do with me. I told you, I can't—'

'Please. It won't take long.' He pushed his card across the table. 'Then ring me on my mobile and we'll arrange how you can return it. Then I'll take it to the police and that, I promise, will be the end of it as far as you're concerned. Will you do that?'

And as Johnnie reluctantly agreed, he gave a sigh of relief and leant back in his chair. 'Now, let's drink to a just and successful outcome.'

Which it very definitely had not been.

Petrie's death made the lunchtime news, and although he'd been expecting it Johnnie felt himself tense. The reporter was stationed in front of the house he recognized, his hair blowing in the wind.

'Martin Petrie, a manager in the building conglomerate Parsons Makepeace, was fatally injured last night in a hit-and-run incident on his way home from work and was pronounced dead at the scene. He leaves a wife and two sons. Police are anxious to hear from anyone who was in the vicinity of Oak Tree Avenue, Blaircomrie around seven thirty last evening who might have witnessed the accident or noticed a car being driven erratically. The number to call is at the foot of the screen.

'Parsons Makepeace are the firm under investigation into the collapse of the Whitefriars Shopping Centre in Blaircomrie just before Christmas that left over a hundred dead and hundreds more injured.'

He'd heard enough, and as the firm's directors appeared on screen to record their shock and appreciation of their employee he pushed his tankard across the bar and requested a refill.

Now what was he going to do? As requested, he'd meticulously gone through the contents of the padded envelope, listened to the recording, examined the photos and documents and concluded Petrie had stated his case clearly and concisely, as he'd intended telling him when he'd phoned the previous evening. But now the picture had changed. Now he was left holding the baby – and a lethal baby it was. *If* Petrie's death hadn't been an accident, and *if* his killers knew he'd passed on information – they might, for instance, have overheard his telephone call arranging their meeting – then what he was holding *was* what Petrie had referred to as 'dynamite' and the sooner he got rid of it the better.

He finished his beer and ordered another. But he couldn't just dispose of what was potentially evidence in a criminal case. Send it to the police anonymously, then? That would be the obvious course of action. But the date of posting would show it couldn't have been Petrie who'd sent it and he couldn't allow the slightest chance of its being traced back to him.

What he needed was time to think, to ensure he didn't act hastily and come to regret it. For the next thirty minutes, therefore, he went over the position from every angle and reached a decision that seemed to cover everything. He would lodge the package, possibly with an explanatory note, at his bank while he considered his best plan of action. And just in case – he shuddered involuntarily – he ended up the same way as Petrie, he'd leave instructions that if the package hadn't been collected within a couple of months, say by his mother's birthday on the twenty-first of July, the box should be opened and the package handed to the police. It was the least he could do for the poor sod.

Decision reached, Johnnie put down his tankard, wiped his mouth with the back of his hand and went back to work.

Beth Monroe skirted the boarded-up ruins of the shopping centre, averting her eyes as she always did. She was meeting Moira for their regular Thursday lunch but her anticipation was tempered, as it had been for the last six weeks, by an undeniable sense of guilt. Because, for the first time in the thirty-odd years of their friendship, she had a secret she could not bring herself to share.

They hadn't been easy years; both women had been widowed relatively young, but while Moira now had a married daughter and two grandsons, Beth and her husband had been childless and she'd felt all the more alone. She'd thrown herself into her job as a dental nurse and it had proved a lifeline, but she still had to return each evening to an empty house, which seemed the more lonely after the hustle and bustle of the surgery. It had been Moira who'd suggested she might take in lodgers.

'But you'd have to vet them carefully,' she'd added warningly, 'and I'd advise you to stick to women.'

It had taken Beth a while to reach a decision, reluctant as she was to share her home with strangers. But, as Moira pointed out, she had three bedrooms, two of which were habitually empty, and the extra money would certainly be useful.

In the end it had been quite exciting; a few alterations needed to be made to the house, the first being the creation of a sitting-cum-dining room for her guests. Once the original dining suite was removed and sent to auction, Beth decorated then refurnished the room with individual tables at one end and easy chairs, a television and a coffee table at the other. Bookshelves and lamps completed the transformation. The lodgers would have to share the bathroom but there would never be more than two of them at any one time, and she sacrificed a corner of her own bedroom to install a small en suite. She was then ready to receive boarders.

That had been six years ago and lodgers had come and gone. For some time she'd kept to the women-only rule, offering accommodation to a succession of students from the local college, women on business assignments and nurses from a nearby hospital. Then, after several months of having one room unoccupied, Eric Barnes had arrived at the door and it had seemed illogical to turn him away. He worked for a local firm but his family was down south and, like all her lodgers, he went home at weekends. He paid his account promptly, was tidy in his ways and friendly without being familiar – in short, the ideal lodger – and had now been with her for two years.

Which brought her to Johnnie, who had also arrived when she had a room free, due to a guest leaving suddenly to nurse a sick parent.

'He was born in Dorset,' she'd told Moira over lunch a couple of months ago, 'but his mother was Australian and when his father left them she decided to return to her family in Adelaide, taking him with her. But he never really settled out there and when he left school he came to university in the UK and has been here ever since.'

Moira had laughed. 'Do your guests usually tell you their life stories?' she'd asked, and Beth had flushed.

'No, but we got talking somehow and it just . . . came out.'

'Did he also give you his date of birth?'

She'd laughed shamefacedly. 'No, but if there's a hidden question there, I'd say he's in his mid-fifties.'

'And now you have two gentlemen under your roof! So much for my dire warnings!'

'Neither is likely to stab me in my bed!' she'd retorted, feeling the need to defend herself.

'But that's not the only danger,' Moira had said darkly.

Even to herself, Beth couldn't explain why she'd not shared her secret. At first it had seemed so amazing, so totally unexpected, that she'd wanted to hug it to herself, uncertain of her own reactions. It wasn't that Moira would disapprove – she'd probably be glad for her – but suppose it didn't last and she was made to look stupid, gullible? Better to play safe, with no one to have to tell when it fell apart.

It had started so innocuously. Johnnie – or Mr Stewart as she'd then thought of him, since she kept her dealings with her lodgers on a strictly business footing – had settled in well, though he was little company for Mr Barnes as he went out each evening after their meal. She had, however, been disconcerted to learn he intended to stay over the weekends, when she enjoyed having the house to herself. 'I sometimes have to work on Saturdays,' he'd said when she'd broached the subject. 'And anyway, where would I go?' And she'd helplessly let it drop.

Possibly because he sensed her reservations, for the next few weekends he'd left the house straight after breakfast on both days and not required an evening meal. Then the status quo irrevocably changed, and it began on one of his free Saturdays while he was still at breakfast.

Beth had stripped all three beds as usual and stuffed the sheets and pillowslips into the washing machine. It was some minutes before she noticed that the machine was leaking, by which time a creeping tide of soapy water was spreading over the kitchen floor. Horrified, she'd flown to the machine and switched it off but when the water continued to gush she ran to Johnnie in the front room.

'I'm sorry to disturb you,' she gasped, 'but can you help me? The washing machine's leaking and I can't stop it!'

He hurried after her into the kitchen. 'Where's the stopcock?' he asked. And, at her blank look, 'The valve that controls water coming into the house?'

'I don't know!' she stammered. 'How stupid—'

'No matter, I'll find it,' he said briskly. And he did. Then, while she watched helplessly, he siphoned the rest of the water from the machine and together, with the help of mops and towels, they soaked up the spilled liquid.

'Thank you so much,' Beth exclaimed, flushed and breathless. 'I'd better phone a repair man to find out what caused it.'

'Before you do,' Johnnie said, wringing the last sodden towel into the sink, 'let me take a look at it; it might be a simple blockage, which I can fix and save you a call-out fee.'

Thankfully, his diagnosis proved correct. Beth made a fresh pot of coffee which they drank together in the restored kitchen, after which, as usual, he went out for the rest of the day. The episode had caused a blip in the balance of their relationship, but now order was re-established she'd assured herself it wouldn't happen again.

Johnnie, however, had other ideas. The following morning he arrived in the kitchen as she was frying his bacon.

'No point taking it through when there's just me,' he said. 'If you've no objection I'll eat in here with you.' And he'd seated himself at the kitchen table.

It would have been churlish to object, Beth told herself, particularly after all his help yesterday. And that was how it started.

Moira looked up with a smile as Beth joined her at their usual table.

'You've had your hair cut!' she exclaimed. 'It suits you – you look a good ten years younger!'

Beth flushed as she seated herself. 'I'd got in a bit of a rut,' she said dismissively.

Moira continued to survey her, head on one side. '*And* you're wearing more make-up than usual!'

'Nonsense.' Anxious to change the subject, Beth glanced at the paper her friend had laid down. 'Anything of interest?'

Moira sobered. 'Yes, actually; a member of that building firm was killed last night in a hit-and-run – you know, the ones who built the Whitefriars Centre. As if they weren't in enough trouble.'

'Poor man. It must have been weighing on his mind, though; perhaps he stepped out deliberately.'

Moira frowned. 'I hadn't thought of that. Do you think it's possible?'

Beth shrugged. 'Could you live with knowing you might have killed a hundred people?'

'Put like that . . . But if he did mean to kill himself, it's a bit hard on the driver.'

'Who didn't stop, you said.'

'He probably thought no one would believe him.'

The waitress hovered over their table and after a belated glance at the menu they gave their order. As she moved away, Moira said casually, 'How's that new lodger of yours? You've not mentioned him lately.'

To her annoyance Beth felt her cheeks burn and Moira gave a low laugh, laying her hand briefly over her friend's. 'Oh, come on, hen, this is me you're talking to! *Something's* been putting a spring in your step these last few weeks, even before the new hair-do. You like him, don't you?'

'You mean I'm behaving like a teenager,' Beth said crossly.

'Not at all. The young haven't a monopoly on falling in love.'

Beth drew in her breath sharply. 'I'm not—'

'Whatever. Something's going on, so tell your Auntie Moira, who has only your best interests at heart!'

So reluctantly at first, then with a feeling of relief, Beth told the story of the flooded kitchen and the consequences it had led to.

'When Mr Barnes goes home at weekends it leaves just the two of us, and soon after that episode Johnnie suggested that instead of him sitting alone in some café and me cooking for one, we should go out for our evening meal. He was already having weekend breakfasts in the kitchen, so I couldn't think of a valid reason to refuse.'

'No reason why you should,' Moira said.

'It's become a regular routine. We usually go the cinema and round the evening off at a Chinese or Indian restaurant. Then on Sunday evening when Mr Barnes comes back we revert to being Mr Stewart and Mrs Monroe. It's – exciting, Moira; like playing a secret game.'

'But while Mr Barnes is away . . .?'

Colour washed over her face, and Moira said softly, 'Oh, dearie, I'm so glad for you.'

'You don't think I'm a silly, middle-aged fool?'

'Not at all. At least – he's not married, is he?'

'Divorced. He told me that at the beginning.'

'Then what possible harm are you doing?'

Beth released her breath in a long sigh. 'I'm sorry I didn't tell you before, Mo. I wasn't at all sure what you'd think and I suppose I was a bit . . . ashamed. After all, I'd never been with anyone but Dougie.'

'I know, hen, but Dougie, bless him, has been gone a long time.'

'You've never . . .?'

'It's just never come up, but then I do have Katrina and the bairns. They were my survival kit, something you never had.'

'So you're not going to cross me off your Christmas card list?'

Moira laughed. 'Not a chance!' she said.

THREE

Foxclere

As he washed his hands, Edward French glanced up and caught his reflection in the bathroom mirror – a lived-in face, he thought, greying hair, lines round his eyes and mouth. Wryly, he recalled the many words that had been used to describe him over the years – entrepreneur, businessman of the year, dynamic. All of them decidedly past tense. Did everyone feel like a knotless thread when they retired?

No, he answered himself, reaching for a towel, because the fortunate majority, unlike himself, had a family awaiting them, with whom, as the cliché had it, they could 'spend more time'. Not only that, it was only recently he'd realized to his dismay how few people he could consider friends, having concentrated over the years on maintaining business rather than social contacts and leaving the latter to his wife. Which was why he was now trying to build a new life for himself, hence this insane idea of learning the piano. Several times he'd been on the point of cancelling the appointment but had been unable to think of a convincing excuse. Why he'd considered it in the first place he couldn't remember. Because he enjoyed music?

As a boy he'd been more interested in outdoor pursuits than in learning an instrument, and since then he'd simply not had the time. In fact, he'd not had time for a great many things that in retrospect were more important than flying round the world on business, chief among them poor Cicely, his gentle, compliant wife who 'hadn't liked to trouble him when he was so busy' and therefore failed to mention the symptoms of what had proved to be a fatal illness. That was something he'd have to live with, as was the likelihood that he'd also lost his daughter, who had roundly condemned his self-centredness, accused him of neglecting her mother throughout their marriage, and, immediately after the funeral, flown to Canada with the express intention of remaining there. And since she'd changed her mobile number he'd had no success in contacting her, despite repeated attempts.

He sighed, turned from the mirror and walked through the echoing rooms to the front door. Lamb to the slaughter, he thought.

Ten minutes later he drew up outside a substantial detached house standing in what looked to be an acre or so of garden. A blackbird was singing lustily in a cherry tree as he walked up the path and rang the bell. It was answered by a small woman with fair hair, who gave him an encouraging smile.

'Mr French? I'm Jill Lawrence. Please come in.'

She stepped aside and he expected to see an impressive entrance to match the exterior; but although a handsome staircase swept up to the right, on the left the rear of the hall had been closed off by a door, now standing open, that presumably led to a private apartment.

'It used to be the family home,' Mrs Lawrence explained, 'but it was too big for me after my husband's death, so now we share it. My daughter and her family live upstairs.'

He could do with a similar arrangement, Edward mused, but regrettably there was no one prepared to share with him. Beyond the door the rear of the hall was furnished with a mahogany coat stand and a monk's bench on which stood a large vase of flowers. Various doors opened off it and he was shown through one of them into a small room where the sun streamed through a bay window that gave on to a patch of lawn at the side of the house. In front of the window stood a piano with its attendant stool and another chair drawn up beside it.

Ridiculously he felt his heartbeat quicken, but his companion was indicating one of the easy chairs that flanked the fireplace. 'Please sit down for a moment,' she said. 'Before we start the first lesson I like to have a chat with new students to learn their interests and help us get to know each other.' She paused, and when he didn't speak, continued, 'You told me you'd recently retired; what line were you in?'

'I was the managing director of a wholesale clothing firm,' he said a little stiffly. Then, since she seemed to be expecting more, added, 'My wife died a couple of years ago and my daughter's now living in Canada, so I felt it was time to make a new life for myself and catch up on things I've missed, such as going to the theatre, reading books I've always intended to . . .'

'And learning to play the piano,' Jill prompted.

'Indeed. If I have a vestige of talent, which is highly unlikely.'

She gave a light laugh. 'Not the kind of attitude I encourage! You never learnt to play at school?'

'No. I was into sport of all kinds – rugby, cricket, swimming, rowing.'

She leant back in her chair and studied him with clear grey eyes. 'So what made you decide on the piano?'

He shrugged, the corner of his mouth lifting in a smile. 'Since our phone call I've been asking myself the same question. I suppose because it's something completely different and I've always enjoyed listening to music.'

She nodded, apparently satisfied. 'One other thing – with my adult students I like to establish at the outset how they prefer to be known.' And at his blank look she added, 'Should I continue to call you Mr French, for instance, or would you feel more relaxed with Edward?'

'Whichever you prefer,' he said unhelpfully.

She shook her head. 'No, it's what *you* prefer.'

Familiarity had never come easily to him and there were now few people who used his first name. However, in for a penny . . .

'I suppose "Edward" is less of a mouthful,' he said.

She smiled. 'Then Edward it is,' she said. 'And I'm Jill.'

'So how was your new pupil?' Georgia asked a couple of hours later. She had knocked at her mother's door on her return from a visit to *Plants R Us*, the commercial flower-arranging firm that she ran, and Jill had invited her to an impromptu lunch.

'Not quite the usual run,' Jill replied, sliding the omelette out of the pan. 'A widower, recently retired and with too much time on his hands, from what I can gather.'

'No family?'

'Only a daughter in Canada.'

'And how did he shape up musically?'

Jill made a little face. 'He was terrified of making a fool of himself, which didn't help. I'll have to get him to relax or he'll lose all interest and give up. The trouble is he hasn't got a piano at home, didn't seem to realize he'd have to practise between lessons and had no idea where he could go to do so. So I suggested he ask Giles Austin, whom he knows and plays golf with, if he could have access to one at school a couple of times a week.'

Georgia helped herself to salad. 'He sounds hard going.'

'I get the impression – I don't know why – that he's rather lost, somehow. He probably lived for his work and now that it's gone he feels he has nothing left.'

'Well, at least he's making an effort,' Georgia said. 'Oh, and talking of making an effort, after our discussion about Richard feeling left out, I thought I'd ask them to dinner – plus you, of course – try to smooth things over. We did invite them to the house-warming when we moved in, but if you remember they weren't able to come.' She paused. 'Or didn't want to. And they've not been to you either, have they?'

'No,' Jill admitted, 'though it's only been five weeks and they're both very busy.'

'The fact remains that they don't know exactly what we've done with the house and could be imagining all sorts of horrors. They – or rather Richard – might feel better once they satisfy themselves that we've not made any major changes – in fact, all we've done structurally is close off the entrance to your flat and put in the en suite.'

'Then do invite them. Apart from anything else, I'd love to see them.'

'Right, I'll phone this evening.'

'That was Georgia on the phone,' Victoria said, coming into the sitting room where Richard was watching the news. 'She's invited us for dinner next Friday.'

'Oh, God,' Richard said, his eyes still on the screen.

'You could sound more enthusiastic. It's nice of her, and it will be interesting to see what they've done to the house.'

'Interesting is one word for it.'

'For God's sake, Richard! You can't go on avoiding them – they're your family!'

'I presume you've accepted?'

'Yes, I have – there was nothing in the diary. We must get them a house-warming present, and your mother too.'

He did not reply.

The next phone call came just after midnight, as they were about to turn off the light. Victoria reached for her mobile to find Nigel on the line.

'Hope you weren't asleep.' His voice sounded jerky, out of breath.

'Nigel! Whatever is it?'

'There's been an attempted break-in at The Gallery.'

'*What?*' She struggled to sit upright and Richard turned enquiringly.

'It's OK – or reasonably OK; they didn't manage to get in. The alarm went off and Beryl phoned to let me know.' Beryl was the owner of the café, who lived above it. 'I'm there now. There's a crack in the glass of the door and starring round about it, but that's all.'

'It must have been that snooper,' Victoria said.

'What's happened?' Richard demanded, levering himself up, but she waved him to silence.

'Him or one of his pals. He didn't look the type, but he could have been – what's the phrase? – casing the joint. As, if you remember, I suggested before.'

'We must get on to the police!'

'And tell them what? They won't be interested if no one was hurt and nothing was taken, and it wouldn't be much help to say a middle-aged man has been seen hanging around. We couldn't even give an accurate description, and it's probably nothing to do with him anyway.'

Victoria conceded that he had a point. 'Do you want me to come down?'

'Lord, no,' Nigel said, to her relief. 'There's nothing we can do but I thought you should know, in case you got in before me in the morning and freaked when you saw the crack.'

'What could they be *after*, though? We don't keep cash there overnight.'

'They wouldn't know that. Anyway, we'll give it more thought tomorrow. See you then. 'Night.' And he rang off.

'What the hell was that all about?' Richard asked.

'Someone tried to break into The Gallery but it seems the alarm scared them off.'

'Good God! What have you got in there, the *Mona Lisa*? And what was that about a snooper?'

'Someone was hanging around there last week.'

'Hanging around how?'

'Looking in the window, pacing about on the street outside and stationing himself at a window table in the café.'

'Doesn't sound exactly criminal behaviour.'

Victoria snuggled back under the duvet. 'Now I probably shan't be able to sleep,' she said plaintively.

'Well, please try,' Richard replied, and reached up to switch off the light.

Victoria felt round the rough edges of the crack with one finger. 'What would you say caused this?' she asked.

Nigel shrugged. 'A jemmy? Isn't that what burglars use?'

'To break glass?'

'Whatever it was it didn't work, for which we can be thankful.'

She shivered, looking round her at the paintings lining the walls. 'I know I dismissed it when you were worried last week, but suppose you were right? There's been that spate of art thefts recently, especially in this area – that big heist in Crowborough last week and a couple of stately homes before that. They took some very valuable miniatures.'

'But as you said before, the stuff we sell is not in that league; none of the paintings is worth more than five hundred max.'

'Then why did someone try to break in?'

'God knows, but there's no point in worrying ourselves sick,' he said philosophically. 'If we see that bloke again we'll make sure we get a good description of him, but it's my bet he won't be back. Not if he's connected with this.'

'But suppose they try again?'

'We can only hope that now they know the thickness of the glass, not to mention the alarm – which presumably they thought they'd have time to dismantle – they won't bother. Now I don't know about you, but I could do with a good strong coffee, so let's put the kettle on before we have any customers.'

And, shrugging aside her worries, Victoria followed him into the room at the back of the shop.

It was the first day back after half-term and Richard had been lunching with the governors. It was as he cut across the playground on his return that he saw the child, a sturdy little boy whose red-gold hair stood out among all the fair and brown heads. There was little doubt whose son he was. He paused for a moment, watching as the children excitedly chased each other, and was about to move on when disaster struck. From one minute to the next the red head disappeared under a heap of tangled arms and legs as the other children fell on top of him, and there was an ear-splitting scream of pain.

He set off at a run towards them, seeing Sue Little, who was on playground duty, running from the opposite corner. Several boys began to extricate themselves, tearfully nursing grazed knees and elbows, but – Toby, was it? – was at the bottom of the pile and his injury looked more serious. White with pain, he was crying in harsh, staccato sobs, one arm bent beneath him.

Richard knelt beside him, and, glancing up at Sue as she reached them, ordered tersely, 'Fetch Nurse, would you, and let his mother know.'

She hurried away and he turned to the circle of children anxiously watching. 'Go back to your classrooms, boys, break's almost over. Those of you with grazes can wait in Nurse's room; she'll be back when she's seen to Toby.' They obeyed in subdued silence and Toby's sobs intensified.

'Try not to move, Toby,' Richard said quickly. 'Your mother's just coming. Don't worry, we'll soon have you right.'

Maria and Joan Pendley, the school nurse, arrived simultaneously, Maria's face even paler as she dropped to her knees beside her son, taking his free hand. A bell was sounding the end of lunchtime break and Sue Little, resuming her duties, began shepherding the rest of the children inside.

Joan, meanwhile, was quietly and calmly questioning the child, whose sobs lessened slightly as he answered her. She looked up at Richard. 'It could just be tissue damage but it might be a fracture,' she said. 'He'll need to go to A&E, I'm afraid. I'll ring for an ambulance.'

'I'll take him,' Richard said. 'It'll save time.'

Maria was saying, 'Oh, we really can't expect—' but he cut across her.

'It's no trouble. It's quicker this way and it would be better if you sat with him in the back rather than driving yourself.'

Joan nodded and turned back to her patient. 'Now, Toby, we'll help you to get up, but you must move very slowly and carefully so as not to hurt your arm.'

Richard watched as the two women gently raised the child, who was again screaming with pain, and helped him to his feet.

'I'll bring the car round,' he said. 'Oh, and Nurse, a few of the other children involved are waiting for you, some with nasty grazes that will need dressing.'

He set off for the car park, using his mobile as he went to inform the head of his temporary absence and arranging for Ben Chambers, who he knew had a free period that afternoon, to stand in for him.

The journey to the hospital, driving extra carefully to avoid bumps, took a good fifteen minutes, during which Richard was aware of Maria's soft voice comforting her son, whose hiccupping sobs punctuated her words.

It was a further ten minutes before he found a parking space in the crowded car park and was able to follow them into the building, where he took a seat in the main lobby. Glancing at his watch, he hoped he wouldn't have too long to wait.

London

The plane began its descent towards Heathrow, and since the film he'd been watching was just ending, Paul Devonshire removed his headphones and glanced out of the window. So here he was, back in old England after two years in the States on a work project. It would be good to be home, but in his absence things had moved on, chief among them the shocking death of his friend Greg in a suicide bombing. One of his first actions on returning from a business trip had always been to phone him and meet for a jar to catch-up.

It was a sobering experience when one's contemporaries died, especially when they were longstanding friends. He and Greg had met at university and had shared digs, girlfriends and pretty much everything else during the time they were there. Later they'd been best men at each other's weddings and, though he and Laura had long since parted, had kept in touch.

One poignant aspect of Greg's death was that he'd never achieved his potential. At uni he'd been an outstanding student and everyone confidently expected a double first, but he was inherently lazy and to his tutors' frustration achieved only a third-class degree. Consequently his succession of jobs, though respectable enough, were well below his capabilities – a point exemplified by the fact that he soon became bored and moved on.

'You could be a brain surgeon or a rocket scientist!' Paul had railed at him. 'The whole world's your what's-it!' But Greg had laughed. The only times he exercised that brilliant mind was to master the game of poker, at which he was virtually unbeatable, and to write a highly regarded column in the *Sunday Chronicle* which he submitted under a pseudonym.

It must be about fifteen years ago, Paul reflected, that, on one of their irregular meetings, they'd been discussing a topic of the day about which Greg held strong opinions. Since he'd been a leading light in the debating society, it was no surprise that he'd stated his case with clarity and perception and Paul had laughingly conceded the point. 'You made me see it in a completely different light,' he'd admitted. 'Why don't you write to the papers? Put like that, it might make people think.'

'And bring a mass of approbation on my head from the opposition? No, thanks!'

'Then use a pen name and get your point across without hassle.'

He'd thought no more about it until a month later, when a copy of the *Sunday Chronicle* had come through the post, with *See Page 4* scrawled in red ink on the front page. And there, under the byline Jake Farthing, Paul had read not the letter he'd half-expected but a complete, well-argued piece.

When he'd phoned Greg to congratulate him, he'd been sworn to secrecy. 'They want me to do a regular column,' he'd said, 'but they don't know my real name and I don't want them to, or anyone else for that matter. Then I can write what I think without having to soothe any ruffled feathers.'

The column had swiftly acquired cult status, being variously described as astringent, perceptive and succinct, and his anonymity added to public interest. No photograph appeared at the head of the column, and the many invitations to appear on TV panels or current affairs programme were always declined. At one time a 'Who is Jake Farthing?' competition was launched, with readers invited to submit suggestions as to his identity, suggestions that afforded Greg and himself much amusement. On one occasion he'd even been quoted in the House of Commons on a particularly contentious issue.

Paul was roused from his musings by the arrival of the flight attendant to collect his headphones, and switched his thoughts to more practical matters such as where he could stop on the way home to stock up with basic supplies.

A voice came over the loudspeaker. 'Cabin crew, please take your seats for landing.'

Home sweet home, Paul thought, and couldn't repress a sigh.

Foxclere

Richard lay awake a long time that night, reliving the drama of the afternoon. He'd been waiting twenty minutes or so before

Maria came to seek him out to report that Toby had been assessed by a triage nurse. He would shortly be seen by a doctor and taken for X-ray but the initial opinion was that there was no fracture. She'd spoken quickly, obviously anxious to return to her son, but though it was clear she'd scarcely been aware of him, every fibre of his body had been concentrated on her, her green eyes distractedly looking about her, her fleeting smile.

God, he thought, a wave of heat washing over him, what was the *matter* with him? This young woman, whom he'd met only twice, was a junior member of the school where he was deputy headmaster. There'd no doubt been raised eyebrows when it was learned he'd taken her and Toby to the hospital, but the fact that he'd actually been on the scene when the accident occurred would be explanation enough. Any further meeting between them – which he found to his consternation he most fervently desired – would be dangerous indeed.

'I seem to spend my time thanking you for coming to my rescue!' she'd said with a smile, briefly laying her hand on his arm.

Enough!

Careful not to disturb his sleeping wife, Richard turned his pillow in the hope of finding a cool patch. Then he closed his eyes and began reciting the French and German alphabets alternately until, at last, he fell asleep.

Blaircomrie

Beth paused in the doorway, surveying the sole occupant of the room.

'Mr Stewart not down yet?' she asked, frowning. It was unlike Johnnie to be late for meals.

Eric Barnes shook his head. 'I've not seen him this morning.' His smile was slightly disapproving. 'Must have been a good session last night.' He was ruffled, Beth knew, by the fact that Johnnie went out each evening, depriving him of company.

'I'd better give him a knock,' she said, 'or he'll be late for work.'

She laid a plate of eggs and bacon in front of him, then ran up the stairs and knocked on Johnnie's door. There was no reply. She knocked again; still no response.

'Mr Stewart?' she called, knowing Mr Barnes would be listening.

Silence. Tentatively she turned the knob and pushed the door open a couple of inches, stopping in dismay when she saw the neatly made bed. Either Johnnie had gone out early – which seemed unlikely – or he'd not slept here last night.

Her heart began a slow, muffled beat. She hadn't heard him come in the previous evening, but then she seldom did. She thought back frantically to the last time she'd seen him, which was after dinner when she'd come out of the kitchen as he was crossing the hall en route to the front door. Catching sight of her, he'd smiled, said, 'See you!', and left the house. He hadn't been carrying so much as a briefcase and there'd been no hint that he didn't intend to return.

She brought herself up short. She was getting ahead of herself. Of *course* there was a simple explanation. He must have spent the night here, got up early and made his bed, then for some reason, possibly work related, left before she was awake. But if so, why hadn't he left a note to let her know? Surely he'd have realized she'd worry?

She made her way slowly down the stairs.

'Did you manage to wake him?' Eric Barnes called from the front room.

Beth hesitated, reluctant to tell him the truth but knowing it was impossible to hide. She paused in the doorway. 'He wasn't there,' she said simply.

Mr Barnes frowned. 'Not there?'

'His bed looked as if it hadn't been slept in, but he might have gone out early for some reason.'

'It must have been very early; I've been awake since five with toothache and I'd certainly have heard his door.'

Beth moistened her lips. 'Well, no doubt he'll explain when he comes back this evening.'

But he didn't come back.

FOUR

Stonebridge, North Yorkshire

Some hundred and twenty miles south a funeral was taking place in a small Yorkshire town. The organ was playing softly as they entered the church and David Gregory, bearing his mother's coffin, caught his breath as a shaft of multi-coloured sunlight filtered through the windows, touching it briefly as though in blessing. He glanced at his brother, wondering if he'd noticed, but Will, concentrating on keeping time with the other pall bearers, was staring straight ahead.

At the chancel steps they lowered the coffin on to the stand awaiting it, then, as the official bearers returned down the aisle, he and Will slipped into the front pews to join their family. Julia, standing between the twins, glanced at him briefly, her face unreadable, while in the pew in front Sylvie reached for Will's hand and Henry and Nina, Sally's parents and his own grandparents, stood unmoving with bowed heads.

The service began but he only half-heard it, still unable to believe this wasn't some terrible nightmare, that he'd wake up to find the last ten days hadn't happened. It was all so senseless, so *avoidable*; if they could only turn the clock back so that Mum *hadn't* taken that particular route home, and the other driver *hadn't* suddenly shot out from a side turning, and . . . But what was the use? It had happened and they were all having to deal with it. His overriding concern at the moment was to get through the eulogy without breaking down.

That prayer at least was answered; he delivered the words he'd rehearsed in front of the shaving mirror recalling his mother's life and her courage in facing its challenges, starting with the death of her husband weeks before Will's birth, the stresses of single motherhood and the gradual building up of her chiropody practice.

'She was brave and cheerful and funny and always there for

us,' he ended quietly. 'We shall miss her more than we can say.'

Some thirty people had accepted the invitation to go to Sally's house after the service, and they gathered a little awkwardly in her light-filled sitting room – patients and ex-patients, colleagues, friends and neighbours. The nine-year-old twins, overawed by the occasion, were handing round canapés and sandwiches as David and Will refreshed glasses, and after the solemnity of the service people began to relax and exchange memories of Sally.

'We'd had a girls' night out the week before,' a former school friend confided. 'I just couldn't believe it when I heard.'

In Sally's kitchen her daughters-in-law filled kettles and set out cups and saucers. 'They'll need tea or coffee before they leave,' Julia said. 'I don't know about you, but wine always makes me thirsty.'

Sylvie smiled. 'I keep telling you, you should dilute it as we do in France.'

Julia glanced round the comfortable, familiar room, at the pots of herbs on the windowsill, the rubber plant in the corner, the memos that were no longer needed pinned to the noticeboard. 'It seems so strange to be here without her,' she said. 'I can't believe she's gone.'

'Anything I can do?'

They turned as Nina Hurst came into the room. Small and grey-haired, she seemed to have aged ten years in the last ten days.

'We're just about to produce tea and coffee,' Sylvie said.

Nina nodded distractedly. 'And then perhaps they'll begin to leave. It sounds ungrateful but I'm not sure how much longer I can last.'

She moved restlessly about the room, rearranging cups on the tray, gazing unseeingly out of the window and coming to a halt at the cork notice board. 'There's a dental appointment down for next week,' she said, her voice unsteady. 'Someone will have to cancel it.'

Sylvie put her arms round her. 'Don't worry about that now. How about coming with me to collect Amélie?'

Will and Sylvie's year-old daughter had spent the day in the care of a neighbour down the road and was due to be picked up at five o'clock.

Nina's face lightened. 'I'd love to.'

And, mouthing, *Back soon* at Julia over her head, Sylvie led her from the room.

It was two hours later. The guests had gone, cups and glasses had been washed and put away and the twins had taken Amélie to play in the garden. The six remaining adults had gathered in the sitting room, postponing the moment of departure in the knowledge that this was probably the last time they'd all be together in this house where they'd shared so many memories. It was to be put on the market at the end of the week.

Breaking a brief silence, Will cleared his throat. 'I was talking to one of Mum's chiropodist friends and he asked what we plan to do with the equipment. He offered to take the workstation off our hands, and he's sure the rest could be disposed of among her colleagues. They'd obviously pay a fair price and it would save all the hassle of having it evaluated then advertising it for sale.'

David nodded. 'That would be one less thing to worry about; we could clear the surgery any time, but I think we agreed to leave the main house clearance till after it's been sold. It'll look much better to prospective buyers furnished.'

'I still think we should cancel the cruise,' Nina said suddenly. The Hursts were due to leave on a three-week holiday the following week, and it had taken the combined efforts of the younger members of the family to convince them that they should go ahead with it.

'We've been through that, Gran,' Will said patiently. 'There's nothing you can do here and you're both in need of a break. It'll do you good to get away and have a change of scene.'

Nina still looked uncertain, but Henry nodded. 'He's right, love.'

'But when the house is sold you'll need help going through everything, deciding what—'

David shook his head. 'It's not even on the market yet, and it'll be months before anything happens. There'll be plenty of time when you get back.'

There was a roar from the garden, and as Sylvie rose to her feet the twins appeared at the patio doors, leading a crying Amélie.

'She fell,' Cassie reported, 'but she didn't really hurt herself.'

'She's tired,' Sylvie said, lifting the child, who promptly stopped crying. 'Time we were going, anyway.' She turned to her parents-in-law. 'If we don't see you before Tuesday, take care, try to relax and send us a postcard!'

'*Lots* of postcards!' interposed Pippa, and her twin nodded agreement.

Everyone stood and emotional hugs and kisses were exchanged as they took their leave of each other. After a last look round David followed them all out of the house, locked the door and put the key in his pocket. The end of an era, he thought sadly.

Foxclere

'Well, the evening didn't go too badly, despite your reservations,' Tim remarked. 'I think they were quite impressed with what we've done with the house. "Sympathetic conversion", wasn't that the expression?'

'Victoria's, yes.' Georgia leant towards the mirror to remove her make-up. 'Richard wasn't so enthusiastic. In fact,' she added, frowning slightly, 'I thought he seemed a bit . . . subdued.'

Tim gave a snort. 'Your brother, subdued? That'll be the day!'

'Didn't you think he was unusually quiet?'

'I can't say I noticed, but as you women were chatting nineteen to the dozen neither of us could get much of a word in.'

She pulled a face at him in the mirror. 'Well, at least we've broken the ice – if there was any to break. Now it's up to them to return the invitation.'

He bent and, lifting her hair, kissed the back of her neck. 'Hurry up and come to bed,' he said.

Stonebridge

David and Julia were also preparing for bed. The raw emotions of the day had given way to a dull ache and overwhelming lethargy. Seeing tears in her eyes, he went to put his arms round her but she shook him off, turning her face away.

'Don't, David,' she said, her voice choked.

'Darling, I—'

'And don't "darling" me!' she added in a low, vicious voice.

'Julia, for God's sake!'

'Exactly!' she said and, slipping off her dressing gown, slid quickly into bed and turned off her bedside light. 'Goodnight,' she said.

He stood looking hopelessly at her rigid back, misery sluicing over him. 'Goodnight,' he echoed dully.

'I worry about them, Henry,' Nina said into the darkness. 'Now more than ever. Don't you think we should tell them?'

Henry sighed. 'We made a promise, love,' he reminded her.

'That was years ago. Things are very different now.'

'But what possible good would it do?'

'My poor girl!' Nina said brokenly. 'My poor, beautiful girl!' And she turned her face into her husband's shoulder, feeling his arm come round her as the tears started again.

Blaircomrie

That Friday evening, as usual, Eric Barnes left straight from the office to go home to Kent, and also as usual Beth had begun to prepare something special for her and Johnnie's supper. Because he'd be back for it, she knew he would, or he'd have told her.

But by the time eight o'clock had come and gone she knew he was not coming and, her throat clogged with unshed tears, she tipped the whole meal into the bin. *Where was he?* Had he dumped her, was that it? But then surely he'd have taken all his possessions, cleared out of the house? She'd seen him go, she reminded herself, and he'd not been carrying anything. Might he have come back while she was at work to collect some belongings – but if so, why not all of them? She'd glanced into his room again that evening, hoping against hope he might be there, and though she couldn't bring herself to go in, she could see his trainers on the floor and his raincoat draped over a chair.

Had something happened to him? Bracing herself, she took out the old telephone directory and fearfully rang all the hospitals in the neighbourhood. No one called Johnnie Stewart or even answering his description had been admitted to any of them in the last two days. Which was something, she supposed numbly.

She longed to phone Moira, but she'd gone to stay with her daughter for a long weekend and Beth had no wish for her concerns to be discussed between them. She'd be back in time for their Thursday lunch, but that was almost a week away and by then, Beth told herself, all this anxiety would be in the past and they'd be able to laugh about it. But, oh God, she wished she could speak to her now!

Anxious and fearful, she made herself a cup of tea, her usual panacea, and sat drinking it at the kitchen table, its heat searing her tongue as she played a game with herself: by the time the hands of the clock had reached the half hour, she'd hear his key in the lock. By the time they'd reached a quarter to, the hour, a quarter past . . .

Never had the house felt so empty. At ten o'clock, shivering despite the warm night, she went up to bed and cried herself to sleep.

London

On the first weekend since his return, Paul's daughter invited him to Sunday lunch. At twenty-nine Vivien was making a name for herself at the BBC and still sharing a flat with her long-time friend Wendy. It had crossed his mind more than once that there might be more than friendship between them, but when he'd ill-advisedly suggested this to Laura, she'd flown off the handle and roundly castigated him for even entertaining the idea.

'Neither of them has found the right man yet, that's all,' she'd declared, and he hastily let the subject drop, having no intention of sullying one of their infrequent meetings with argument. For himself, he'd no strong feelings on the subject, and since he'd known Wendy since she was a schoolgirl, regarded her as almost another daughter.

They both greeted him warmly, small, curly-haired Viv and tall Wendy with her smooth golden pageboy – a hairstyle that hadn't changed since she was fourteen.

'Welcome home, Pops!' Viv cried, throwing her arms round his neck. 'Lovely to see you in the flesh instead of on Skype!'

'Likewise.'

She stepped back and surveyed him critically. 'A little greyer and a little plumper round the jowls!' she pronounced.

'That's American food for you! I have to say neither of you has changed an atom.'

'Flatterer! Now, sit down and let me get you a drink. Still Scotch? You haven't succumbed to bourbon, have you?'

'Scotch it is, thanks.'

Wendy excused herself to check on something in the kitchen and Viv asked, 'Seen Mum yet?'

'No; how is she?'

'Blooming.' She handed him his glass. 'It was she who told me about Uncle Greg.'

He sighed. 'Yes, really bad news. I shall miss him.' He'd also, he thought privately, miss reading the Jake Farthing column in the *Sunday Chronicle*, though he couldn't admit as much.

'Well,' Viv said philosophically, 'he always liked living on the edge, didn't he? He probably went out the way he'd have wanted to.'

Paul smiled crookedly. 'With a characteristic bang? I suppose that's one way of looking at it.'

Wendy returned, and the conversation switched to an exchange of news which continued over lunch. Then there were photographs to show and exclaim over, among them Paul's skiing trip in the Rockies and Viv and Wendy's holiday in Thailand. Viv also produced photos of her half-brothers, now, incredibly, aged fourteen and sixteen. She glanced affectionately at her father.

'Ever thought of marrying again, Pops?' she asked.

He smiled, raising his hands in mock-surrender. 'Once was more than enough!' he said, adding, since it might have seemed strange not to, 'What about you two? Any Prince Charming on the horizon?'

They both shook their heads. 'We're career girls, Pops. We work hard and play hard.'

'As long as you're happy,' he said.

It was after six by the time he got back to his flat, where he poured himself a glass of whisky before settling down with the Sunday papers – and received a severe shock. For there, on its accustomed page, was an article by Jake Farthing.

Briefly he wondered if Greg had supplied copy in batches to be used as and when, but that couldn't be it; this week's column, like all the others, was concerned with current news. As he ran his eye disbelievingly down the page, a more likely explanation occurred to him. When the monthly articles had inexplicably stopped arriving, the paper must have guessed something had befallen its anonymous author, and, reluctant to lose one of its most popular features, commissioned another journalist to take it over. The old Peterborough column in the *Daily Telegraph* had, he remembered, passed to successive authors over the years.

This, however, was altogether more personal, and as he started to read it Paul prepared to be highly critical. But to his grudging surprise it seemed the baton had passed seamlessly and the words he was reading were, both in style and content, much as he remembered them. The substitute writer had studied his predecessor assiduously and proved himself a worthy successor. Nonetheless, it made painful reading and, on coming to the end, Paul decided not to repeat the exercise. Albeit with reluctance, for he was a creature of habit, he would change his Sunday newspaper.

Foxclere

It had been decreed that Toby should have a week at home in order to recover from the shock as well as the pain he'd suffered, and as her family were up north and unable to help, Maria took a leave of absence to look after him. Meanwhile, the accident report form had been completed and filed and running in the playground was being more closely monitored. As far as the school was concerned the incident was virtually closed.

At the end of lessons the following Monday there was a tap on Richard's door, which opened to admit Maria and Toby himself, looking pale and somewhat reluctant.

'We're sorry to disturb you, Mr Lawrence,' Maria said, with the smile that always caught him unawares, 'but Toby would like to thank you for being so kind when he fell over.'

Richard rose from behind his desk. 'I was glad to help. Are you feeling better now, young man?'

The child's eyes dropped to the floor. 'Yes, thank you, sir,' he murmured.

'He made something for you,' Maria added, gently pushing him forward, and Richard saw he was holding a folded sheet of paper which he shyly handed over. The picture on the front depicted a small stick figure lying on the ground, a lopsided car and an uneven oblong painstakingly labelled *Hospital*, all executed in various coloured crayons. Inside, someone had faintly pencilled in *Thank you for helping me. From Toby*, which had been laboriously traced over.

'That's lovely, Toby,' Richard said warmly. 'I shall put it on my desk. But be careful not to fall again, won't you.'

He nodded and returned to his mother's side.

'And I'd like to add my own thanks,' Maria said warmly. 'I hope I thanked you at the time, but I don't remember – all I could think about was Toby. It was really extremely kind of you to run us to the hospital.'

'It seemed the most sensible thing in the circumstances.' He paused, suddenly unwilling to let them go and, ignoring the clarion of warning bells in his head, added rashly, 'You were a very brave boy, Toby, and I think you deserve a reward, don't you?'

Aware of Maria's puzzled glance, he was careful to keep his eyes on her son. 'School's finished for the day, and I know a place where they sell particularly nice ice cream. Would you like one?'

'Mr Lawrence—'

He turned to her. 'Do you know Angelino's in the High Street? I have a couple of things to tidy up, but I'll meet you there in fifteen minutes.' And as she hesitated, he added humbly, 'Please.'

After a moment she nodded, and, Toby's hand in hers, they left the room. As the door closed behind them Richard sank back on to his chair, his heart pounding. What in the name of heaven was he thinking? Suppose someone from school saw them? He'd instinctively picked a café some distance away but there was still a chance another child would be taken there. Well, too late to do anything about it now. The die was cast.

What exactly he hoped to achieve from this ill-considered invitation was a point he was not prepared to consider.

'So,' Mike Chiltern said, coming into the kitchen where his son was having tea, 'how did his first day back go? Did Mr Lawrence like his card?'

Fortunately Toby had a mouthful of shepherd's pie and Maria was able to forestall him. 'Very much; he said he'd put it on his desk, didn't he, Toby? As for the rest,' she went on quickly, 'Sue Little said he seemed nervous at playtime and kept very much on the edge of things, but that's all to the good. He's been excused games and PE for the rest of term.'

Toby swallowed his mouthful. 'Daddy, we went—'

'And they had a nature walk in the afternoon, didn't you? Tell Daddy about seeing the baby rabbit.'

And as he happily embarked on the story, Maria silently blessed the distractibility of children. It would not do for Mike to know Mr Lawrence had singled them out in any way; after the episode at her last school, which had resulted in Mike's applying for a job transfer and removing the whole family from lingering gossip, he understandably remained distrustful.

Staffroom opinion was that Richard Lawrence was a self-contained man who never gave a hint of what he was thinking, which made approaching him with any kind of problem somewhat daunting. 'Brilliant academically, by all accounts,' Stephanie James had volunteered, 'but a bit of a cold fish, if you ask me. Can't help feeling sorry for his wife, though as they say she's on the arty side perhaps it suits her. No kids, if that's any indication.'

But suppose staffroom opinion was wrong and there were hidden depths to Richard Lawrence, depths she herself had stirred? She was pretty sure he fancied her; she'd seen that expression in men's eyes often enough not to mistake it and his kindness with the ice-cream treat had surely been beyond the call of duty. Not to mention the fact that he'd seemed more interested in her than in Toby – asking where Mike worked, how they were settling in, and so on.

A stab of conscience reminded her that she'd promised Mike there would be no repetition of her unfaithfulness, which she knew had hurt him deeply. He was a good, reliable husband but there was no denying he was dull. Landing the 'cold fish' would be an exciting challenge, one that would spice up her rather lacklustre marriage and if it fulfilled her, surely Mike would reap the benefit?

His voice reached her from the top of the stairs. 'Ready for the bedtime story!' he called, and abandoning her thoughts along with the washing-up, Maria dried her hands and went upstairs.

FIVE

Blaircomrie

I t was the most interminable week of Beth's life and she lived each day in an agony of worry and indecision. Eric Barnes had been incredulous when he'd returned on Sunday evening to find Johnnie still absent.

'I don't know what to do, Mr Barnes,' she'd said tremulously. 'I did phone the hospitals but none of them had seen him. Do you think I should get on to the police?'

He'd shaken his head decidedly. 'No, Mrs Monroe, I don't. He's a grown man and it's not as though he's family. To be frank, I've often wondered if he was involved in something shady, and if so he wouldn't thank you for bringing in the police, would he?'

'Shady?' Fresh fears assailed her.

'Have you ever wondered what he gets up to every evening when he's out of the house from half seven till bedtime and beyond?'

Yes, she'd wondered, but she'd never dared ask him. 'I . . . thought he was meeting friends,' she'd said feebly, attempting to conceal the extent of her worry since as far as Mr Barnes knew, Johnnie was just another lodger.

He grunted derisively, then, as something occurred to him, asked sharply, 'He *has* paid you till the end of the month?'

She nodded.

'Well, if he's still not turned up by then, you'd be within your rights to remove his things and advertise the free room. No reason why you should lose out because of his thoughtlessness.'

'But that's three weeks away!' she'd exclaimed. 'Surely we'll have heard something by then?'

'Then there'll be nothing to worry about, will there?'

'I suppose not,' Beth said miserably, and by tacit agreement the matter wasn't referred to again.

*   *   *

Unable to concentrate on her work at the dental practice, she twice handed Bruce the wrong instrument, and compounded her error by spilling water over a patient when handing her the cup for a rinse.

'Not like you, Beth,' Bruce had said in mild reproof when they were alone, and she'd apologized profusely, pleading a migraine.

Tuesday was her evening at the bridge club, and she wouldn't have gone had it not been that she played in a regular four and they'd be expecting her. But she couldn't remember the sequence of cards, and unforgivably trumped her partner's ace. Again, a migraine was pleaded as an excuse. Her only consolation throughout all this was that apart from Moira no one knew of her liaison with Johnnie, so there were no knowing remarks to contend with.

Then, at very long last, Thursday arrived, and she set off with a dry mouth and thumping heart to meet her.

As usual, Moira was there ahead of her, looking tanned and happy, and as Beth seated herself she pushed a small packet across the table towards her.

'A present from the seaside!' she said gaily. Then, as Beth made no move to open it, her eyes narrowed. 'Beth, what is it? Has something happened?'

With an overwhelming flood of relief, Beth poured out the whole story.

Moira stared at her aghast. 'And he never gave any hint he was thinking of leaving?'

'No, but he can't have left, Moira, not really, or he'd have taken his things, wouldn't he?' Her eyes filled with tears. 'You think he's dumped me, don't you?'

'No, I don't; as you say, he'd have taken his things.'

'Then where is he?' Beth wailed.

'Can I take your order?' said a disapproving voice, and they hastily made their choices.

When the waitress had moved away, Moira said, 'You said your lodger mentioned shady dealings.'

Beth made a dismissive gesture. 'He's miffed that Johnnie's no company for him, that's all.'

'But where *does* he go every evening? You must have asked him?'

'Actually, I didn't. If he'd wanted me to know he'd have told me, and . . . I suppose I didn't want to rock the boat.'

'In case he was spending them with his wife?' Moira's tone was playful but Beth's eyes widened.

'He could have been! Oh, Moira, what a fool I've been!'

'Don't be daft,' Moira said briskly. 'If his wife was near enough to visit in the evenings, he'd have been living with her and not you, wouldn't he? You're sure he wasn't carrying anything when he left?'

'Positive. When he left the front room he went straight out of the house. He didn't even take a coat.'

'Then, unlike your Mr Barnes, I think you should go to the police.'

'You think something's happened to him?'

'Well, *something* must have, mustn't it, and as his landlady you're entitled to make enquiries.'

Beth felt suddenly sick. 'Will you come with me?'

'Of course I will. We'll go this evening after work. Then at least they can advise you whether there's any need to worry. Ten to one they'll say people are always disappearing and in most cases turn up again. And now that that's settled, you can open your present!'

They met as arranged outside the police station at six o'clock. It was a sultry evening but Beth's hands were ice cold. Moira took her arm and marched her firmly inside and across the foyer to the desk. The man behind it looked up from his papers.

'Evening, ladies. What can I do for you?'

Moira nudged her and Beth cleared her throat. 'I thought I should let you know that I run a B and B and one of my lodgers went out last Thursday evening and hasn't returned. All his things are still in his room.'

'I see. And I'm guessing he never said he was leaving?'

She shook her head, her mouth dry.

'Owe you any rent, does he?'

'No, he . . . he's paid till the end of the month.'

'Very well, madam, let's start at the beginning. You are . . .?'

Beth automatically answered his questions, including Johnnie's name and a brief description.

'And Mr Stewart's home address?'

Beth stared at him blankly. 'I don't think he's got one. I mean, I think it's with me.' She thought a moment. 'When I asked if he'd be going home for the weekends, he said, "Where would I go?"'

The man looked back at her for a long moment, tapping his pencil against his teeth. Then he said, 'Excuse me a minute.' And, lifting a phone, he moved away slightly, spoke into it in a lowered voice, then turned back to them.

'If you'd like to take a seat, ladies, DS Grant will come down and have a word with you.'

Exchanging a puzzled glance they seated themselves, looking apprehensively about them.

'At least he didn't seem to think we were wasting his time,' Moira said encouragingly.

'Is that a good or a bad thing?'

They didn't have long to wonder. A door further down the hall opened and two men came through it, one carrying a file under his arm. The desk sergeant nodded in their direction and they both came over.

'Good evening, ladies. I'm DS Grant and this is DC Coombes.' The man with the file nodded. 'I believe you want to report a missing person?'

'Yes, I suppose we do.'

'Then let's go to an interview room.'

He tapped on a door to their left, opened it and glanced inside, then waved them in ahead of him. The room was small and bare, containing only four chairs and a table bearing a recording device. They seated themselves on the chairs indicated, DC Coombes laid the file on the table and the two policemen sat down opposite them.

Grant leant back in his chair. 'So which of you ladies is reporting the disappearance?' Beth raised a hand. 'Then let's start with your name and address.'

She complied, supplying Johnnie's name when requested.

'Can you give me a description of Mr Stewart? Age, height, and so on?'

'In his fifties, I'd say. Not particularly tall – certainly under six feet. Dark hair going grey.'

As the questions progressed she became increasingly embarrassed by how little she actually knew about Johnnie, having to admit she'd no idea of his next of kin or last known address, nor even where he worked. 'I believe he's divorced,' she added inadequately.

DS Grant surveyed her thoughtfully and she wondered for a panic-stricken moment if he'd guessed about their affair. But all he said was, 'How long has he been with you, Mrs Monroe?'

She thought back. 'It must be about eight weeks now.'

'And his references were satisfactory?'

She flushed. 'I didn't ask for one. I never have, with my guests.'

He shook his head disapprovingly. 'One of the first rules of running a guest house. Suppose the applicant was a criminal on the run? You should always run checks and credit searches before allowing anyone to live in your home. Only common sense.'

'I've never had any trouble,' she said defensively. Before, she added silently.

Grant upended his pencil and righted it again, an action he repeated several times. Then he said slowly, 'You say you last saw Mr Stewart on the evening of Thursday the fifth?'

'That's right.'

'Exactly a week ago?'

She nodded. 'I kept thinking he'd come back,' she said feebly.

'How did he seem when you last saw him?'

'Well, he'd just had his dinner. He was . . . the same as usual.'

'He hadn't seemed any different over the last week or so? As though something was on his mind, perhaps?'

'No, he—' Beth broke off, coldness spreading over her. 'Actually, he did seem a bit on edge,' she said, aware of Moira turning to her in surprise. 'A couple of times he didn't hear when I spoke to him, and he was very anxious not to miss the six o'clock news – I did notice that. He got quite angry once when Mr Barnes, my other lodger, switched channels before it had finished, and insisted he change back again.'

'And this was unusual?'

'Well, yes. He's usually very easy-going.'

'They get on well, do they, your two lodgers?'

She moved uncomfortably. 'Well, they're not exactly *friends*; they really only meet at mealtimes.'

'They don't spend the evenings together, both being away from home?'

'No; Mr Stewart goes out straight after his meal.'

Grant looked up in surprise. '*Every* evening?'

'Yes.'

'And he never mentions where he's going?'

Beth flushed. 'I've never asked him.'

Grant looked at her frowningly. 'What about weekends?'

Dangerous ground. She said carefully, 'Mr Barnes goes home to his family in Kent.'

'And Mr Stewart?'

Her hands twisted in her lap. 'He stays here. He works most Saturdays.'

'Where is that?'

Again, Beth had to confess she didn't know. It felt as though she was taking an exam and failing miserably and Grant's face expressed his exasperation. 'He never speaks of his home or family?'

Miserably she shook her head.

He resumed upending and righting his pencil, an action that grated on her fraught nerves. Then he said, 'You say he seemed on edge recently; apart from being anxious to hear the news, did he do or say anything else unusual?'

'Not that . . . oh!' She put a hand to her mouth.

Grant leant forward. 'Yes?'

'He did ask me to sign something.'

'What was that?'

She flushed. 'I don't know; it wasn't a formal document or anything,' she added in mitigation.

'So what was it?'

'Just a single sheet of paper with a ready-typed sentence at the bottom which said "I, Elizabeth Monroe of . . . and my address . . . swear this is the signature of the above-named as witnessed by me" – something like that.'

Grant said carefully, 'And what name had he signed?'

Beth moistened her lips. 'He said he'd fill it in later.'

Grant swore under his breath. 'And you didn't ask what it was about?'

'I did, but he said it was something to do with work, so I didn't pursue it.'

There was a long silence, during which Beth castigated herself for her stupidity. *Why* had she been so trusting? She knew the answer, of course – because she loved him – but she must look a complete idiot to the police, and no doubt she was.

Finally Grant cleared his throat. 'I don't want to alarm you, Mrs Monroe,' he said slowly, 'but I'd like you to take a look at this photograph.' He leant forward, removed a print from the file on the table and handed it across.

Moira gripped her arm and they both stared down at the print of a man lying with closed eyes, a sheet up to his neck – a man aged in his fifties, with dark, greying hair.

Beth's sharply indrawn breath was answer enough for Moira. She raised anguished eyes. 'What's happened to him?' she whispered.

'Can you identify that man, ma'am?'

She nodded. 'He's my lodger, Johnnie Stewart.'

'You're quite sure?'

'Quite,' she said, the word almost strangling her. 'He's . . . dead, isn't he?'

'I'm afraid so, yes.'

'How did he die?'

'I'm not—'

'For God's sake!' she broke in roughly.

A pause, then, 'He was found in the early hours of last Friday but had apparently died some hours earlier. There was no wallet or any form of identification, and despite extensive searches we've so far drawn a blank.'

Only one word had registered. 'Found?'

'In the street; he'd been stabbed.'

A jolt went through her, dispelling her fleeting hope of a heart attack. *Something shady*, Mr Barnes had said. But innocent people got stabbed – you were always hearing about it. Just not people you *knew*.

So he'd not left her intentionally after all. She felt numb, disorientated. Soon, she knew, the truth of this, however bizarre, would hit her and the pain would begin. She could only be thankful it was suspended.

DS Grant was saying gently, 'You have identified the deceased as the man you knew as Johnnie Stewart?'

Beth nodded. 'Yes.'

'Would you be prepared to go to the mortuary for a formal identification?'

She heard Moira gasp, clamping down on her own instinctive refusal as she realized this was the last thing she could do for Johnnie. She owed him that.

'Very well,' she said.

Viewing the body was a surreal experience, a procedure familiar from TV crime dramas, and Beth was able to detach herself as though she too was an actress playing a part. Nonetheless, as she turned away she began to shake uncontrollably, and when they were settled again in the interview room someone brought her a glass of water.

'Thank you for that, Mrs Monroe,' Grant said as she sipped at it. 'I appreciate it can't have been easy for you, but at least we now have an identity to work on.'

'What happens next?' she ventured.

'I'll have to report to my boss, but I'm sure he'll want a forensic team to go over Mr Stewart's room and bag up any potential evidence.' He looked at her sharply. 'Have you been in yourself this last week, ma'am, perhaps hoping for a clue as to where he might be?'

She shook her head. 'I looked in twice, once that first morning, expecting to have to wake him, and again in the evening, hoping he'd returned. But I didn't go into the room – it didn't seem right, somehow – and since then I've not even opened the door. It's exactly as he left it.'

DS Grant nodded in satisfaction. 'How many people are living in the house?'

'Only myself and Mr Barnes.'

'Might he have gone in for any reason?'

'I'm quite sure he wouldn't.'

He began playing with his pencil again, his eyes following its rhythmic movements. 'Did you come in your own transport?' he asked suddenly.

Beth blinked at the change of subject. 'No, we took the bus because of parking.'

'Then we'll run you home. Presumably Mr Barnes will have returned from work?'

She glanced at her watch, suddenly aware of the time. 'Yes, and he'll be wondering what's happened to his dinner.'

'We'll need to take his statement.' He turned to Coombes. 'Bring the car round, will you, Jamie?'

Moira went with her in the police car, and while Eric Barnes was closeted with the police Beth cooked the chops she'd bought for supper. She'd have to call at the station herself the next day to read through and sign her statement. It was odd, she reflected; during the past week she'd instinctively avoided entering Johnnie's room, but now that it was forbidden she had an almost irresistible urge to do so, to look at, perhaps finger, his possessions, the last of him that was left to her, before it was all removed by the police.

When eventually Mr Barnes joined them in the kitchen he was considerably shaken, both by the news of Johnnie's murder and by the police questioning, seeming to regret his previous suspicions.

'I shouldn't have dissuaded you from reporting it earlier,' he said more than once. And each time Beth replied wearily, 'It wouldn't have made any difference.'

They ate their belated dinner round the table, Moira taking advantage of the extra chop that, ignoring all logic, Beth had bought in case Johnnie had returned. It was a subdued meal. At one point Beth remarked that she'd phone in sick the next day so she could be there when the police arrived, but Moira shook her head.

'Tell them the truth, that one of your lodgers has been murdered and the police are coming to search his room. It'll be in the papers and they'd wonder why you didn't mention it.' She laid a quick hand over Beth's, aware that she must temper her sympathy in the presence of Eric Barnes. 'It'll be pretty bloody tomorrow and I'm sorry I can't take the day off to support you, but there's an important client coming in and I have to be there.' Moira worked for a building society. 'I'll come and collect you after work,' she added, 'and you can spend the weekend with me. Mr Barnes will have gone home and you won't want to be alone.'

Beth nodded, wondering how long this numbness would last. She resolved to live one day at a time – as, she remembered with a jolt, she had done after Dougie's death. The memory brought her up short. Dougie had been her beloved husband for twenty years, whereas she'd known Johnnie for eight short weeks and imagined herself in love, she supposed, for about half of them. But surely she'd not known him well enough to love him for himself? Had it, then, been simply a strong physical attraction that, after years of celibacy, had gone to her head?

Dougie had died peacefully in his bed with his hand in hers, whereas Johnnie had been stabbed to death in a dark street. It was shock as much as grief that had unbalanced her, and it was as well to get things into perspective.

She looked up at the two worried faces watching her. 'I'll be fine,' she said.

Foxclere

Victoria was still jumpy. During the last two weeks there'd been no sign of the man who had been so much in evidence, but she couldn't put the attempted break-in out of her mind.

'Forget it,' Nigel advised. 'They found we were harder to get into than they expected, so they've gone after easier pickings.'

'Or they're lulling us into a false sense of security,' Victoria countered. 'If only we knew what they were after, Nige.'

He shrugged, losing interest, but between customers she spent her time moving from one painting to the next, though as far as she could tell there was nothing unusual about any of them. As always, a few were by local artists who were grateful for the opportunity to display their work and who usually sold out at the twice-yearly exhibitions, partly because their friends and relatives flocked in to support them but also because their paintings were lower priced than those of better-known artists. It was unlikely, she thought, that any of them would have been the target for their unwelcome visitors, nor any of the small sculptures, pottery ornaments and hand-carved wooden figures which were also on display. Though decorative, they were not valuable.

Nigel was right, she decided. She'd no way of knowing who or what had sparked that interest and perhaps, as he said, having tried and failed, they wouldn't risk another attempt.

*   *   *

By the third week, and rather to his surprise, Edward was beginning to look forward to his piano lessons. The focus and determination that had furthered his business career was standing him in good stead and he quickly learned to correct mistakes, seldom making the same one twice. Having overcome his embarrassment, he even enjoyed his twice-weekly visits to the school music rooms, where he diligently practised for an hour at a time, and had already decided to continue with his lessons when the trial period came to an end.

Jill was delighted with his progress. 'I wish all my pupils were as quick to learn,' she said. 'We'll have you on the concert platform yet! And speaking of concerts, did you see that Ludmilla Kranz is coming to the Elizabeth Hall next week? I'd give anything to hear her, but even though I phoned the day booking opened they were sold out by the time I got through.'

Edward hesitated. 'Actually, I'm going to hear her,' he said.

'You managed to get a ticket? Oh, well done! I'll expect to hear all about it!'

He cleared his throat. 'Actually, my wife belonged to Friends of Elizabeth Hall; we had reserved seats for the first night of every performance, though sadly, because of business commitments, I was seldom able to go with her.' He paused, then went on: 'Since her death I've been releasing them, but now I've retired I intend to make full use of at least one ticket.' Another pause. 'And on this occasion, I should be delighted if you'd accompany me.'

Jill stared at him, conflicting thoughts milling round her head. Of *course* there was nothing she'd like better than to hear her favourite pianist, but she'd always vowed never to mix business with pleasure. On the other hand, it would be ungracious to refuse; Edward was lonely, he'd mellowed considerably since his first stiff lesson and she'd even begun to enjoy his company. She should put her prudish principles aside and accept his invitation in the spirit in which it was offered.

'Provided you allow me to pay for my ticket,' she said, 'I'd be delighted.'

'There's really no need—'

'It's a condition of my acceptance.'

He smiled, and she was reminded how seldom he did so, and how much more approachable it made him seem. 'Then you leave me no option,' he said.

Stonebridge

'I was so sorry to hear about your mother-in-law,' said one of the regular customers, and Julia burst into tears. Horrified, Alexa took her arm and hurried her to the back of the shop, while Charlotte reassured the embarrassed customer.

'She's come back too soon, that's the trouble,' she confided. 'We tried to persuade her to take longer, but she was desperate to get back to work. Said it took her mind off things.'

'I'm so sorry,' the woman stammered, clearly distressed. 'The last thing I wanted was to upset her.'

'I know, and she's grateful for your sympathy. Please don't worry about it – she'll be fine in a minute.'

Alexa, meanwhile, passing Julia a packet of tissues, was thankful that the only other customers at the moment were in the basement looking at cookware; tears were not a recommended selling point. But Julia, mortified, was already blowing her nose.

'I'm so sorry,' she said. 'That was unforgivable.'

'Of course it wasn't.' Alexa looked at her shrewdly. 'But it's not only Sally, is it? Even *before* she was killed, something was wrong.'

Julia made an impatient gesture. 'I must apologize to Mrs Carson,' she said.

The three women, who had met on a Cordon Bleu course, had opened Jac's Books and Cookware – known simply as 'Jac's' – ten years ago, and it had been an instant success. The ground floor was given over to recipe books from around the world, with a couple of sofas and a coffee-making machine to make browsing more pleasant. The basement held an extensive range of the latest cookware and the first floor was used for cookery demonstrations and weekend courses. The shop's name was composed of the initials of its three owners.

Driving home at the end of the day, Julia remembered Alexa's perceptive comment. She was right, dammit; she'd been feeling hurt, angry and upset for some weeks now since, quite by chance, she'd learned of David's affair, and his protestations that it was over were little consolation. To add to her misery Sally, in whom she'd always confided, had clearly been out of bounds on this occasion. After a wearying round of excuses, rows and subterfuges, she had finally, three days before Sally's fatal accident, reached the decision to leave him, and been planning the best time to tell him. Which, of course, was now impossible, at least in the near future. In any case, she'd no idea where she would go; her parents had retired to a town on the south coast that was awash with grey hair and wheelchairs, and her sister, to whom she'd never been close, lived in Wales and was unlikely to welcome an influx of family. There was also the girls' schooling to consider.

The reason she'd not confided in Charlotte and Alexa was largely a question of pride, though no doubt they'd offer helpful advice. Charlotte was divorced herself but on incredibly cordial terms with her ex, and Alexa, who was now living with a TV chef, had survived a couple of break-ups. The fact that they both congratulated her on her stable marriage did not make things easier.

None of this, though, was responsible for her embarrassing tears earlier; it was simply that Mrs Carson's unexpected though well-intentioned sympathy had touched a raw nerve. Julia had always felt closer to her mother-in-law than to her own parents; Sally had made her welcome from the moment David first introduced them, and on their wedding day had declared with satisfaction, 'At last, I have a daughter!'

Julia's eyes filled again at the memory. She really must pull herself together before she reached home. Turning her mind to more prosaic matters, she hoped Lisa had remembered to put the lasagne in the oven; she was a nice girl and the twins loved her, but she did sometimes have her head in the clouds.

Ten minutes later, when she opened her front door, she was reassured by the savoury smell that assailed her nostrils. Dropping her bag on the hall table, she walked down the hall to the kitchen, where the twins were halfway through their tea.

'Any more replies to your invitation?' she asked after the usual greetings.

'Florence and Lily gave me theirs,' Cassie volunteered, gesturing at two crumpled envelopes on the side, but Pippa shook her head and Julia gave an exclamation of annoyance. There was just over a week to the twins' tenth birthday party and so far there had been few replies. Last year she'd had to phone to ascertain whether three or four of the invited guests could be expected at the party.

She prided herself on the fact that Pippa and Cassie, though they complained vociferously, were required to send replies and, later, thank-you letters, within a few days of receipt.

'What shape will the cake be, Mummy?' Cassie enquired. A loaded question, since both girls had submitted requests.

'You'll have to wait and see,' Julia said, and, leaving her daughters to Lisa's ministrations, went up to take a shower before David came home.

SIX

Foxclere

For some reason she'd not bothered to define, Jill hadn't mentioned she was going to the concert with Edward. However, on the day before Georgia called in with a library book she'd offered to collect for her, and over a cup of tea remarked casually, 'Too bad you weren't able to get tickets for Ludmilla Kranz; she's getting rave reviews.' And she had felt bound to confess.

'Actually, I'm able to go after all,' she admitted. 'My new student Edward French has reserved seats for every performance and invited me to go along.'

Georgia looked at her in surprise. 'Well, you kept that pretty quiet!'

To her annoyance, Jill felt herself flush. 'It was only arranged on Friday; I mentioned I'd been unable to get a ticket and he said he had a spare one. It's all perfectly innocuous.'

'I never suggested otherwise,' Georgia said solemnly, and after a moment they both laughed. 'Seriously, Mum, I'm delighted you're going. I know she's one of your favourites.' She paused. 'How's his playing coming along? Still afraid of making a fool of himself?'

Jill poured another cup of tea. 'No, actually, he's doing quite well. He's been practising at the grammar school and made good progress.' She paused. 'His late wife was a member of the Friends of Elizabeth Hall, which explains the reservations, but I don't think he's made much use of them since she died.'

'Perhaps you should join yourself. At least it would ensure you a regular seat.' She flashed her mother a wicked glance. 'Unless, that is, you're going to cash in regularly on Edward's spare ticket!'

'You see!' Jill exclaimed. 'Is it any wonder I didn't volunteer the news?'

Georgia laughed. 'Only teasing.' She glanced at a folded newspaper on the chair beside her and picked it up, sobering abruptly. 'God, Mum, have you seen this? They've actually attacked someone this time!'

'Who have? What are you talking about?'

'The latest country house burglary. Haven't you read the paper?'

'No, I save it till lunchtime when I can give it my full attention. But what's happened?'

Georgia's eyes flew down the page. 'The owners were at home. They heard a noise and the husband, a Mr Donald Lancing, went down to investigate while his wife phoned the police. The brutes bashed him over the head before escaping empty-handed. He's in hospital in a coma.'

'Oh, that's terrible – the poor man! The robberies were bad enough, God knows – all those irreplaceable antiques – but at least no one's been hurt before.' She drew a sharp breath. 'You don't think there's any connection with that break-in attempt Victoria was telling us about?'

Georgia looked up. 'Of course not – how could there possibly be? As you said yourself, it's priceless antiques they're after, not the sort of knick-knacks The Gallery sells.'

'Nevertheless, she was worried and this certainly won't help.'

'It was just an opportunist attempt, Mum – probably some drunk on the way home from the pub.'

'I hope you're right,' Jill said uncertainly, 'and that poor Mr Lancing or whatever his name is makes a full recovery. At least after this the police will be redoubling their efforts to catch them.'

Edward had regretted his impulsive offer of the spare seat. Not that he didn't like Jill – he did – but he knew a lot of Cecily's friends would be at the concert and might put the wrong interpretation on seeing them together. There was also a point of etiquette that was troubling him; the concert began, as always, at eight o'clock, and on the relatively rare occasions he'd gone with Cecily they'd had a pre-theatre supper in the hall's restaurant, as had a large proportion of the audience.

Should he also invite Jill to that? Or would it put too much emphasis on the evening, make it more of a 'date'? He winced at the word. And if he did ask her, she'd probably insist on paying for her meal as she had for the ticket, which could be embarrassing. In the end he flunked it, reckoning it was better to be thought mean than forward, and called for her at seven thirty to allow time for a drink in the bar before the performance.

To his relief she made no fuss about reimbursing him, merely handing him an envelope as she got into the car. 'I really do appreciate this,' she said.

She was looking subtly different, wearing a dress and high heels in place of the casual clothes he was used to. The effect was oddly unsettling, as though they were meeting for the first time, and as they entered the bar he couldn't help noticing that men's eyes followed her, prompting him to see her as an attractive woman rather than simply his long-suffering music teacher.

Nonetheless, that was how he introduced her when people he knew came up to greet him. 'She wants me to hear how the piano should be played!' he added. But he hadn't foreseen – though he should have – that Jill would also know some of the concertgoers and, following his lead, she introduced him as one of her pupils, which illogically annoyed him.

Once they were alone he decided to put them on a more social footing, even if temporarily, and said lightly, 'At our first meeting you asked a few questions about my background; now if I may I'd like to do the same. I believe you said your daughter lives in the flat above you?'

Jill smiled. 'I don't think of it as a flat, but I suppose you're right. Yes, we converted the family home after my husband's death. My son was somewhat ambivalent about it but we're hoping we've won him round.'

'Does he live locally?'

'A few miles away. He's deputy headmaster at Briarfields.'

Edward raised his eyebrows. 'An eminent institution. Was your husband also in the teaching profession?'

'No; when we met he was doing project work for an IT firm which entailed working away from home all week, but he moved on to other things.'

Edward waited, and when she didn't elaborate, prompted, 'He must have died tragically young?'

'He was fifty-six.' She paused, then ended flatly, 'He was killed in a suicide bombing.'

Edward's eyes widened. 'Good God – how horrific! I'm so sorry – I've no right to interrogate you like this. I'd no idea—'

She raised her hand with a faint smile. 'It's all right, it's common knowledge. I'm used to talking about it.'

'Nevertheless, it was very intrusive of me—'

'Please, Edward, forget it. It doesn't matter.'

He was saved from further grovelling by the sound of the bell intimating the performance would shortly begin. Thankfully he was able to take her elbow and lead her into the auditorium.

The following morning, Nigel and Victoria were discussing the latest report on the coma victim when The Galley door pinged open. The newcomer looked to be in her early forties, with a Riviera tan shown to advantage by her short skirt and sleeveless top. Her hair was dark and cut close to her head and she nonchalantly swung her sunglasses as she moved from picture to picture.

Victoria glanced at Nigel, raising her eyebrows, and he lifted his shoulders in reply. Since there was no one else in at the moment, she smilingly approached her.

'Are you interested in any particular artist, or just browsing?' she enquired pleasantly.

The woman, who had jumped at her approach, turned, her blue eyes vivid against her tan. 'Just browsing, thanks,' she said. Then, 'Are these all by local artists?'

'Oh, no, most are by established names. There are only two or three local ones.' Victoria waved a hand towards the far right-hand wall.

'Could you show me which they are?'

'Of course.' They walked together down the room while Nigel busied himself at the counter. 'The artist of this seascape lives locally, as does Francis King, who painted the still life.'

The customer glanced briefly at the two pictures indicated. 'My friend was in about week ago and said you had several by local artists.'

'There might have been a couple more, but they're popular and sell well.'

Which was sales talk rather than the truth.

'So they could have been sold in the last week?'

'I can check if you tell me the subject or the artist you're looking for,' Victoria offered. Though what good it would do, she couldn't imagine.

'I can't remember exactly, though I'd recognize the names if I heard them. Could you look up those that were sold and who bought them?'

'I'm sorry,' Victoria said smoothly, 'we don't pass on customer details. But if it's local work you're interested in you should come to one of our exhibitions, where you'd have much more choice. We hold two a year and they're advertised in the local press. In the meantime, if you'd like to leave your name and address and the name of any artist you particularly like, we'd be happy to contact you when we have some of their work.'

The woman shook her head. 'No, it doesn't matter; it was just a spur-of-the-moment thing as I was passing.' And she turned and walked quickly out of the shop.

'Well!' Nigel said, emerging from behind the counter. 'What do you make of that?'

'Prices higher than expected?' Victoria suggested.

He shook his head. 'It went further than that; she seemed more interested in who'd bought paintings than in the paintings themselves.'

'Wanting to keep up with the Joneses, perhaps. Well, win some, lose some. I doubt if we'll see her again.' And she turned to greet a new customer.

Blaircomrie

Beth had just returned from work when the doorbell rang and she was surprised to find the two detectives on the step.

'Good evening, Mrs Monroe,' DS Grant said genially. 'Sorry to bother you, but may we have a word?'

'Yes, of course.' She moved aside to let them in. 'Have you found out who killed him?'

He didn't reply immediately so, since Mr Barnes wouldn't be back for another hour, she showed them into the front room. 'Sit down,' she invited, and as they gingerly did so, she seated herself on one of the dining chairs.

Grant leant forward, his hands between his knees. 'To answer your question, ma'am, no, we haven't found the perpetrator, but unfortunately we've been experiencing some problems.'

'Oh?'

'To recap, you identified the deceased as Johnnie Stewart?'

Beth looked surprised. 'Yes, of course.'

'Had you any proof that was his name? A driving licence, for instance?'

'No,' she said slowly. 'Why?'

'You see, ma'am, our difficulty is that we've been unable to trace him.'

Beth looked at him blankly. 'I don't understand.'

'We started by searching missing persons records but drew a blank. Then as the search progressed it emerged that there's no John Stewart fitting his particulars on the electoral roll or any of the civil registers, so no birth or marriage certificate on file. He doesn't appear in medical or employment records, nor those relating to national insurance, rent, mortgage or tax. Nor does he appear to have had either a driving licence or a bank account.' He sat back, looking at her expectantly. 'Which is where we're hoping you can help us: firstly, did he own a car?'

She frowned, trying to process the information with which she'd been bombarded. 'Not as far as I know,' she said after a moment. 'I don't offer garaging and the only one that's ever been parked at the gate belongs to Mr Barnes.'

Odd how that had never struck her when they were out together; but then they'd never ventured far afield and it had seemed natural to walk. Grant was leaning forward again, his eyes intent on her face.

'So now we come to the crux of the matter: tell me, Mrs Monroe, how did he pay for his lodgings?'

She met his eyes almost defiantly. 'In cash,' she said.

Grant stared at her disbelievingly. 'He paid weekly?'

'No, monthly in advance.'

'That must have been a considerable amount; didn't you think it strange?'

'Not really. I simply banked it as I would a cheque.' She paused, moistening her lips. 'Are you saying he was some kind of criminal?'

'Not necessarily; the national police, fingerprint and DNA data-bases were also searched without success and he's not served a prison sentence. Quite frankly, Mrs Monroe, we've drawn a total blank. To all intents and purposes, Johnnie Stewart simply didn't exist.'

Beth stared at him, suddenly frightened. 'I don't understand,' she said again.

'Nor do we, ma'am.'

'But – I mean, that's ridiculous. Of course he existed!'

'Tell us again everything you know about him.'

Her eyes filled with sudden tears and she slammed down her hand. '*Nothing!*' she said in a choked voice. 'It seems I know absolutely nothing about him!'

'Did he never speak of his family, or where he used to live?'

She tried to force her mind back. 'When he first arrived he told me he was born in Dorset—'

'So he wasn't Scottish?' Grant interrupted.

'No; his mother was Australian and he grew up there.'

Grant cast his eyes at the ceiling. 'So he had an Aussie accent?'

'No, just . . . English.'

'Regional?'

She shook her head and continued, 'He returned to the UK to go to university—'

'Which one?' he broke in eagerly. Then, seeing her face, 'Don't tell me – he didn't say.'

'I'm afraid not.'

'And you're sure you don't know where he worked? He must at least have mentioned what line he was in?'

Again she shook her head, fumbling for a handkerchief.

Grant thought for a minute. 'You said before that he worked on Saturdays, which would rule out most office work. Could it have been manual, perhaps?'

'I don't *know*, I tell you! Please don't keep asking me!'

The two policemen exchanged a resigned look and rose to their feet.

'We should also warn you,' Grant said, moving towards the door, 'that from tomorrow an artist's impression – what is known as an e-fit – will be shown on TV and in the press asking for information. Damn it, *someone* must know who he was!'

Beth saw them out in silence, closed the front door and collapsed against it as a storm of trembling seized her. After a minute she drew a deep breath, brushed her hand across her eyes and went to phone Moira.

'What do you make of him paying his rent in cash, Sarge?' Coombes asked as they walked down the path.

'Same reason as she had to verify his signature before he'd actually signed, Jamie. Didn't want her to know his real name.'

Foxclere

Owen Jackson, a one-time business associate of Edward's, slid on to the stool beside him in the golf club bar, and, having ordered a drink, surprised him by asking, 'Am I right in assuming that was Gregory Lawrence's widow you introduced me to at the concert?'

Edward raised an eyebrow. 'She's never mentioned his name, but it's possible.'

'He was blown to smithereens in Egypt last year.'

'Ah. That was something she did mention.' He glanced at Owen curiously. 'Did you know him?'

'Not well, but I came across him now and again – the last time, actually, in Cairo shortly before his death.'

'What was he like?'

Owen shrugged. 'Good company, amusing, always on the *qui vive* and usually had a good-looking woman with him. Couldn't help liking him, but that's not to say I'd have trusted him too far.'

'Really? Why's that?'

'Just a gut feeling. He was something of a jack of all trades – in a different job every time we ran into each other, none of them top of the range. I had the impression he was operating well below his potential. Not that he was ever short of the odd buck, mind you. Family money, I suppose.' Owen drained his glass. 'I'd never met his wife, though. Attractive woman.'

'She's teaching me the piano,' Edward said, and Owen laughed. 'Sure!'

Before he could reaffirm the position they were joined by a couple of friends and the conversation dropped, but thinking it over later, Edward resolved to reinstate it when he got the chance. He was interested in finding out more about Gregory Lawrence.

Blaircomrie

Beth gazed at the drawing of Johnnie until the pixels separated into dots and danced in front of her eyes. Somehow, seeing it in black and white provided the final confirmation of his death, eliminating even the faintest possibility of his walking through the door, laughing at all the fuss.

He'd done a good job, the police artist. Only the eyes weren't quite right, no doubt because, she remembered with a shudder, they'd have been closed when he did the sketch. The clock in the hall chimed the half-hour and she recollected herself with a start. If she wasn't careful she'd be late for work.

Leaving the paper on the kitchen table, she hurried out of the house.

London

Paul Devonshire sat on the tube, numb with shock and oblivious to the noise around him, the strap-hangers who swayed into him, the rattling, shaking motion of the train. Someone, somewhere, was guilty of the most enormous cock-up, because he was ready to swear that the drawing in the paper in front of him was of Greg Lawrence. God dammit, he'd known the man almost from boyhood.

But how the hell could it be? Greg had been killed in Egypt almost a year ago. Had there been a misunderstanding of some kind? Had he got hold of the wrong end of the stick? But no, Viv had referred to his death, said it was Laura who'd told her – he couldn't have imagined it. With an effort, he dragged his eyes from the sketch to reread the paragraph beneath it, only the odd word penetrating his understanding. *Known locally as Johnnie Stewart.* Where the hell was 'locally'? He forced himself to concentrate. Somewhere in Scotland, apparently.

Obviously it *couldn't* be Greg, but they say everyone has a doppel-gänger . . . He stood up as the train drew into his station, and it was minutes later as he was jammed on the escalator, a conveyer belt packed with commuters, that another thunderclap struck him. *The Jake Farthing column!* Had Johnnie Whatshisname been responsible for that too, or was that stretching coincidence just too far?

Foxclere

'Georgia?'

'Richard! This is a surprise! It's usually Victoria who phones! How are you?'

'It's not a social call. Have you seen this morning's paper?'

'No, I'm just back from the school run. Why? Has World War Three broken out?'

'The equivalent. Have you got it to hand?'

'Yes, it's here on the table.'

'Then turn to page two.'

'You *are* being mysterious!' He imagined her tucking the phone under her chin and picking up the paper. 'Why don't you just tell me—' She broke off with a little gasp, and he waited, knowing she'd found the requisite page. 'My God, Rich, he looks just like Dad!' She ran her eyes rapidly down the print. '"Johnnie Stewart". What does it mean, "known locally as" – that it's not his real name?'

'I don't know what the hell it means. Where's Mother?'

'Downstairs, I presume. Her first pupil must be almost due. But she won't have seen this; she saves the paper till lunchtime.'

'Thank God for that. Can you get to her before one of her friends rings to remark on the resemblance?'

'And say what?'

'Use your initiative.'

'But it obviously can't *be* Dad.'

'Obviously.'

'Where are you?'

'In the school car park but I must go in; it's almost time for assembly. It's just that it'll be a shock for her, that's all, and it's best if you're with her when she sees it.'

'Very well,' Georgia said, her mouth dry.

*   *   *

Jill, answering the tap on the inner door, looked at her daughter in surprise.

'Can I come in for a minute, Mum?'

'Oh darling, this isn't a good time; Edward's due any minute. In fact, I thought—'

'Please. It's important.'

Jill sighed. 'Very well, but it'll have to be quick.'

She stood aside and Georgia went past her into the rear hall while her mother waited impatiently, her hand still on the door knob as though ready to open it again and usher her outside.

Georgia said gently, 'Come and sit down for a minute.'

'Georgia, I—'

Georgia took her arm and led her firmly into the sitting room. 'I have something to show you. It's nothing to worry about, but I'm afraid you'll find it upsetting.' And she pushed her gently into an armchair.

Jill's impatience gave way to alarm. 'Whatever is it? What's happened?'

Silently her daughter handed her the newspaper, folded to display the sketch of the dead man. Jill stared at it in total silence, the colour draining from her face.

'Obviously it isn't Dad,' Georgia said quickly, 'but it certainly looks like him. Did he have a brother? I don't remember him speaking of one, but—'

The clarion of the doorbell interrupted her and they both jumped. Before Jill could get to her feet Georgia hurried out to the main hall and opened the front door. The man on the step, preparing to enter, paused on seeing her. Georgia said rapidly, 'I'm so sorry but my mother has just had a shock. Would you mind postponing—'

'It's all right, Edward, please come in,' Jill said from behind her. 'This is Edward French, Georgia. My daughter, Edward.'

They nodded uneasily at each other, then Georgia turned to her mother. 'Mum, you really should—'

'I'm perfectly all right, darling, as you see. We'll speak later.'

And Georgia, dismissed, had no option but to return upstairs. Edward watched her go.

'Look, Jill, if you're not—'

'Come through, Edward. I've a new piece for you to try.'

Since she was obviously not prepared to discuss what had happened, he followed her down the hall. It was the first time they'd met since the concert and he'd been wondering if the evening spent together would affect the atmosphere between them. It seemed not; whether it was the shock her daughter had referred to or just a natural return to their pupil–teacher relationship, it was clear that it was to be very much business as usual. Edward was uncertain whether he was disappointed or relieved.

SEVEN

Foxclere

Jill was thankful that Edward's difficulties in playing the new piece took all her concentration, blotting out the memory of the folded newspaper in the sitting room. She'd written to thank him for the concert and felt no need to mention it again, for which, unsure of her self-control, she was also grateful. A strictly formal atmosphere was as much as she could handle.

When, at the end of the lesson, she had seen him out, she returned to the sitting room and, with shaking fingers, retrieved the paper. The face that looked back at her, while being, as Georgia had said, uncannily like Greg, was after all only a drawing; any resemblance must therefore be purely fortuitous. Her eyes moved to the paragraph below it.

Blaircomrie police are anxious for any information about the man shown in the above e-fit, whose body was found near the Stag and Thistle public house in the early hours of Friday 6 June. In particular, they would like to hear from anyone who might have seen him the previous evening, Thursday 5 June. Known locally as Johnnie Stewart, he is described as being in his fifties, of stocky build and with dark, greying hair. Police stress that any information will be treated in the strictest confidence. They can be contacted . . .

She dropped the paper back on chair and walked to the window, her arms hugging her chest as she gazed unseeingly at the sunlit garden. Hopefully someone would recognize a missing husband or father and come forward to claim him, putting an end to possibly months of worry. The fact that he'd been killed over two weeks ago and was still unidentified pointed to a longer absence than popping out for cigarettes and never coming home. And, curiously, he seemed to have been in the area long enough to become known, even if presumably not by his real name.

She turned away, glancing at her watch. She had half an hour until her next lesson; time for a cup of coffee. Georgia would be at *Plants R Us* until lunchtime, collecting Millie from play school on her way home. Until then she must marshal her whirling thoughts as best she could.

'Who could he possibly be, to look so like Dad?' Jill's voice was shaking.

'It's just one of those weird flukes, Mum,' Georgia said reassuringly. 'In the flesh the resemblance wouldn't be nearly as strong. I'm sorry I showed it to you now, but Richard wanted to be sure you had someone with you when you saw it.'

'That was thoughtful of him.'

Georgia handed her a glass of sherry but Jill hesitated. 'I don't usually drink at lunchtime,' she demurred.

'Medicinal purposes,' Georgia said firmly.

'Dutch courage, more like.'

Georgia raised an eyebrow. 'Is it needed?'

'I'm going out this evening – a fortieth anniversary party – and no doubt everyone will have seen the paper.'

'Did they know Dad? After all, he wasn't around that much.'

'Some of them certainly did.'

'Well, play it by ear. Don't bring it up, but if they mention it, just agree it looks quite like him. Now, you are staying for lunch, aren't you?'

And Jill, grateful for her daughter's common sense, accepted her invitation.

With Greg so often working away from home, Jill had become used to being the odd one out at dinner parties even while he was alive, and had long since overcome any feelings of awkwardness.

She had a wide circle of friends and was comfortable in her single-ness, whether as wife or widow.

This evening, however, was different, and despite Georgia's advice she felt apprehensive. The sketch in the paper had unsettled her, bringing her husband very much to mind, and as she prepared for the party she felt unaccountably close to tears.

The phone rang as she was putting on her lipstick. 'Hi, Jill, it's Daphne. We wondered if you'd like a lift to the Trents'? We'll be passing your door and as Bill has foresworn alcohol for the evening, it would leave you free to imbibe.'

Jill felt a surge of gratitude. 'That would be great, Daphne; thank you.'

'Pick you up in twenty minutes, then.'

So at least she wouldn't have to walk in by herself, wondering if the assembled company had been discussing the e-fit and her reaction to it.

In the event, it was dealt with as painlessly as Georgia had predicted.

'That murdered man in Scotland must have given you a jolt,' someone commented casually as they went through to eat. 'From what I recall, he had quite a look of your husband.'

'There was a resemblance, certainly,' Daphne cut in quickly, 'but Greg was much better looking!' And with smiles of agreement, the subject was dropped.

Stonebridge

The twins' birthday party was in full swing and Amélie, who had been petted by a succession of motherly little girls, had begun to wilt.

'Take her into the sitting room, Will,' Julia suggested. 'The noise should be fairly muted there and with luck she'll fall asleep on the sofa. Here, take the paper with you. Sorry it's yesterday's; we've not had time to look at it yet.'

'Thanks, we didn't get round to it either,' Will admitted. 'I sometimes wonder why we bother, with the news on TV and the Internet so much more recent. Would you mind if I had a go at the crossword?'

Julia laughed. 'Feel free. We're just about to have tea,' she added. 'I'll send David in with a cuppa and a plate of sandwiches.'

It was ten minutes later that David pushed open the sitting room door, a mug of tea in one hand and a piled plate in the other. Amélie was lying on the sofa, thumb in mouth and eyes closed. Will, standing by the window holding a newspaper, looked up as his brother entered.

'You've not seen yesterday's paper, have you?'

David set the cup and plate down quietly so as not to wake the baby. 'No, didn't have the time. Why? Something interesting?'

'The weirdest thing; there's a picture of a guy here and he's the spitting image of Dad.'

David went to join him. 'God, he is, isn't he? Who is he?'

'He's been calling himself Johnnie Stewart, but the implication is that it's not his real name.'

'What's he done?'

'Got himself stabbed.'

David frowned. 'Dead, you mean?'

'Yep.' They stood together looking down at the sketch.

'It would be interesting to do a comparison,' Will said. 'He might be a long-lost uncle. Have you got Mum's old albums?'

'Yes, we brought them back when we removed her personal things last weekend. They're in one of the boxes in the spare room.'

'Let's dig them out after the party, though I seem to remember there weren't many of Dad, presumably because he had the camera. But there's the framed photo she had by her bed. Did you bring that as well?'

'Must have done. Julia dealt with the bedroom; she's sure to have packed it.'

'Oh, there you are.' Julia herself was in the doorway. 'The twins are about to cut the cake; can you come and record the event? You too, Will; Amélie will be all right for a minute or two, won't she?'

Will nodded and, having anchored the sleeping baby with a couple of cushions, followed his brother out of the room.

It was as the last little guests were leaving that Henry and Nina phoned from Naples to wish their great-granddaughters happy birthday. After the traditional song had come over the line and the girls had recited a list of the presents they'd received, constantly interrupting each other, David took the phone from them.

'Hello there! Naples coming up to expectations?' The couple had rung several times during their holiday, Nina still feeling guilty at leaving her family and needing the reassurance that all was well.

'It's fantastic!' she enthused. 'We've seen Vesuvius and had a day trip to Pompeii. I warn you, we'll bore you rigid with photographs when we get back!'

'Can't wait! And talking of photos, there's an extraordinary picture in the paper today of a man who's been stabbed in Scotland, and you wouldn't believe it but he looks just like Dad! I'll save it to show you. The police are asking if anyone can identify him. Hang on, Julia wants a word.'

He passed the phone to his wife and turned to the twins, who were rolling on the carpet in a fit of giggles. 'Take Amélie into the garden and show her your new toys. But remember she's only little and be gentle with her.'

As Julia ended the call, Sylvie said curiously, 'What was that about a picture in the paper?'

'We've not had a chance to tell you,' Will replied. 'Come and see if you think this looks like photos you've seen of Dad.'

The two women dutifully studied the grainy paper. 'The only one I've seen is the framed one by Sally's bed,' Julia said, 'and though I packed it with everything else last week, I didn't really look at it.'

'And I don't think I've even seen one,' Sylvie added.

'Then come upstairs and we'll dig Mum's albums out of the boxes and look through them. And while we're at it, we'll see if there's one of Dave on a bearskin rug!'

They sat in a group in the spare room, the two women perched on the bed, the men squatting on the floor as they pulled item after item out of the boxes and carrier bags that surrounded them. At the bottom of one box they found three or four albums and seized on them eagerly, but the first few contained only snaps of the brothers growing up, from babies to toddlers to schoolboys. However, the last, and earliest, one had some half-dozen pages filled with shots of Sally laughing up at the photographer in various locations, interspersed with a few of a young man titled *Larry at Castle Howard, Larry at Whitby, Easter 1977* and so on. And though all four of them peered intently at the fading prints, it was impossible to make out his features with any clarity.

'Where's the wedding album?' Julia asked suddenly. 'There must be one, surely?'

The men looked at each other, frowning. 'I don't remember one,' Will commented.

'They hadn't much money at the time,' David said slowly. 'Perhaps they did it on the cheap and asked friends to take photos.'

'Then where are those photos?'

'There's nothing else in this box,' Will said. 'Perhaps it got separated and ended up somewhere else.'

A further search produced the framed photograph Julia had mentioned, but it hadn't been taken professionally and it too had started to fade. Even so, they were able to detect a definite likeness to the newspaper print.

David pulled a carrier bag towards him. 'These are the things I cleared from Mum's desk – let's see if they help.' He began to extract them. 'Here's her passport . . . and a stack of bank statements . . . and some invoices for surgical supplies. Ah, this envelope looks more hopeful; it's full of certificates.'

He drew them out, glanced quickly through them and frowned. 'That's odd; Mum's birth certificate is here and another copy of her will and various nursing and chiropody qualifications. But no marriage certificate or, come to that, anything relating to Dad.'

They looked at each other in bewilderment. 'Perhaps your father kept them himself?' Sylvie suggested.

'Not his own death certificate,' David pointed out. 'There has to be another box or bag somewhere, but it's odd they're not all together. Mum was pretty efficient. Dad certainly left a will, because we each got a very welcome lump sum when we reached eighteen.'

'We're sure to come across them,' Julia said soothingly, 'but I think we'd better call a halt for the moment; it's time to bath the twins and get them ready for bed. They're over-excited and it will take a while to calm them down.'

'And we must be going,' Sylvie said. 'Amélie's nap revived her, but it's past her bedtime.'

The men got to their feet, easing their cramped legs. 'Not a very fruitful exercise,' David commented. 'Far from satisfying our curiosity, it's raised further questions.'

'All will be revealed, no doubt,' Will said, and with those unanswered questions circling in their heads, they went back downstairs.

Foxclere

Richard Lawrence had always prided himself on being a man of moderation, in control of himself at all times. Love was a word that seldom entered his thoughts; if pressed, he would say he loved his mother, by which he meant he felt deep affection for her and a desire to protect her. He was also 'very fond' of his wife and enjoyed their rather sedate love-making without being in any sense swept away by it. Until now he had presumed, without thinking too deeply about it, that she felt the same.

But though ridiculing any idea of being 'in love', a sensation he doubted he'd ever experienced, there was no denying that Maria Chiltern had turned his world upside down. It was now a month since he'd stopped for her at the bus stop, little realizing the consequences of his actions, and two weeks since their trip to the ice-cream parlour. In that time she'd pervaded his every thought like an insidious illness. He woke sweating from dreams of her – dreams that on waking shamed him – and he was obscurely worried that if he found himself alone with her he might not be able to resist her.

This inner turmoil and its outward manifestations had not passed unnoticed; Victoria, he knew, had been surprised by the sudden change in and frequency of their love-making.

'I'm . . . sorry,' he had stammered after one particularly tempestuous coupling, and she'd been quick to reassure him.

'Darling, don't apologize – it was wonderful!'

'Really?'

'Of course!'

Her reaction had surprised and disconcerted him, and he had briefly wondered if he'd been disappointing her over the years by his lack of passion, before shying away from further analysis.

That Monday afternoon he'd been about to leave his room when there was a tap on the door, and on opening it, as though his thoughts had conjured her up, he came face-to-face with Maria herself. Disconcerted by her sudden appearance, he stared at her in silence, uncomfortably aware of a flush creeping up his neck.

'I'm sorry to disturb you, Mr Lawrence,' she said quickly, little knowing, he thought wryly, how much she did indeed disturb him, 'but I was wondering if I could ask you a favour?'

He cleared his throat. 'I've a class almost due.'

'I'll make it brief, then. It's my husband's birthday in a week or two and I'd really like to arrange some golf lessons for him.' She gave a little laugh. 'Depending on how much they cost, of course. You mentioned playing at a club and I was hoping you might be able to advise me the best one to approach?'

'It's purely a matter of choice,' he blustered, 'but I really haven't—'

'I'm sorry,' she broke in, 'bad timing! Perhaps we could have a word after school? Toby's going to tea with a friend so he won't need collecting.'

Richard's mouth was dry. 'As I said, it depends on various factors, but I have played at several of the local ones; I suppose I could take you . . .' His voice tailed off uncertainly but her face lit up with that enchanting smile.

'That's so good of you! Thank you so much! I'll wait in the car park, shall I?'

He nodded, edging past her with a mumbled, 'Now you really must excuse me . . .' and hurried down the corridor. Maria stood looking after him for a moment. Then, with a little nod of satisfaction, she turned in the direction of her own classroom.

God, he must be out of his mind! Richard was thinking as he made his way to the hall. What hope had he of freeing himself from what was rapidly becoming an obsession if he kept meeting the girl on a social footing? He should simply have told her to go online and phone whichever club seemed the most convenient; there was absolutely no necessity to become involved. As things were, he was laying himself open to an unspecified amount of time alone with her and God only knew what that would do to his equilibrium, already in a state of flux over that bloody man in the paper who looked so unnervingly like Father.

Why, he wondered despairingly, had life suddenly become so complicated?

Stonebridge

David's mobile vibrated in his pocket and he swore softly at the interruption. He was drawing up a complicated will for a wealthy client, endeavouring to incorporate all his stipulations while at the same time ensuring there could be no room for misinterpretation.

Pulling out his phone, he was surprised to see his grandfather's name on the screen. It was only two days since he'd called during the party.

'Grandpa?'

Henry's voice was grave. 'David: I don't want to worry you, but I need to speak to you and Will as soon as possible.'

David's chest tightened. 'What's happened? It isn't Gran, is it?'

'No, no, your grandmother's fine.'

'Then I don't understand. You're due back in another week; surely—'

'Actually we're home now; we cut short our trip and flew back yesterday.'

Foreboding closed over him. 'But – why?'

'We'll explain when we see you. Could I leave you to arrange with Will to come round this evening, at about seven? I know it's short notice, but it really is urgent.'

'Yes, of course, but can't you give me—?'

'Till this evening, then. Goodbye, David.'

Foxclere

She was waiting by his car, as she had said she would. He'd stayed on an extra few minutes to finish some marking and to allow the main exodus of staff to disperse so there was no one else around. He nodded to her briefly, unlocked the car, and the minute she'd fastened her seat belt switched on the engine and accelerated out of the car park on to the road.

'I really do appreciate this,' Maria said. 'I know I could have made enquiries myself, but I'm not sure what questions to ask.'

'Depends what you want to know,' he replied, more curtly than he'd intended, and felt her quick glance.

'I did look up some clubs, but I still don't know the area very well and I wasn't sure which would be the most convenient.'

'They have websites setting out what's on offer and where they're located,' Richard said. And suddenly knew beyond doubt that she'd already checked this for herself, which could only mean that she was aware of his interest and playing him for her own amusement. Rage spread over him that he should have fallen so easily into her trap.

'So why are you really asking for my help?' he added coldly.

There was a long silence. Then she said very quietly, 'Please could you pull over? I'd like to get out.'

'Changed your mind already?'

'Why are you being like this?' she asked softly, a catch in her voice. 'You were so kind and helpful before that I hoped you wouldn't mind—'

'—if you took advantage?'

'I've obviously completely misread the situation,' she said in a low voice. 'I can only apologize. It was just . . .' She broke off, biting her lip.

'Just what?'

'That I haven't many friends here and I'd fooled myself – but I should have known better. After all, you have a position to maintain and I'm just – well, a lowly member of staff. Obviously you—' She choked to a halt. 'Please pull over. Please!'

He swerved to the side of the road, startling a driver about to overtake him, and skidded to a halt, sitting with his hands gripping the steering wheel as she fumbled with the catch of her seat belt and opened the door. Out on the pavement she bent down to look into the car but he stared straight ahead.

'I'm . . . sorry,' she said, and turned blindly away. He watched her in the rear-view mirror as she hurried back along the pavement. Then he closed his eyes, waiting for his breathing to slow down. Suppose he'd misjudged her? he thought in anguish. Suppose after all she really did want his input, and because of his paranoia he'd thrown it back in her face?

For a wild moment he considered getting out of the car and going after her. But traffic was building up and he appeared to be on a yellow line. Mind churning and heart thundering, he started the car.

Blaircomrie

Beth could hear the phone ringing as she returned from work and hastily fumbled to open the door and reach it before it stopped.

'Mrs Monroe? This is DS Grant, Blaircomrie police.'

'Yes?' she said breathlessly.

'I'm just calling to let you know *Crimewatch* will be featuring a reconstruction of the stabbing on Tuesday the first of July. Let's hope it leads to someone coming forward.'

'Do you think it might?'

'It's our best chance at the moment. I suppose nothing's arrived for him in the post, from relatives, say, who've been unable to contact him?'

'No, nothing, but he never had any post.'

Grant's sigh came over the wire. 'Why am I not surprised?' he said.

EIGHT

Stonebridge

'I don't *know*, Will!' David said for the second time.

'But it must be something serious for them to fly home early,' Will said worriedly. 'They were all right on Saturday, weren't they? Something must have happened since, but what?'

'Your guess is as good as mine. By the way, I phoned Mum's solicitors this morning and asked them if they were holding any certificates relating to Dad, but they're not.'

'They must be in one of those boxes,' Will said.

David had collected him as arranged in a quick phone call and they were now driving through the early evening traffic towards

Harrogate, on the outskirts of which their grandparents lived. The day had been close and airless and now purple clouds were banking in the east.

'Looks as though we're in for a storm,' he added.

'Not metaphorically, I hope,' David commented. He switched on the radio and they drove in silence for a while. 'He said Gran was OK,' he remarked suddenly, 'but I never thought to ask about *him*, and he did have that heart scare last year. You don't think . . .?'

'We'll soon know,' Will said grimly.

The first heavy drops of rain were falling as, twenty minutes later, they turned into their grandparents' drive, and Henry was at the open front door to greet them. He was tanned from his holiday, but there were bags under his eyes and he looked strained.

'Come in, come in,' he said. 'Gran has some sandwiches ready in case you didn't have time to eat.'

Nina came bustling forward, hugging them tightly in turn. 'It's so good to see you,' she said, her voice shaking, and their alarm deepened. 'Come and sit down; there's some food on a tray and—'

Will spoke for both of them. 'Gran, we won't be able to eat till we hear what all this is about.'

Henry indicated the sitting room and they went in and seated themselves expectantly. Having furnished them with drinks he sat down and leant forward, his hands clasped between his knees. 'There's no easy way to say this,' he began, 'but we have reason to believe that the man who was stabbed in Scotland was your father.'

Into the shocked silence the hall clock started to chime, making them jump. When no one spoke, Henry continued, 'We feared the worst when you mentioned the artist's impression on the phone, and immediately checked online. Seeing the e-fit for ourselves left little room for doubt.' He paused, then continued heavily, 'Obviously we had to come home at once in case his real identity came to light before we'd a chance to speak to you.' He brushed a hand across his face. 'I wish to God I didn't have to tell you all this.'

David forced himself to speak, his voice seeming to echo round his head. 'He was killed in a train crash in France, just before Will was born.'

'No,' Henry said gently, 'he wasn't.'

Will said in a low voice, 'You're saying Mum lied to us all these years?'

Nina made a sound, her hands going to her mouth.

'She wanted to shield you from the truth,' Henry said sadly. 'Made us promise never to tell you, and in normal circumstances there'd have been no need for you to know.'

'So what *is* the truth?' David asked in a new, hard voice.

Henry gave a deep sigh. 'Your father was at Durham University in the seventies and Sally met him at a party during her nursing training. They started going out together and for a year or so were very close. She even brought him to see us once. He was handsome and charming, and it might be hindsight but I believe we had our reservations even then.'

'So what happened?' Will prompted, when his grandfather came to a halt.

'What happened was that he graduated and went back down south. Sally was heartbroken, but they were both young and we told ourselves she'd get over it. And she seemed to: she passed her exams and started work at the hospital and a couple of years went by. Various young men were mentioned but she never brought them home and none of them lasted very long.

'Then one day she rang up, bubbling with excitement. "Guess what?" she said. "Larry's back! He'll be working up here for the next couple of months. Isn't that great?"

'Well, we didn't think it was great, but told ourselves that perhaps it would work out this time. The next we heard he was staying at her flat – saving on digs, no doubt. Then his stint of work ended, he returned home, and a few weeks later Sally told us she was pregnant. I was all for contacting Larry and making him face up to his responsibilities, but she wouldn't hear of it. "It's no good unless he wants to," she said. So in due course David was born and your grandmother looked after him while Sally continued working at the hospital.'

'But what about me?' Will broke in. 'I was born thirteen months after Dave.'

'He came back, didn't he?' Henry said bitterly. 'Another stint of work. Quite proud of his baby son, by all accounts, so he repeated the exercise.' His voice hardened. 'He was still around when Sally found she was pregnant again, and this time she did suggest they marry.' Henry sat back in his chair, looking round at his audience. 'At which point he calmly informed her he was already married.'

'The bastard!' David said softly.

'Don't think too harshly of your mother,' Nina begged. 'Whatever our opinion of him, Larry was the love of her life and she was prepared to take whatever he offered until she learned he was married. Then she sent him packing and never saw him again, but to give him his due he paid a considerable amount into her bank account, on the understanding it should be divided between the three of you. She invested your portions until you each reached eighteen.'

A handful of rain rattled against the windows and thunder growled in the distance. Nina got up to switch on the light and they blinked in the sudden brightness. There was a short silence while they tried to digest what they'd heard. Eventually David said, 'If he was married why hasn't his wife identified him, and why is he calling himself Johnnie Stewart?'

Henry lifted his shoulders. 'I've no idea.'

'But there's still the possibility he *isn't* the man in the paper?' Will pressed.

'A faint one, I suppose.'

'Could he have had a brother, perhaps?'

'He could.'

'Poor Mum,' David said softly. 'What a slap in the face for her.'

'Yes; we decided a fresh start was called for, so we all upped sticks. She left Durham, we left Thirsk and we moved down here. Sally changed her surname to his, largely for your sakes, and re-trained as a chiropodist so that, with two small children, she could work from home. We'd suggested we all live together, at least for a while, but she was used to having her own place and determined to be independent.'

Nina looked from one grandson to the other. 'Darlings, we're so sorry you've had to find out this way, especially so soon after her death.'

Will made a dismissive gesture. 'The question is what do we do now? Tell the Scottish police we can identify him?'

'So from nobody knowing the truth about Dad, including us, now everyone will – our friends, our business colleagues, our kids . . .' David's voice tailed off.

Nina laid a hand over his. 'I'm so sorry,' she whispered again.

Henry stood up. 'Will's right, we must contact the police. I made a note of the number so I suggest we get on to them straight away, tell them what we know and find out what – if anything – is required of us.'

Foxclere

Nigel was late returning from lunch and Victoria, busy with some customers, was aware of his concealed excitement. However, she'd no option but to contain her curiosity since the couple she was dealing with were choosing a ruby wedding present. Several times they'd been on the point of deciding on a painting when another had caught their eye and the whole process began again.

It was another half-hour before the definitive choice was made and the customers left to collect their car and drive to the rear of the premises for their purchase to be loaded into it.

'Now,' Victoria said, as they folded corrugated cardboard round the corners of the frame and carefully wrapped it in brown paper, 'why were you looking so smug when you came back from lunch?'

'I've been playing detective,' he said. 'You'll never guess who I saw downtown.'

'Then I won't waste time trying. Come on, tell me.'

'Our friend from the café over the road.'

Victoria paused, sticky tape in hand. 'Really? Where was he?'

'Coming out of the office block next to the bank. So on the spur of the moment I decided to tail him.'

'Go on.'

'Well, he went into the White Horse, obviously for a pub lunch, so I followed him and sat down at the next table.'

'Suppose he'd recognized you?'

Nigel shrugged. 'It wouldn't have mattered if he had; it would never have occurred to him that I was following him. *However*,' he went on, his voice heavy with portent, 'you'll never believe who joined him.'

'Will you stop being so annoying!'

Before he could continue there was the agreed toot from the yard behind the shop and he carried the unwieldy package out to the car. Victoria was waiting impatiently for his return.

'So, who was it who joined him?'

'The woman who claimed to be interested in local artists.'

Victoria stared at him. 'My God! So they're in cahoots!'

'It looks like it, though to what end I can't imagine. Anyway, *she* might well have recognized me, so I kept my face turned away after that.'

'I don't suppose they said anything incriminating?' Victoria asked hopefully.

'Hardly; they were discussing some meeting they had to go to. But I did get their names – their first names, anyway. He went to order their drinks and she called after him, "Bernard – better make it a small glass." And later when they were arguing about something, he said, "I told you before, Tina, that won't work."'

'Well done, Sherlock,' Victoria said dryly. 'That's not going to get us very far.'

'I just thought you'd be interested to hear that they know each other.'

'Oh, I'm interested, all right. The point is, of course, we've no way of knowing, let alone proving, that they had anything to do with the break-in attempt.'

'Well, I did glean something else; the meeting they were discussing apparently concerned a disputed insurance claim, so when I left the pub I went back to the building Bernard had come out of and looked at the brass plates outside. And guess what? One of the occupants is Selby and Frodsham, Insurance Brokers.'

'Ah! Now that *could* be useful.' She took out her mobile, searched for the number and then called it.

'What are you doing?' Nigel hissed, and she made a shushing gesture.

'Yes, hello,' she said into the phone. 'Could I speak to Bernard, please? I'm sorry, I can't remember his surname. Davies? Yes, that's it.' She gave Nigel a thumbs up. 'It's Mavis Trilby calling.'

Mavis Trilby? he mouthed with exaggeratedly raised eyebrows.

'Yes, I'll hold,' Victoria said blithely and cut the connection. 'Bernard Davies. Now we can look him up on the local register.'

'Hey, slow down!' Nigel protested. 'For all we know the man hasn't done anything except buy his girlfriend a pub lunch!'

'But if anything else suspicious happens, at least we'll have something to go on,' Victoria said with satisfaction.

Stonebridge

Two Scottish detectives drove down to Stonebridge the next day, where David and Will, having arranged time off work, awaited them. They brought with them photographs of 'the deceased' and seemed disconcerted that, not having known their father, neither man could make a definite identification. There was, though, as they all agreed, a notable resemblance to the man in Sally's album.

'And he has quite a look of you too, sir,' the more senior officer, who'd introduced himself as DS Grant, said to David.

'I'm sure you'll appreciate this is highly embarrassing for us,' David replied, pouring coffee and handing it round. 'Until last night we believed our father had died over thirty years ago. We still haven't got our heads round it.'

'And now?' queried Grant.

David glanced at his brother. 'It seems likely the photos are of the same man.'

'What can you tell us about your father?'

'Virtually nothing. His name was Laurence Gregory; he met our mother at Durham University and . . . they fell in love.'

'We were told he died in a train crash just before I was born,' Will intercepted. 'Which we now learn isn't true.'

'What about his family?' the detective asked, stirring his coffee. 'Where did he come from originally?'

'I can ask my grandfather but I doubt if he'll know; he just said he went back "down south".'

'There was no mention of his having lived in Australia?'

The brothers looked surprised. 'Not that we heard.'

'But you must know *something*!' Grant said a little impatiently. 'Your mother must have spoken of him, surely?'

'She said he was clever and witty and made her laugh, and she told us stories of things they did together and how he used to fool around, but there was nothing . . . concrete.'

'And that satisfied you?'

'We thought it upset her to speak about him – which it probably did.'

'So you've no idea if he has any other living relatives?'

'None whatsoever.'

'Or what he's been doing for the last thirty years?'

'Obviously not.'

'Not even what line of work he went into?'

'No.'

The two policemen exchanged an exasperated look.

'So what happens now?' David asked after a pause.

'We'll need you to make written statements.'

'Both of us?' Will objected. 'They'd be identical – we were told at the same time.'

'Nonetheless, sir. Whatever you may suppose, no two accounts are ever the same.'

Unconvinced, the brothers sat at the dining table and recorded what their grandfather had told them, handing the signed accounts to DC Coombes as requested.

Grant cleared his throat. 'The only conclusive way of proving the deceased is or is not your father is by comparing your DNA with his. Would you be prepared to give samples?'

David hesitated. 'What would that involve?'

'Accompanying us to your local police station where we can obtain mouth swabs.'

David glanced at Will, who nodded. 'Then yes, of course; we need to know.'

'Suppose one of us matches and the other doesn't?' Will asked uneasily.

'That would be something you'd have to deal with, sir,' Grant said impassively.

An hour later the policemen were on their way back to Scotland and the brothers went for a pub lunch before returning to their respective offices.

'No wonder there was no marriage or death certificate,' Will said bitterly. 'I can't believe we never suspected anything.'

'No reason why we should,' David pointed out. 'His name's on our birth certificates – I checked mine last night when I got home.'

'You'd think he'd have shown *some* interest in us – how we were growing up, what we were doing and so on.'

'From what Gran said, it sounds as though he and Mum didn't part on the best of terms after she found he was married, but at least he made provision for us. We'd have had a much tougher time at uni without it.'

Will's thoughts moved on. 'I wonder why he was stabbed.'

'And what he was doing in Scotland, masquerading as Johnnie Stewart.'

'A man of mystery, our father. And I can't help wishing he'd remained so.'

Foxclere

By Wednesday morning Richard could stand it no longer. He had spent two wretched nights tossing and turning, and at school was permanently braced against the possibility of seeing Maria and the ensuing embarrassment.

By now he had convinced himself that he'd behaved unforgivably and not at all as she'd had a right to expect after their previous encounters. *You were so kind and helpful before*, she'd said. What had got into him? And how could he rectify it? In the normal course of the school day their paths never crossed, which was why he'd barely recognized her at the bus stop that day. So how could he engineer a meeting in order to allow him to apologize?

Hoping to corner her he went to the staff dining room for lunch, but to his chagrin she didn't appear. However, returning to his room afterwards, he turned a corner and almost bumped into her. She looked upset, and to his horror on seeing him her eyes filled with tears.

'Maria!' he exclaimed involuntarily, forgetting they were not on first name terms. 'Has something happened?'

She shook her head, obviously flustered, and made to pass him but he caught hold of her arm. 'You don't look well,' he said. 'Come and sit down for a while and get your breath back.'

She made a token resistance, then allowed herself to be led to his room where he closed the door and stood looking at her. 'What's wrong?' he asked quietly.

Tears spilled down her cheek and she brushed them impatiently aside. 'I'm sorry, I'm being extremely silly. You just . . . caught me at a bad moment.' He waited and after a pause, not looking at him, she continued. 'The Head sent for me just before lunch and I . . . I foolishly got in quite a state about it. I thought you must have reported me for harassing you and he was going to ask me to . . . leave.' She looked up then, meeting his startled gaze. 'Of course, it wasn't that at all, so thank you for not doing. The tears were only of relief, I assure you.'

She turned swiftly towards the door but he caught her arm.

'I behaved very unreasonably,' he said. 'I'd no call whatever to speak to you the way I did and I was intending to apologize, but I never dreamt it could cause any upset.' He could feel her trembling under his hand and his throat was dry. He forced a smile. 'So let's put the clock back to Monday and yes, Mrs Chiltern, of course I'll show you the local golf clubs—'

He broke off as she made a little choked sound and shook her head. 'The point is you were right,' she whispered.

'Right?' His voice clogged in his throat.

'I *had* already researched the clubs, I was just using them as an excuse to . . . to see you.' She looked up at him then, tearfully defiant. 'So perhaps you *had* better report me.'

'But I don't . . . it was because . . .' he stammered, and broke off with a gasp as she caught hold of his face and kissed him on the mouth. Then, before he could collect himself, she turned and fled.

Having shown out the last pupil of the afternoon, Jill went into her sitting room, opened the bureau drawer and took out the cutting of the dead man, experiencing, as she did each time she looked at it, a shock of recognition. Yet of *course* it couldn't be Greg; he'd died last year and his estate had been wound up. It was pointless to keep torturing herself like this, but the sketch was so unnervingly like him that she knew she'd have no peace till she learned who this man was. Where was his family and why hadn't they made contact? She shuddered. No one deserved to lie for weeks in a mortuary with no one to mourn them.

The e-fit had been shown on TV as police widened their appeal, and several of her friends had commented on the likeness, sympathizing with her over the distress this must cause and commenting that everyone was supposed to have a double but you didn't expect to come across him.

Stories of doppelgängers and identical twins separated at birth, a favourite ploy in fiction, had fluttered briefly in her head and been impatiently dismissed. Greg had been an only child and she couldn't count on any bizarre theories to provide a solution. A hitherto unknown cousin was the farthest she'd allow herself to consider.

Should she, she wondered, mention this remote possibility to the Scottish police? They would already have been inundated with possible identities from the usual cranks and those craving attention; an unknown cousin would doubtless come into the same category.

With a sigh she replaced the cutting, closed the drawer and went to make herself a cup of tea.

Stonebridge

'Charlotte and I decided it's time for another girls' night out,' Alexa said brightly as they prepared to open the shop. 'How are you fixed tomorrow, Jules?'

'Oh . . . I don't know,' Julia procrastinated. 'Things are a bit topsy-turvy at the moment.'

'All the more reason to escape!' Charlotte said. 'Come on, Jules, it's ages since we had one. You've got a live-in nanny so you've no excuse and there's that new Thai restaurant I've been wanting to try out. Shall I book a table for about eight o'clock?'

Julia smiled a little reluctantly. 'OK, I suppose I could do with a break; things have been rather getting on top of me lately.'

Her friends exchanged knowing glances and behind her back Alexa gave a thumbs up.

'Consider it done,' Charlotte said with satisfaction.

The good food and wine combined with low lighting were conducive to relaxing, and this in turn led to an exchange of confidences. Charlotte started the ball rolling with the news that her ex, with whom she'd remained on good terms, was about to re-marry and she'd been surprised how much this had upset her.

'It's not as though we were ever going to get back together,' she said, 'but we still phoned each other if there was a film we wanted to see or a garden to visit. It feels like being single all over again.'

'Have you met her?' Alexa enquired.

Charlotte pulled a face. 'No, but I've seen her. She's a good fifteen years younger than I am – heels like stilts and that casual, expensively coiffured hair.' She smiled self-mockingly. 'I took an instant dislike to her, but in all seriousness she's not his type and I don't see it working.'

'I hope you didn't tell him that!' Julia said.

'Not in so many words, but I made some throwaway comment about age differences. I must have sounded like a shrew.'

'I know what you mean,' Alexa remarked, refilling their glasses. 'I felt like that after both my break-ups.' She smiled. 'This is where Jules looks superior!'

Julia shook her head.

'Oh, honey!' Charlotte laid a quick hand on hers. 'Is that what's been upsetting you these last weeks – apart from your mother-in-law's death, I mean?'

But Julia was after all not ready to talk about David. 'It's not that,' she said quickly, 'but there's been complete upheaval in the family; it turns out David and Will's father didn't die years ago as they thought. In fact, he was probably that man in Scotland whose stabbing has been in the news.'

Her friends stared at her aghast. 'How on earth could that happen?'

Julia took a fortifying sip of wine. 'When that e-fit or whatever it's called was in the paper, we all thought he looked incredibly like the photo of Larry that had always stood by Sally's bed. And when David mentioned it to his grandparents the whole story came out, about them being illegitimate and his mother changing their names and God knows what else.'

'But . . . is there any way to prove this? I mean, have they told the police?'

She nodded. 'Two detectives came down yesterday to take their DNA for comparison with the dead man's. We won't get confirmation one way or the other for some time.'

'But what was he doing in Scotland calling himself Johnnie whoever it was?'

Julia shrugged. 'I haven't the faintest.'

There was a pause while they all thought it over. Then Alexa said, 'How are David and his brother taking it?'

'They feel their whole life has been a lie, with both their mother and their grandparents keeping the truth from them. Apparently she made her parents promise not to tell them and didn't see any reason for them ever to know. And they probably never would have, if this man hadn't got himself stabbed.'

'So all you can do now is wait for the results?'

Julia nodded. 'Though what good it will do I really don't know; I doubt if there's a family fortune waiting to be claimed.'

'One can always hope!' Charlotte said, and the subject was tactfully dropped.

Foxclere

Maria was absent the next day, and a casual enquiry elicited the information that she'd phoned in sick and Toby's father had delivered him to school.

After a third sleepless night and knowing he couldn't afford a fourth, Richard checked the website to confirm her address, and when the bell for lunch sounded he quickly collected his car and drove to her home. Having delivered her there that first day he'd no trouble finding it and pulled in a few yards short of her house. His heart was crashing around his chest and his breathing laboured, but, he told himself, this situation had to be settled one way or the other, and screwing his courage to the sticking point, he got out, walked along the short stretch of pavement and turned in her gate.

She opened the door almost at once, catching her breath at the sight of him.

'Are you going to invite me in or do we have to sort this out on the step?' he asked, and she stood silently to one side, closing the door behind him. They stood facing each other in the narrow hallway and since she made no attempt to speak, he said, 'I hear you're not well; what's wrong?'

'Do you really have to ask?' He had to lean forward in order to hear her. 'If you've come to demand an apology, you're more than welcome to it.'

'That isn't why I've come.'

She continued as though she hadn't heard him. 'I'm an idiot, I know that, and I'm truly, truly sorry I made such an exhibition of myself and put you in this embarrassing position. But unless you're going to dismiss me – and I certainly couldn't blame you if you do – I'll be back in my classroom tomorrow, all calm and collected, and won't trouble you again.'

All the speeches he had so laboriously rehearsed deserted him and the best Richard could manage was 'Maria . . .'

A fleeting expression of what looked surprisingly like relief crossed her face but before he could analyse it she made an incoherent murmur and moved swiftly into his arms.

They hadn't had long; after a frenzied coming together Richard had dressed hurriedly and left with no further caress.

Maria lay where he'd left her on the guest room bed, reflecting on the past twenty minutes. Cold fish Richard Lawrence most definitely was not – at least not in the physical sense. Emotionally he was still a closed book to her. There had been no words of endearment – barely any words at all – but she had the impression that she'd been as necessary to him as he was to her, and on that basis she was certain their unbalanced relationship would continue.

But she'd had a bad fright when he had challenged her in the car, sure she'd misinterpreted his feelings and fearful he would report her and she'd have to explain to Mike why she'd been so ignominiously dismissed. The relief of seeing him on her doorstep had been overwhelming but she was still far from sure of his opinion of her. One thing at least she could count on; he would not be reporting her to the Head. He had too much to lose himself.

NINE

The following Tuesday a reconstruction of 'Johnnie's' last evening was aired nationwide on *Crimewatch*, and throughout the UK viewers watched the reconstruction as a middle-aged, dark-haired man in jeans and a blue T-shirt left Beth's house at eight fifteen p.m. and made his way to the Stag and Thistle, where he was known to have spent the evening of Thursday 5 June. At just after eleven he was shown leaving the pub and turning into the narrow street where, shortly after midnight, his body had been found.

His landlady, a Mrs Monroe who knew him as Johnnie Stewart, had reported he'd seemed the same as usual, an opinion echoed on screen by people from the pub who had spoken to him that evening. No one could recall any disagreement or whether anyone had left at the same time as he did or soon afterwards.

A continuously moving tape along the bottom of the screen gave the *Crimewatch* studio phone and text numbers together with the date of the incident being covered and the reminder that officers wanted to hear from anyone who might have been in the area at the crucial time and seen anything suspicious. Numbers were also given for those who wished to remain anonymous. It was in the lap of the gods as to whether any useful information would result.

Blaircomrie

The next morning the detectives on the case met for a briefing.

'So let's recap on what we have,' DI Mackay began. 'Sandy, you go first. What do we know for definite about this slippery character?'

'Still precious little, boss. Admittedly this Yorkshire lot came forward but frankly I shouldn't pin your hopes on them. The whole story sounded concocted to me and the ID was far from conclusive. Neither man had ever seen their father and the photos they produced bore only a passing resemblance. We can probably write them off when the DNA results come through.

'For the rest, according to Johnnie-boy's landlady he was *allegedly* born in Dorset and grew up in Australia. He *allegedly* went to uni somewhere in the UK. He doesn't appear in any records and paid for his lodgings in cash, though the digital shop he worked for, who came forward after the e-fit, say they made out their cheques to J Farthing, and he was known to his colleagues as "J". I don't have to tell you *he* doesn't officially exist either.

'His landlady says he went out every night, and we've established he regularly played poker in the upper room of the Stag and Thistle in Forfar Street. He usually left with the night's winnings and it seems a fair bet someone followed him, attempted a mugging and it went wrong. But the crowd at the pub are a taciturn lot and getting anything out of them is like the proverbial.'

Mackay nodded and the discussion turned to the replies already streaming in from the television programme. Surely, they told themselves, something would break soon.

Thursday had come round again, and Beth was meeting Moira for lunch. It was now three weeks since they'd gone together to the police station and identified Johnnie's body, and the police seemed no nearer learning his real name.

'How did it feel, being mentioned on telly?' Moira enquired.

'It was weird, especially seeing that man walk out of my gateway and next door's cat sitting on the fence watching him.'

'Did he look like Johnnie?' Moira asked.

'A bit, but it could have been half the population of Blaircomrie.'

'No doubt there'll be the usual flood of phone calls claiming to identify him,' Moira remarked, 'but the programme does have a high success rate. In the meantime, the press are having a field day with two big local stories to work on – Johnnie's identity, of course, and the mall disaster. I read yesterday that relatives of the victims are demanding more action to identify those to blame for the collapse – it's been over six months now and compensation still hasn't been agreed. Some of the families are on the bread line.'

'Poor souls.' Beth poured water into their glasses. 'Talking of the press, I've got a reporter coming to interview me this evening; I tried to dissuade him but he talked me round and I obviously won't get any peace till I see him.'

'Be careful what you say,' Moira warned. 'They have a way of twisting your words.'

'I haven't any to twist,' Beth pointed out.

'I meant about your relationship. You don't want it noised abroad.'

Beth flushed. 'I was very foolish over that – lost my head completely. I'm hardly likely to mention it.'

*   *   *

Several hours later, as he perched on a chair in her living room, she regretted her capitulation. There was something about the man, with his slicked-back hair and the sweat marks under his arms, that she instinctively distrusted.

'You must have known him better than most, Mrs Monroe,' he wheedled. 'After all, he'd been living here for – what – two months?'

'I maintain a business relationship with my lodgers,' Beth said stiffly and untruthfully. 'He was always pleasant and polite and paid his rent on time, which was all that concerned me.'

He was watching her closely and she had the absurd notion that he could see through her. To interrupt his train of thought she said quickly, 'The police don't seem any nearer finding out who he was.'

'Ah, well now.' Jim Scott, as he'd introduced himself, leant back in his chair and crossed his legs. 'That might not be quite accurate; there's a story going round, unconfirmed, mind, that they've managed to trace his family – they're just waiting for DNA results before announcing it.'

Beth gave in to her curiosity. 'Really? Who are they, do you know?'

'The word is they live in Yorkshire, but that's as far as it goes. Yorkshire accent, had he?' he asked hopefully.

'I wouldn't have said so, but I'm not good at placing English accents.'

He looked disappointed. 'I was hoping the police might have updated you, but perhaps they're waiting till it's for definite.'

'There's no reason why they should tell me; I'm not a relative.'

Since there was patently no more she could – or was willing to – tell him, he got to his feet, stretching. 'Well, I won't keep you any longer, Mrs M.' He handed her a card. 'But if you do hear anything, I'd be grateful if you'd tip me the wink.'

Foxclere

The *Crimewatch* programme had been replaying itself in Jill's head ever since she'd seen it on Tuesday evening. The man acting the part of 'Johnnie Stewart' hadn't borne much resemblance to

Greg, but there was no comfort in that – he was, after all, just an actor playing a part. Yet the man in the paper *had* looked frighteningly like him, and she was beginning to accept that she wouldn't rest until she could satisfy herself that the likeness was pure coincidence.

An idea began to form in her head; the landlady's name had been mentioned, a Mrs Monroe. With luck there wouldn't be too many with that name in Blaircomrie. Quickly, before her courage could fail her, she reached for her phone.

Blaircomrie

In view of public interest and the stalemate they'd encountered so far, permission had been granted to speed up the Gregory brothers' DNA results, so when DS Grant knocked at his door DI Mackay was hopeful that the case was about to take a giant leap forward. There had been the usual calls from folk whose relatives had disappeared years ago and who were clutching at straws, and these had doubled since the *Crimewatch* programme. They all had to be looked into but so far none had held water; despite Sandy's reservations, this latest ID sounded more hopeful, and with luck the DNA results might clinch it and restore his rightful name to their presently anonymous body.

However, Grant's face as he entered showed no sign of elation. 'Well, Sandy? What news?'

'Good and bad, boss, the good being that the Gregory brothers are definitely related to the deceased.'

'Excellent! But if he's Laurence Gregory, what possible bad news can there be?'

'Except that he isn't, boss,' Grant said flatly. 'He bloody didn't exist either!'

Mackay leant back, his eyes narrowing. 'What the hell do you mean?'

'Just that, same as Johnnie Stewart. We trailed through all the channels again, and none of the Laurence Gregorys we came up with fitted the bill.'

He ran a hand through his sparse hair. 'It's a bummer, boss. If you're as confused as I am, let me recap. When his landlady ID'd our body as Johnnie Stewart we thought we were home and dry, but by God we soon learned different. There are lots of Johnnie Stewarts, but all alive and kicking and scattered all over the British Isles.

'So then the e-fit goes public and the shop who employed him comes forward saying they made out his cheques to J Farthing, but that was no help because he also proved to be non-existent, though Johnnie must have banked his cheques somewhere. Then, to crown it all, we're presented with Laurence Gregory, who turns out to be as insubstantial as the rest. How many more phantoms are going to materialize? Hell's teeth, boss, we assumed he was the usual drunk stabbed in a back alley, but he's turned out to be the mystery man of the century!'

'Let me get this straight,' Mackay said slowly. 'You're saying there's no trace of Laurence Gregory either? But there has to be, man! For God's sake, he's got two sons!'

'The guy in the morgue has,' Grant said heavily, 'but he's not Laurence Gregory.'

Foxclere

Jill was holding her breath as she punched out the number she'd looked up on the Internet, and as soon as a voice answered she rushed into her prepared speech.

'You don't know me, Mrs Monroe, but my name is Jill Lawrence,' she began. 'Please forgive me contacting you, but the sketch of your lodger in the paper looks very like my husband, who died overseas last year.'

Mrs Monroe's soft Scottish voice interrupted her. 'Mrs Lawrence, I'm sorry about your husband but it's the police you should be contacting, not me.'

'Please hear me out; I need to speak to you not because I believe this Johnnie Stewart is my husband, but because I'm sure he's *not*. I just have to have proof.'

'And why should you think I could provide it?'

'He lodged with you for two months, the paper says. All I'm asking is for you to spare me ten minutes or so and confirm the photograph that I'll show you is not the same man. I promise you I'm not mad or dangerous or unhinged in any way, and I'm quite happy to meet you in a public place rather than your home if you'd prefer that. It's just that all this publicity and the artist's impression or whatever it was have been exceedingly difficult for me and my family, rekindling our grief.' Despite herself, Jill's voice trembled.

'Of course, I do understand.' The tone had softened. 'And if it means so much to you, of course I'll see you. I lost my own husband, and I know how it feels.'

'That's so good of you, thank you so much.'

'Will you be coming alone?'

'Yes; I . . . don't want to put anyone else through this.'

'Then of course you must come to the house. Have you the address?'

'Yes, I looked it up.'

'When would you like to come?'

'Tomorrow?' Jill held her breath; she'd already booked a seat on the morning plane. 'After lunch some time?'

'Very well, Mrs Lawrence, I'll expect you about two thirty.'

'Forgive me for saying so, Jill, but you seem a little distracted this morning! In that last piece I played at least three wrong notes and you didn't even notice!'

Jill wrenched her thoughts from anticipation of her trip. 'I'm so sorry, Edward. If you wouldn't mind playing it again, I promise to give it my full attention.'

'I'm not complaining,' he said, 'just concerned that you seem to have something on your mind.'

He deserved some sort of explanation. 'It's just that I have to make an unexpected trip tomorrow, and there are various things to plan.'

'You should have cancelled the lesson.' He studied her flushed face. 'Can I be of any help? Run you to the station or airport or anything?'

'Oh, I wouldn't dream—' She broke off. Truth to tell, she'd been concerned about leaving the car overnight in the long-stay car park, but there was no way she could ask her family's assistance; they'd only talk her into not going.

He was watching her. 'Really, it would be no trouble.'

'It's very kind of you,' she said hesitantly.

'Where are you off to?'

'Scotland, just for one night.'

'A long way to go for one night!'

Jill abandoned her reticence; there was no reason not to tell him the truth. 'The point is that this man who was stabbed up there and whose photo is everywhere you look is very like my husband.'

He looked shocked. 'The one who was featured on *Crimewatch*?'

She nodded. 'You must think I'm mad, because it can't possibly be, but I have to satisfy myself that it's not him.'

'How will flying to Scotland help you do that?'

'I'm taking a photograph to show his landlady. She'll be able to give me a definite answer and then I can relax.'

'You poor thing,' Edward said gently. 'This must all be very difficult for you.'

She gave him a shaky smile. 'Don't be too sympathetic or you'll make me cry! But if you really mean it, it would be wonderful if you could run me to the airport.'

'Of course I will, and meet you on your return. So now you can stop worrying and sit back and listen to a perfect rendition of my homework!'

London

Paul Devonshire was frying sausages for his supper when his phone interrupted him and he was pleasantly surprised to find an old university friend on the line. Barnie Reid had been one of the group who went round with him and Greg, but since he'd remained in the north they kept in touch only spasmodically by email.

'Barnie! Great to hear from you! How are things?'

'Not so bad, old pal. But before we start exchanging news, I presume you've seen pictures of this bloke found dead in Scotland?'

Paul stiffened. 'Yes?' he admitted cautiously.

'Remind you of anyone?'

'You must know it does.'

'Yep, but there's something else. For the last week or so a pal of mine up here has had something on his mind and it all came spilling out over a pint last night. It boils down to the fact that he thinks this bloke might be his father, who allegedly died years ago. And to crown it all his father's name was Larry – or Laurence

– Gregory.' He paused and when Paul didn't speak – because he couldn't – he went on: 'Laurence Gregory – Gregory Lawrence. Coincidence or what?'

Paul moistened dry lips. 'Like Greg being known at uni as "Larry" Lawrence? It took me a while to remember to call him Greg, like everyone else down here.'

'I still think of him as Larry.' Barnie paused again. 'We lost touch after we graduated; did he marry Sally Hurst?'

Sally! 'Oh my God!' Paul breathed. 'I've not thought of Sally in years, but your mentioning her in this context rings a bell. We were out in a foursome one time, Larry and Sal and me and Rosie Teal, who I was going around with at the time. I don't know how it came up but we got on to talking about names and Sal was teasing Larry because his was interchangeable. "You can't know if you're coming or going!" she said. And Larry said something to the effect that we might laugh, but it gave him a dual personality, which could come in useful one day! It was a throwaway line,' Paul ended flatly. 'A joke.'

'But as you say, oh my God.'

'Logically it can't be either of them,' Paul insisted a little desperately. 'Lots of people have the same name – you only have to look on the Internet – and you said this Larry Gregory died some time ago.'

'*Allegedly* died. As did Greg Lawrence. *Allegedly*. But since he was blown up there wouldn't have been a body, would there?'

Numbly, Paul recalled his first sight of the e-fit, when he'd briefly wondered if this Johnnie Stewart could conceivably have written the Farthing piece. Now, incredibly, it seemed possible that Greg himself had been alive and writing his anonymous column until a few weeks ago. The *Sunday Chronicle* knew him only by that name: the fact that someone called Gregory Lawrence had died would, even if they'd heard of it, have meant nothing to them. But where, for God's sake, did Johnnie Stewart come in?

'To answer your question,' he said slowly, 'no, he didn't marry Sally; he married a girl called Jill and I was his best man.'

'So what do you make of it all?'

'God knows. Why is your friend so sure it's his father?'

'Photo comparisons. They got in touch with the Scottish police who drove down and took DNA samples from him and his brother, so they must be taking it seriously.'

'Did you tell him he also looked like someone you knew?'

'No; I was on the point of it, but it didn't seem the right moment. So now the poor bloke's on tenterhooks waiting for the DNA results.'

'Then we'll have to do the same,' Paul said. And though there was undeniably relief in the sentiment, he couldn't help feeling he was shirking his responsibility.

Foxclere

Jill also received a phone call that night, from Daphne Harris.

'I know it's rather short notice, dear, but we were wondering if you'd like to come for supper tomorrow? Nothing formal, just pot luck.'

'That's sweet of you, Daphne, but I'm going away for the weekend.'

'Oh, well, that's fine; as long as you have something pleasant to look forward to, after that *Crimewatch* business.' She hesitated. 'You carried if off magnificently at the Trents', but I had the feeling you were more upset than you were letting on about that picture in the paper.'

Jill smiled. 'Very astute of you; I was.'

'But you're over it now?'

'Not really. Actually, I'm flying up to Scotland tomorrow to speak to that man's landlady.'

Daphne's gasp came down the line. 'Do you think that's wise?'

'What possible harm can it do? She must have known him better than anyone else up there and, if I take a photo of Greg with me, she'll be able to tell me definitely that it wasn't him and then I might get some peace.'

'Is Georgia going with you?'

'No; she's as upset as I am, though neither of us will admit it. It wouldn't be fair to put her under the strain, and when I come home I'll be able to tell her it's not her father.'

'But you're not going up alone?'

'I'll be fine; it's just a quick trip. I've booked in for the night at a hotel and will fly back the next day.'

'I could come with you if you like,' Daphne offered diffidently.

'Bless you, but this is something I have to do alone.'

'Well, if you're sure. And you'll let me know the outcome?'

'Of course I will. Over a pot-luck supper, if I'm lucky!'

Edward was as good as his word and Jill was grateful for his company on the drive to Gatwick. Her courage was fast running out and she kept asking herself what on earth she was doing, flying four hundred and fifty miles on a whim. But she'd committed herself now and the peace of mind that would result was worth a king's ransom.

At the airport Edward found her a trolley and escorted her as far as the check-in desk, where he took his leave.

'Good luck,' he said. 'I'll be waiting in the arrivals hall when you land, but you have my mobile number if you can't see me immediately.'

'Many thanks again, Edward; you've made this so much easier,' Jill told him.

'My mission in life!' he said with a rare grin, and she knew he was trying to cheer her. She smiled back and, as the man in front of her moved away, went forward to collect her boarding pass.

Richard was well aware of the risks he was running, not only to his marriage but to his career, appalled to discover that having considered his self-control unassailable, it had withered at the first challenge. With Victoria, 'love' had been a pleasantly undemanding background to life – a watercolour in muted shades, whereas his feelings for Maria were altogether more strident, highly coloured and impossible to ignore. Since he'd met her life had taken on a feverish intensity he had never experienced before – colours deeper, music louder, food more flavoursome. It was a startling and uncomfortable experience.

They'd made love again during the lunch break on Thursday, and, arriving at her home ahead of him, she'd awaited him in her dressing gown, naked beneath it. At least, he consoled himself, he'd never mentioned the word 'love' to her, even at the height of passion. To do so would have been the ultimate betrayal of Victoria, who had responded to his now frequent approaches with undisguised pleasure, intensifying his guilt.

During the intervening week he'd waged an internal battle, arguing that, having discovered himself capable of passion, he could now gratify it with his wife. But the vision of Maria, her copper-coloured hair spread on the pillow, her alabaster body inviting his caresses, was too powerful and he wasn't yet ready to give her up. There were only three more Thursdays till the end of term, which would provide a natural break. He would indulge himself till then, and by September would long since have freed himself from her spell.

Meanwhile, his sense of guilt spread from his wife to his mother, and he realized he'd not checked how she'd coped with that disturbing newspaper picture. On the Saturday morning, therefore, after Victoria had left for The Gallery, he rang her number, only to be greeted by the answerphone. Her mobile also went to voice-mail and, with an exclamation of annoyance, he phoned his sister.

'You never let me know how Mother reacted to that sketch,' he began accusingly.

'You never rang to find out,' Georgia replied.

Richard bit his lip. 'I've been feeling guilty about that.' Though only for the last few minutes. 'Was she very upset?'

'I think so, though she tried to hide it. She came up for lunch that day and was going to some do in the evening. She seemed more worried that people there would want to discuss it.'

'I've just tried both her phones but couldn't get through. Do you know where she is?'

'She's gone away for the weekend.'

'Oh? Where?'

'I don't know; some friend she wanted to see but she didn't give any names.'

'Didn't you ask?' Richard demanded impatiently.

'No, brother dear, not believing in the third degree, I didn't. If she'd wanted me to know, she'd have told me.'

There was a pause, then: 'When's she due back?'

'Sometime tomorrow.'

'Right, I'll try again then.' Another pause. 'All well with you?'

'Yes, thank you. Millie fell off a swing in the playground yesterday and gave us a fright, but thankfully she escaped with a grazed knee.'

A vision of the red-haired Toby Chiltern lying under a clutch of children flashed into Richard's mind and he hastily dismissed it. 'These things happen,' he said.

'Indeed,' Georgia agreed dryly.

'Salaams to Tim, then, and have a good weekend.'

'You too.'

Not a very satisfactory conversation, Richard thought, going in search of his golf clubs, but at least he'd made an effort.

Blaircomrie

Having paid the taxi, Jill turned and surveyed the neat stone house outside of which it had deposited her. Heart in mouth she opened the gate, murmured a greeting to the ginger cat that was regarding her balefully from the fence and walked up the path.

Jill's first impression was that Mrs Monroe must be about her age, though she seemed older. Her fair hair was greying and there were lines round her deep-set hazel eyes.

'Mrs Lawrence?' she said with a smile, holding out her hand. 'I'm Beth Monroe. Come away in. I thought a cup of tea might be welcome after your journey?'

'It would indeed,' Jill assured her, though she'd just finished a bar lunch in the hotel where she'd left her case. She was led into a room at the back of the house where a tea tray with a plate of obviously home-made scones stood on a low table.

'Have you come far?' her hostess enquired, indicating an easy chair.

'Quite a way, yes,' Jill acknowledged, seating herself. 'From Sussex, actually.'

Beth Monroe, teapot in hand, turned to look at her in surprise. 'On the south coast? My goodness, that *is* a long way. I'd somehow thought you were fairly local. That makes me feel—'

'I must apologize again for this imposition,' Jill broke in nervously. 'It's just that ever since that newspaper came out—'

'Of course, I quite understand.' She poured tea into one of the china cups, offered milk or lemon, and handed it to Jill together with a plate and a prettily patterned paper napkin.

'Now, help yourself to a scone. They were only made this morning.'

'They look delicious.' And, lunch notwithstanding, Jill took one.

'You want to know about Mr Stewart, of course,' Beth went on, seating herself, 'but I fear there's little I can tell you.' She smiled ruefully. 'The police gave me a lecture about not vetting my lodgers.'

Greg's photo was burning a hole in Jill's handbag but she allowed her hostess to steer the conversation. 'Didn't he offer any background information?' she asked.

'Only that he was divorced and had spent some years in Australia—' She broke off at Jill's sharply indrawn breath as some tea slurped out of her cup on to the saucer. She hastily set it down on the table.

'I'm sorry, that's a rather horrible coincidence. My husband also grew up there.'

Beth said quickly, 'Well, please don't worry; I was about to tell you earlier that the police have apparently traced his family. They live in Yorkshire, I believe.'

Jill released her breath, only aware as she did so of the tension that had gripped her.

'Really?' she said shakily. 'Well, that's certainly good news.'

'I should have mentioned it on the phone,' Beth went on apologetically, 'but you took me by surprise and I didn't think of it until later. Though if I'd known you were coming so far, I'd have made some effort to stop you taking the trouble.'

'I think I'd still have wanted to come, because of his resemblance to my husband.' Jill bent down to retrieve her bag and, withdrawing the photo which she'd extracted from its bedroom frame, she passed it across. And watched with growing fear as the colour left her hostess's face.

Beth looked up at last, her haunted eyes meeting Jill's. She moistened dry lips. 'I . . . don't know what to say.' Her voice was a croak.

Jill leant forward, hands gripped tightly together. 'Well, for God's sake say something.'

Beth looked down again at the photograph in her shaking hand. 'I can't explain it, Mrs Lawrence, but without a shadow of doubt this is my lodger, Johnnie Stewart.'

TEN

After leaving Beth Monroe, Jill walked the streets of Blaircomrie in a daze, its grey stone houses a sombre backdrop to her mood. How could Greg possibly have been alive all this time and not let them know? Despite her seeming certainty, could Mrs Monroe be mistaken? And what of that family in Yorkshire? Myriad questions circled her brain, all without answers. The only acceptable solution was that he'd been left with amnesia following the bomb blast – though admittedly selective, as he'd remembered living in Australia. And he'd said he was divorced – another sharp stab of pain. In effect she was grieving for him all over again, this time with the added bitterness of abandonment.

Beth, almost equally shocked, had done her best to offer comfort, ending by asking if Jill would go straight to the local police. She'd shaken her head, knowing she needed time to think, time to discuss it with her family. Yet how, she wondered achingly, could she subject them to the level of pain and betrayal that she was feeling?

Barely registering them, she walked past children playing in the street, queues waiting at bus stops, a bridal party coming out of church. She passed what appeared to be a boarded-up shopping precinct, graffiti scrawled all over the hoarding, and, farther on, a park with couples strolling down its paths arm in arm. A normal Saturday afternoon.

When exhaustion finally claimed her she caught a taxi back to the hotel where she ordered herself a large whisky in the bar. It was not her normal choice, but was supposed to be the antidote to shock. Not that it was much help.

Aware that she should eat, she ordered room service but was unable to manage more than a mouthful as she stared at the moving pictures on the television. And over and over came the tortured query: *why?* Greg had loved her, she was sure of it, though she doubted that he'd been entirely faithful; his lifestyle argued against that, with so much time spent away from home. He was an attractive and virile man and she'd chosen not to ask questions to which she might not like the answer. But consciously to deny her existence and that of his children – that she couldn't accept or forgive. Not unless there was some overwhelming reason for it that was beyond his power to withstand.

As the hours passed and she listlessly undressed and prepared for bed, she waited for the tears to come but to her surprise remained dry-eyed; there were too many conflicting emotions to allow the release of tears. Lying in the strange bed, she heard a church clock chime one hour after another through the long night before finally falling into a restless doze around four o'clock.

She had ordered a wake-up call to ensure she caught her flight, and it seemed she'd only just closed her eyes when she was jerked awake. A hot shower helped to revive her and she made a cup of tea from the facilities in the room. It was pointless to attempt breakfast; there was a heavy weight at the base of her throat that made the thought of food nauseous.

An hour later the taxi she'd ordered conveyed her to the airport. Her feeling of disorientation was similar to jet lag, no doubt due to lingering shock and a lack of both food and sleep, and as she made her way on to the plane she was profoundly grateful that Edward would be meeting her and she'd have his company on the twelve-mile drive home; she'd had more than enough of her own.

And there he was, head and shoulders above those around him, hurrying to take her arm and lead her back to the car park. A glance at her face prevented him asking any questions until they were both seated in his car. Then he turned to her and said quietly, 'Well, how was it?'

And without warning Jill burst into tears, deep, painful sobs shaking her whole body. His arm came comfortingly round her and she leant against him until they lessened in intensity, when, embarrassed, she straightened and he handed her a large, clean handkerchief.

'I'm so sorry,' she said, her breathing still ragged, 'but I think I needed that.'

Still he didn't question her, letting her take her time.

'They're one and the same,' she said then, 'the man in the paper and Greg. There's no shadow of doubt.'

He waited, letting her choose her words. 'His landlady couldn't believe it,' she went on, 'because she'd heard the police have just traced him to a family in Yorkshire.'

'Then perhaps it's possible . . .?'

'No,' Jill said decidedly, and blew her nose. 'There must be a mistake somewhere along the line, and I'm sorry for that family if it had got their hopes up, but Johnnie Stewart was definitely my husband.'

She turned to look at him and he thought how vulnerable she seemed, her eyes swollen with tears. 'Yet how could he be?' she demanded. 'We held his memorial service, Edward; probate was granted. There was no doubt in anyone's mind.'

He said gently, 'Why was it assumed he'd been in the blast?'

'He'd just been seen walking into the hotel when the bomb went off in the doorway. He couldn't have got any further than the foyer.' Her voice caught. 'A lot of people were killed but it was . . . impossible to identify them. There was no reply to our increasingly frenzied emails and phone calls and as time went on without hearing from him, he was officially listed among those who'd lost their lives.'

'Who was it who saw him going into the hotel? Could they have been mistaken?'

'No, it was someone he'd been talking to. The man himself was flung to the pavement by the blast.'

'This must be most distressing for you. I'm so sorry.' Edward paused. 'You're shivering; you need some hot food inside you.'

She gave a half-laugh. 'I've not eaten since lunch yesterday – my throat just closed.'

'Then we'll stop somewhere on the way home. I'm sure you could manage a bowl of soup.'

He started the car and they drove out of the airport in companionable silence, wrapped in their own thoughts. Minutes later he turned into the car park of a pleasant-looking pub. It was shortly after noon; this time yesterday, Jill thought, she'd just landed in Edinburgh, confident that Johnnie Stewart would after all bear only a passing resemblance to Greg.

She gave a little shudder and allowed Edward to help her out of the car.

'Is your daughter expecting you home?' he asked as they began their meal.

'I told her sometime today, that's all.'

'Have you thought what you're going to say to her?'

Jill sipped her soup, surprised to find she was hungry. 'I'll tell them together; I couldn't go through it twice and Richard needs to hear at the same time. The trouble is, as soon as I get home Georgia will come down to ask about my trip. Bless her, she'll probably invite me to supper and I . . . don't think I can face her just yet.'

'May I make a suggestion?'

'Of course.'

'Then what I propose is that you come back to my house for the rest of the day.' He lifted a hand at her instinctive protest. 'You've had enough of an ordeal in the last twenty-four hours without facing the immediate prospect of another. You could phone her and say you'll be late back but would like to see both her and her brother sometime tomorrow. Then you could ring your son to arrange the meeting, and by the time you see them you'll be over the initial shock and will have had a chance to decide how best to handle it. How does that sound?'

'It's very kind of you, but I've already taken up quite enough of your time; I really can't impose on you any further.'

'It would be a pleasure to have your company.' He gave one of his rare smiles. 'And I have some excellent recordings of Rubinstein and Brendel, among others, that I think you would enjoy. Then we could have a spot of supper and I'll drive you home.'

It was an infinitely tempting prospect; she'd been dreading facing Georgia while having to conceal her news, and there was no denying she felt exhausted. The thought of being able to relax and listen to music was more than she could resist.

'Then if you're quite sure, I'd be very grateful,' she said.

Stonebridge

'I wish to God those DNA results would come through,' David remarked that evening. 'It's like living on a knife-edge.'

'Oh, for pity's sake, stop moaning!' Julia snapped. 'It won't make them come any faster – and anyway, what difference will it make? Do you really *want* to know that the man who deserted you as a baby was stabbed in the street like some low-life?' She glanced at his startled face. 'Or are you hoping the results will be negative?'

'I know you've not much time for me at the moment,' he said after a minute, 'but surely I deserve some understanding over this?'

'My understanding where you're concerned is in short supply.' She was breathing quickly, hating herself for the way she was behaving but full of resentment at not being free to leave him. First she'd had to postpone her departure because of Sally's death and now there was this further complication. It was as if, albeit unwittingly, he was binding her to him with strands of cobweb.

'I made one stupid mistake,' David said bitterly. 'Am I going to have to pay for it for the rest of my life?'

'You destroyed my trust, David; that's what I can't forgive.'

'But I've learned my lesson – surely you can see that? Give me another chance, please; the kids are beginning to sense something's wrong.'

'We've never rowed in front of them.'

'No, but you're so formal with me – it just isn't natural. I love you, Julia; I've always loved you. I lost my head for a few months but it was never anything serious.' He put an arm round her, feeling her stiffen. 'Because you only found out shortly before Mum died it still seems new, but it had already been over for some time.'

She said slowly, 'When Sally died I was on the point of leaving you.' And saw that she had shocked him.

'God, were you really?'

'Obviously,' she went on, suddenly close to tears, 'I couldn't go through with it when you'd just lost your mother. Now you've learned your parents weren't married and your father abandoned you rather than dying in an accident, but now he really is dead, or at least you think he is, and . . . Oh, God!'

'Oh, darling, I'm so sorry!'

'It's not your fault, damn it!' she said through angry tears. 'I'm not saying you arranged it on purpose!'

'No, but perhaps these traumas could have one good outcome if they keep us together.' His arm tightened round her and she turned her face into his shoulder, feeling him kiss her hair. Still hurt and angry, she wasn't yet ready to forgive him, but for the first time she wondered how much of this intransigence was due to pride. And if the price it was demanding was perhaps too high.

Foxclere

When they had reached Edward's house that afternoon, Jill's lack of sleep had been catching up with her, and at his suggestion she went straight upstairs for a rest. He showed her into a musty-smelling bedroom, and when she wearily flopped down on top of the covers he draped her coat over her, closed the curtains and left her. She was asleep within seconds and it was two hours before she stirred and made her way downstairs.

It was a large, echoing place he lived in, cool even in the heat of summer. He made her a cup of tea and they sat listening to music and carrying on a disjointed but wide-ranging conversation, and she learned more about him in those few hours than she had during all their previous time together. Inevitably they discussed the position with Greg, looking at it from all angles, with the result that she felt considerably calmer about the prospect of passing on the news to her family.

When it was time to eat he took a ready meal out of his freezer. 'Sorry I can't offer you haute cuisine,' he said with a wry smile, 'but I'm ashamed to say this is my usual fare. I've never been one for slaving over a hot stove – in fact, it takes me all my time to boil an egg! Thank God for convenience food!'

'Perhaps I should be giving you cookery lessons too!' Jill said.

'I'd be more than grateful if you would.'

She glanced at him quickly, unsure whether he was serious, but was unable to tell.

It was a quarter to eleven when he dropped her off at the gate of Woodlands, brushing aside her repeated thanks. 'I haven't enjoyed myself as much for a long time,' he said.

As she closed the inner door behind her, Jill saw the answer-phone blinking and pressed the button to hear the message. She was considerably surprised when the caller identified himself as Paul Devonshire, and had to think for a moment to place the name:

of course, Greg's friend who'd been their best man. She'd had a condolence note from him the previous year.

'It's a long time since we met,' he began, 'but as you probably know I was in pretty regular touch with Greg and was appalled to hear of his death. The last thing I want to do is upset you, but something has come to light that I think you should know, and I'd be most grateful if you could call me back when you get this message. It doesn't matter how late it is – I'm a night bird. My number is . . .'

Jill frowned. After a pleasantly relaxing evening, the last thing she wanted was to have her emotions stirred up again at this late hour. On the other hand, curiosity gnawed at her and she knew she wouldn't sleep till she'd heard what he had to say.

She took her overnight bag into the bedroom, the empty frame on the dressing table reminding her of Beth staring disbelievingly at Greg's photo. Before going to bed she'd restore it to its rightful place. In the meantime, she braced herself to call Paul Devonshire, and, picking up the cordless phone as she passed, she went into the sitting room, drew the heavy curtains against the darkness and sat down in her favourite chair.

'Oh, Jill! Thank you so much for calling back.'

'You did say no matter how late.'

'That's right.' He paused. 'Before I start, needless to say I saw the artist's impression in the paper, like everyone else.' He waited but she made no comment. 'However, that's only marginally what I wanted to talk about.' She heard him take a deep breath. 'Did Greg often speak of his writing?'

Whatever she was expecting, it was not that. 'His writing?'

'His articles for the newspaper.'

'Oh, that. No, he hardly ever mentioned it. It amused him to make a mystery of it; he wouldn't even say which paper he was writing for or the pseudonym he was using.' She hesitated. 'Why do you ask?'

'Because without wanting to sound dramatic, I believe I'm the only person alive who knows what it was; it was I who first encouraged him to put his very stringent views down on paper.'

'Oh?' She had no idea where this was leading.

'Jill, he wrote for the *Sunday Chronicle* under the name of Jake Farthing.'

She gasped. 'Not *the* Jake Farthing, who was quoted in the House?'

'The very same. He swore me to secrecy because he didn't want to become embroiled in personal contact either with the pundits or the public, and, to put it crudely, felt freer to say what he felt without having to face the consequences. But I have a reason for telling you this: I returned a few weeks ago from two years in the States, and was considerably startled to find his column was still running.'

Jill sat motionless in her chair, clutching the phone. 'Go on.'

'Well, I told myself the name was generic and someone else had taken over the column, as often happens for one reason or another, though the style was very definitely Greg's and I concluded his successor must have studied him very closely. Then I saw the drawing of this man in Scotland.' He paused. 'But I probably still wouldn't have risked upsetting you if it hadn't been for a phone call from a friend who lives in Yorkshire, who told me someone he knew, who'd thought his father died long since, was now convinced he was this dead man. And the father's name was Larry – or Laurence – Gregory.'

Jill drew in her breath sharply,

'Jill, at uni Greg was known as Larry Lawrence, and he once joked about being able to turn his name round to give himself a dual personality.'

There was a long silence. She felt icy cold: the shock that Greg had been Jake Farthing, the man whose opinions were so widely discussed, had been superseded by a still more incredible revelation, which she was not yet ready even to consider.

Eventually she said, 'It *was* Greg, Paul, the man in the paper. I've just been to Scotland to see the landlady and she confirmed it. She also mentioned a family in Yorkshire, but not . . . the name. That's just . . . bizarre. I was convinced they were mistaken, but . . .' Her voice tailed off. *Greg had had another family in Yorkshire all these years? No! I will not believe it!* And following the instinctive denial came the swift thought: *I wish Edward was here.*

Paul said anxiously, 'God, Jill, my timing leaves a lot to be desired, doesn't it? Are you all right?'

'No, but I shall be. It was good of you to phone.'

'If you want the name and address of the family, I can find out for you.'

'No, thank you.'

'I should have asked – are you alone in the house?'

'Only in my part of it; Georgia and her family are upstairs.'

'Could you go to them, have someone with you?'

She gave a choked little laugh. 'They'll all be sound asleep, but I'll be speaking to them tomorrow. I think I can survive till then.'

'I'm sorry,' he said, cursing himself for his thoughtlessness; he'd been so anxious to put her in the picture that he hadn't given enough consideration to the effect his news would have, with lonely hours of darkness stretching ahead of them.

'If there's anything I can do . . .'

'Thank you for telling me; it can't have been easy. Goodnight, Paul.'

She broke the connection, tucked her legs beneath her and resigned herself to another long night.

As it happened, Georgia was not asleep. She had heard her mother come in but respected her wish to delay their meeting till the following day, when she'd said she wanted to see both herself and Richard but not, apparently, Tim or Victoria. It must be about that man in Scotland, she thought apprehensively. Though she'd played it down for Jill's sake, Georgia was almost convinced he was her father, even while knowing he couldn't possibly be.

And there was another reason for her wakefulness: the previous Thursday she'd been delivering some house plants to an address in the Briarfields area when, to her surprise, she'd seen what looked very much like Richard's car parked a little way down on the other side of the road. She was still puzzling about it – surely he'd be at school? – when the front door of one of the houses opened and Richard himself came out, turning to speak to a young woman who'd appeared briefly framed in the doorway behind him – a young woman wearing what looked suspiciously like a dressing gown.

Georgia had stared disbelievingly as her brother got into his car and drove off in the opposite direction. What the *hell* was he doing? Why wasn't he in the staff dining room having lunch? And, most importantly, why was the woman wearing a dressing gown at that time of day? The implications seemed all too obvious.

She had told Tim what she'd seen and asked his advice, which, put simply, was 'Forget it; it's not your business.' But she was fond of Victoria, prickly though she could be, and feared for Richard's recklessness when his entire career could be at stake. There might, of course, be a perfectly innocent explanation, but it was hard to imagine what it could be.

Now she had the prospect of facing him tomorrow while the incident was still very much on her mind, let alone whatever it was their mother had to tell them. It was little wonder she was finding sleep elusive.

As he made his way to his study the next morning, Richard was also wondering, slightly uneasily, why his mother wanted to speak to them. He imagined it could only be about their father who, it must be admitted, had been rather pushed to the back of his mind thanks to Maria. It had been arranged that he would drive over to Woodlands straight after school, and in the meantime he must try not to second-guess the reason for their summons.

There was the usual pile of papers on his desk and he leafed through them, pausing when he came to a plain white envelope addressed simply to Mr Lawrence. He took his paper knife, slit it neatly open and drew out the single sheet of paper. Printed in the centre of the page was one line:

How do you solve a problem like Maria?

Richard stared at it, coldness spreading over him as a dozen wild thoughts collided in his head. They'd been so careful – or so he had thought. Surely this didn't date back to his driving her and Toby to the hospital? The only other time they'd left together was to look at golf clubs – an aborted mission – and he could swear no one had been around at the time – unless, of course, they'd been sitting in one of the few remaining vehicles in the car park.

Feverishly his brain replayed their time together: she had come to his room on three occasions, once with Toby to thank him for the hospital ride, when he'd unwisely taken them for an ice cream – where, of course, they might easily have been spotted – and again to request his help over the golf clubs. And he'd taken her there himself when he found her distressed in the corridor, which with hindsight mightn't have been wise either, especially since it had led to such an unforeseen escalation in their relationship.

He glanced again at the paper, his heart thudding. For whatever reason, their names had now been coupled; by how many people and who were they? God, if this became public the repercussions could be devastating.

There was a tap on the door and he jumped. The school secretary put her head round it. 'You asked me to remind you about the governors' meeting this morning, Mr Lawrence.'

'Yes. Yes, thanks, Polly,' he said distractedly, and after a curious glance she withdrew. He must be careful, Richard reminded himself, and not allow any change of demeanour to give rise to possible speculation. The obvious course of action was to break it off with Maria straight away but there were only two weeks of term remaining and, as he'd reasoned before, all would be forgotten by September. He just couldn't sacrifice their last couple of times together.

He ran a hand through his hair, drew a deep breath and sat down to compose himself for the governors' meeting in an hour's time.

Blaircomrie

'Detective Sergeant Grant?' Beth's voice shook a little.

'What can I do for you, Mrs Monroe?' There was a note of resignation in the policeman's voice.

'I hope I'm doing the right thing, but there's something I think you should know.'

'Go on.'

'A lady came to visit me on Saturday and she had a photo with her of . . . of Johnnie Stewart, who she claimed was her husband.'

'Oh . . . my . . . God!' said DS Grant.

'It was definitely him, Mr Grant, no doubt whatever. And I'm phoning because I heard you were linking him with some family in Yorkshire.'

'And that's not where this lady's from?'

'No, she lives in Sussex.' Beth paused and, receiving no encouragement, added tentatively, 'Her name is Mrs Lawrence and her husband's name was Gregory.'

The phone slipped in Grant's suddenly sweaty hand. 'Say that again.'

'Mrs Gregory Lawrence. She gave me her card in case I needed to contact her. Would you like her address and phone number? I did suggest she go straight to you but she wanted to discuss it with her family first.'

'And what,' Grant asked heavily, 'had she previously thought had happened to this husband of hers?'

'That he'd been killed in a terrorist attack in Egypt last year.'

'Not abducted by aliens, then?'

'I beg your pardon?'

'Nothing, nothing.' Grant sighed heavily. 'Yes, I'll take that information if you have it to hand. And thank you for getting in touch, Mrs Monroe.'

Beth replaced the phone, wondering if she had done the right thing. She wasn't sure Jill Lawrence would appreciate it, yet surely she'd want to get to the bottom of this business as much as, if not more than, anyone? Beth and Moira had discussed it over the phone for nearly half an hour before deciding Beth should phone Grant. Well, the deed was done, she thought philosophically, and the outcome was out of her hands.

ELEVEN

Blaircomrie

D S Grant was jubilant. 'We've checked, boss, and guess what! Gregory Lawrence actually existed! What's more, the details coincide with what Mrs Monroe reported. I reckon this could be the end of the rainbow!'

'Before you claim that pot of gold, Sandy,' Mackay said dryly, 'we need to be sure this woman is who she said she is. In this case, we can only believe someone's identity if they produce a birth certificate.'

'Well, the name "Laurence Gregory" hasn't appeared in the press,' Grant reminded him, 'so she can't have been trading on that, and she did say he grew up in Australia, which ties in with what he told Monroe. And, of course, she had his photo. Monroe was convinced it was Johnnie and I'd say we can accept that; the man lived under her roof for eight weeks. Also, the similarity of the name has to be significant, surely.'

Mackay slammed his hand on his desk. 'What the hell was he up to?' he demanded irritably. 'Damn it, we've got a DNA match to this other family; where do they fit in?'

'Search me, boss.'

Mackay considered for a moment. 'Where did you say this woman comes from?'

'East Sussex. A place called Foxclere.'

'Well, it sounds as though she's looking for answers, so if she and her family are willing to comply, let's check *their* DNA. Fancy another trip south, if the SIO's agreeable?'

'Why not? Gets me out of the office. At this rate we'll be awash with DNA samples.'

'It'll be pricey, especially if we want to expedite them, but this shambles has gone on long enough and the top brass are getting restive; I think we can bank on authorisation for the trip. And it's time we called the press in for help – publicize the various names he lived under and see what comes up. But before that we should put the Gregorys in the picture and let them know first that the man in the morgue *is* their father and, secondly, that he wasn't who he said he was.'

'Right, boss, I'll get on to it. Oh, and in the meantime, some good news for a change: traffic say there's a fresh slant on that hit-and-run. A new witness has come forward – been abroad for a few weeks – and his testimony could be really useful. Says this car cut him up and he was so incensed he recorded its registration number on his phone. He'd intended to report it but was going abroad the next day and never got round to it.'

'Thank God for small mercies,' Mackay said morosely. 'Keep me informed.'

Foxclere

They sat in silence for some minutes when Jill finished speaking.

'I don't know which is the biggest shock,' Georgia said eventually. 'The fact that Dad was Jake Farthing, that he might have another family in Yorkshire, or that he was alive until recently.'

'Allowing us to go on grieving for him,' Richard added. 'I find that difficult to forgive.'

'It must have been amnesia,' Jill insisted a little desperately. 'He's unlikely to have escaped that bomb blast completely unscathed, when he'd been seen entering the hotel only seconds before it went off. I'm quite sure he'd never have let us go on believing . . .'

Her voice tailed off and Georgia went to sit beside her, taking her hand. 'I still can't believe he was Jake Farthing,' she said, subtly side-stepping. 'It was the column Tim and I always turned to first.'

But Richard doggedly returned to his father's failings. 'I knew he compartmentalized his life,' he said tightly, 'but I little guessed to what extent. Another family closeted away, for God's sake! It seems barely credible. No wonder he was away so much!'

Jill winced and Georgia sent her brother a warning glance. 'Plenty of men are unfaithful,' she said pointedly. 'He just carried it one step further.'

Richard gave her a quick look before deciding he was being paranoid. 'A bloody big step,' he replied. 'God, the publicity this will stir up!'

Jill didn't seem to be listening. 'I suppose we should go to the police,' she said.

Richard stood up abruptly. 'I'll do it. I have the *Crimewatch* recording and they give the number to call. Try not to worry, Mother, I'll sort it out but I must be getting home now; Victoria will be worrying.'

He bent and kissed her cheek, nodded to his sister and took his leave.

'Come up and spend the evening with us,' Georgia said gently, and Jill was only too happy to accept.

Stonebridge

'Mr Gregory?'
 'Yes?'
 'DS Grant, Blaircomrie CID.'
 David's hand tightened on the phone. 'Yes?'

'The DNA results are through, sir, and I can confirm that you and your brother are a match with the deceased.'

David released his breath. 'Well, I suppose that's something.'

'But not all, I'm afraid. I also have to tell you that we've made extensive searches on all the Laurence Gregorys listed in various databases and none of them comply with the facts we have on your father.' He paused and when David didn't speak, added, 'In other words, that particular Laurence Gregory never existed.'

David frowned, shaking his head impatiently at Julia, who was hovering at his side. 'What the hell does that mean?'

'Presumably that he was using a pseudonym.'

'Then who *was* he, for God's sake?' David burst out. 'Johnnie Stewart, after all?'

'No, sir; Johnnie Stewart never existed either.'

There was a pause. Then: 'So . . . where do we go from here?'

'Our enquiries are continuing and of course we'll keep you informed. In the meantime, we've learned of another family who might have a connection—'

'With Laurence Gregory?' David interrupted incredulously.

'All I can tell you at this stage is that there'll be an appeal in the press shortly, when all the names that have come up in the case will be made public.'

'Have you found out yet who killed him?'

'The investigation is continuing,' Grant answered smoothly, 'and we're hopeful that the correct identification will be of assistance. In the meantime, I'm sure you'll want to contact your brother and pass on the news. Goodnight, sir.'

'What is it, David? What did he say?' Julia demanded, but he shook his head again, punching numbers into his phone.

'Grandpa? You'll never believe this! Our DNA matches the man in Scotland but his name wasn't Laurence Gregory.'

Julia gasped.

'God knows,' David replied in answer to his grandfather's exclamation. 'But it seems someone else has come forward . . . I don't know, that's all they'd say.' He ran a hand through his hair. 'This business is getting more bizarre by the minute. Look, we must meet as soon as possible. We need to go through everything we have and somehow get to the bottom of it. I appreciate it's too late now, but is it OK if Will and I come over tomorrow evening?

Perhaps you could dig out anything you might have on . . . this man, and I'll do the same.'

He put down the phone and rubbed his hand across his eyes.

'Oh, David!' Julia said softly.

He turned to her, and as the stress of the last weeks reached breaking point, tears came into his eyes and he went blindly into her arms.

Blaircomrie

Richard's phone call to the police coincidentally confirmed Beth's report about her visitor and vindicated the planned trip to Sussex.

'And that's not all,' Grant ended. 'It seems Gregory Lawrence wrote a column in one of the London broadsheets under the pen name Jake Farthing, which ties in with what his workplace told us. He must have had a bank account in that name for his news-paper cheques, so he needed to be J Farthing at work in order to bank his wages up here.'

'Then where the hell does Johnnie Stewart come in?'

'Search me. By that time he'd have been used to having several names on the go and it did make him harder to trace, as we know to our cost. Question is why was he so anxious not to be traced?' Grant ran a hand over his thinning hair. 'And we're no nearer finding who did for him, as one of his other sons was careful to remind me. We can but hope clearing up this tangle of names will point us in the right direction.'

Ever since Jill Lawrence's visit Beth had suffered from a feeling of guilt, illogical though she knew it to be. After all, she hadn't *known* Johnnie wasn't who he said he was, still less that he'd been reported dead and his family was grieving for him. But the sight of Jill's face when she'd confirmed his identity continued to haunt her, eliminating the last of her own feelings for Johnnie.

It was time for her to put the whole episode behind her, and the best way to do that was to advertise for another lodger. But first she needed to expunge all trace of his occupation and that meant redecorating his room. It was due for refreshing anyway; it had last been decorated when she let it out to her first lodger over six years ago.

Determined to put her plans into immediate effect, she spent her lunch hour buying ready-made curtains and a matching duvet cover in a pretty design of red poppies on a cream background. She then phoned the young man who had done jobs for her previously and whom she trusted to work in the house while she was out, delighted for herself if not for him that he'd no work in prospect and could start right away. He would also give the furniture in the room a fresh coat of paint. Beth was tempted by the thought of a new carpet, but reined in her enthusiasm; there were years of wear left in the one already down.

'I'll have it done for you in the week, Mrs M!' Charlie assured her cheerfully. And then, she thought, feeling happier and more positive than she had for weeks, she could advertise for her new lodger, who would very definitely be female.

Foxclere

Nigel said, 'What's the matter, honey? You look as though all your rabbits died.'

'We had rather a shock last night,' Victoria admitted reluctantly.

'Well? Going to tell me about it?'

She looked at him uncertainly, but she desperately needed to talk it over with someone other than family and Nigel had proved himself trustworthy on many occasions.

'It's a long story,' she said, 'about my father-in-law.'

'Who was killed in Egypt?'

'Who we *thought* was killed in Egypt. God, Nigel, I never felt I really knew him, but believe me I didn't even know the half of it – none of us did.'

'Sounds intriguing. Go on.'

'You realize all this is confidential?'

He grinned. 'When isn't it? Come into the back and we'll sneak a coffee before the first customer arrives.'

So it all came pouring out – the secret other family and the fact that Greg had still been writing the Jake Farthing column months after he was supposed to have been killed.

'Jake Farthing?' Nigel interrupted at that point. 'God, was that him? It was brilliant!'

'So now we feel we didn't know him at all,' Victoria finished. 'How could he have done that to us, to Jill particularly? It's badly shaken us all.'

'I bet it has. And what about this other family? Are they hypothetical or do they really exist?'

'I don't know; it's very complicated and all seems to hinge on the veracity of a phone call from Paul someone, a friend of Greg's.'

'So it's possible you're worrying unnecessarily?'

'Possible but not probable. Looking back, it has the ring of truth about it.'

'How would you describe your father-in-law?'

'Amusing, witty, impossible to tie down.'

'Tie down how?'

'Oh, I don't know. He didn't like committing himself, and even if he did – promising to take the family somewhere, for instance – something would be sure to "come up" at the last minute to prevent it, though if you challenged him he'd always have a plausible excuse. I don't think I ever really trusted him, but, having said that, I could count on one hand the number of times I met him, so perhaps I'm being unfair.' She paused. 'What I most blamed him for was the way he treated Richard. He never seemed to have any time for him, dismissing any comment he made and so on, while heaping praise on Georgia. It was grossly unfair and largely accounts for Richard being the way he is.'

Nigel lifted an eyebrow. 'Which is?'

But that was carrying confidentiality too far. Anyway, Richard had been far less repressed in the last few weeks, with wholly delightful results.

'Interesting!' she said.

It was when Nigel had gone to lunch and she was alone in The Gallery that the mysterious Bernard put in another appearance. Victoria felt a stab of alarm before remembering he'd no idea she knew who he was or that she might recognize him.

'Can I help you?' she asked above her quickened heartbeat.

'I hope so. I'm interested in local artists and wonder what you have in that category.'

Same old question. 'Any artist in particular?' she asked, leading him down the room.

'Alison Lockhart? Ronald Frobisher? Martin James?'

Well, at least he seemed to know what he was talking about
– unlike his girlfriend. 'We have one or two Lockharts but none
of the others at the moment, I'm afraid.'

They had come to a halt in front of a large abstract painting in
strong colours. He shook his head. 'I don't want to appear a phil-
istine, but I fear that's too big for the available space.'

'The seascape is smaller,' Victoria said, moving to the next
painting.

He frowned at it for several minutes. 'That would be more
suitable, certainly.' He paused. 'May I ask how long you've had
it in stock?'

Victoria gave a little laugh. 'An unusual question!'

He smiled briefly. 'My wife was in here a few weeks ago and
mentioned a painting she particularly liked, and stupidly I've
forgotten which it was.'

'Couldn't you ask her?'

'I could, but that would spoil the surprise – it's for her birthday.
So, would it have been here then?'

'We've had that particular painting for some time, yes.'

'And that?' He indicated the next one by the same artist.

'Much the same.'

He paused, looking from one picture to the other. 'Have you
sold any paintings by local artists in the last few weeks?'

Again, the same question 'Tina' had posed. 'One or two,' she
said guardedly.

'About that size?'

'Pretty much, from what I remember.'

'I wonder, could you possibly put me in touch with the buyer
or buyers? Perhaps if I offered an increased figure they might be
willing to sell them to me.'

Victoria shook her head. 'I'm sorry, we don't pass on customer
details.'

He sighed. 'It really is important. Is there any way I can persuade
you to bend the rules a little?'

'I'm afraid not,' she said coolly.

'Then could you take it down so I can check the back?'

Victoria raised her eyebrows. 'If it's the title you're wondering about, it's called *Market Scene*, and as you can see, the artist's signature is in the bottom corner.'

'Nevertheless, you sometimes learn more from labels on the back. Let me help you to lift it down.' He moved forward but Victoria swiftly intercepted him.

'I'm sorry; pictures are only taken down once they've been bought.'

He turned suddenly to face her, an almost desperate expression in his eyes, and she thought for a moment that he was going to seize hold of her. *God, Nigel, where are you?* Then he turned away, apparently defeated.

Hastily she went back into sales mode. 'There's nothing else I can interest you in? I'm sure your wife would be equally pleased—'

But he shook his head and turned to the door. Victoria watched him go. Curiouser and curiouser, she thought.

'It struck me afterwards that he wasn't consistent,' she reported to Nigel on his return. 'First he wanted a picture of a certain size, then the questions started: how long had it been in stock? Could his wife have seen it "a few weeks ago"? Who had recently bought a painting by a local artist? Could he have their addresses? And finally he was all for taking it off the wall – possibly in the hope of making off with it.'

'Tina also asked about local artists,' Nigel said thoughtfully.

'Exactly. We know they're working together but what on earth can they be after? And do you think they were behind the attempted break-in?'

'Almost definitely, I'd say. Not them in person, but I'm willing to bet they arranged it.'

'Well, they're not giving up. I wonder what they'll come up with next.'

'No doubt we'll soon find out,' Nigel replied.

The news that evening, however, drove their nebulous suspicions about Bernard out of their minds. Donald Lancing had died in hospital without regaining consciousness. What the press had dubbed *The Stately Homes Robberies* had metamorphosed into a murder enquiry.

Stonebridge

Once again, David and Will Gregory drove to their grandparents' home, but this time it was their own startling news they'd come to discuss.

'This is an extraordinary turn of events,' Henry said gravely, sitting down opposite them. 'We'd been keeping a secret all these years, but it appears we knew only half the story.'

'Have you come across anything significant?' Will asked hopefully.

'I'm afraid not. As I said, we only met . . . your father once, and we've been searching our joint memory but we're pretty sure his surname was never mentioned. He was introduced to us simply as "Larry", and of course when Sally took the name Gregory we assumed it was his and that she wanted his sons to have it. It now looks as though she just plucked it out of the air.'

'There's another complication,' David said. 'As I mentioned on the phone, apparently someone else has come forward – possibly the legitimate family surfacing at last. We know he was married – you said he told Mum when he left her – but it hadn't occurred to me that he'd have other children – half-brothers or sisters we know nothing about. DS Grant wouldn't give me a name but he said there'll be an appeal in the press shortly, asking for info on all the identities they've come up with, so no doubt we'll learn it then.'

'God, what an infernal mess,' Henry murmured. 'Did you find anything of significance yourselves?'

'No, just the old photos and our birth certificates, where our father's name is plainly stated as Laurence Gregory.'

'Then hard though it is,' Nina said gently, 'all we can do is leave it for the police to unravel.'

Will hadn't spoken for a while, but now he said suddenly, 'Obviously Dad's been on my mind these last weeks and I've been getting more and more keen to find out all I can about him – research him, like that programme *Who Do You Think You Are?*, where you can trace your family back and get to know them.' He looked down at his hands, avoiding eye contact. 'If his other family does come forward, I'd like to meet them.'

David stared at him. 'You're not serious?'

'I am, but the trouble is I very much doubt they'd want to meet us.'

'God, Will—'

'Just think for a moment: they could tell us all the things we've always wondered about – his favourite food, how he liked to spend his holidays, what books he read. We could form a picture of him as a living man, not restricted to an image in a photograph.'

There was a brief silence, then Henry said, 'Well, time enough to think about that if and when they come forward. I just wish to God Sally had been more open with us.'

'Was she ever going to tell us the truth?' David asked.

'I don't think so,' Nina said sadly. 'She thought it would be kinder not to.'

'Or she was ashamed,' he said bluntly.

'That too. Unmarried mothers were far less common in those days and still frowned upon.'

'But when we'd grown up and times had changed, she could have—'

'The truth is I doubt if she ever thought of him any longer.'

There seemed nothing else to say, and shortly afterwards the brothers left to go home.

'You will tell us the minute you hear anything?' Nina said anxiously.

'Of course we will, Gran. Surely this can't go on much longer.'

'Amen to that,' said Henry Hurst.

Foxclere

The appeal was in the press and on television news the next day, requesting information on anyone using the names Laurence Gregory, Gregory Lawrence, Johnnie Stewart or J or Jake Farthing, with the assurance that all information would be held in the strictest confidence.

Georgia, reading the paper over her mother's shoulder, said suddenly, 'What was Dad's full name, Mum?'

Jill looked up, understanding dawning in her eyes. 'Gregory John Stewart Lawrence,' she said slowly. 'My God, why did I never think of that?'

'Well, he made full use of them in various permutations, but heaven alone knows where Jake Farthing comes from. I suppose in the interests of anonymity he didn't want anyone tracing it back to him.'

Blaircomrie

'An immediate result of the appeal, boss, though it doesn't get us far.' There was an undercurrent of excitement in Grant's voice. 'The London paper's been in touch, in a flat spin over their revered columnist ending up dead in a Scottish alley; but it seems he was an enigma to them too. They'd no idea of his real name; their cheques were made out to J Farthing, as we'd supposed, and the last one was cashed on the fourth of June, the day before he died. So he'd had that account long before he did his disappearing act – which was lucky for him in the circumstances, because the one in his real name would have been wound up at his supposed death.'

Mackay nodded. 'It would be interesting to know,' he remarked, 'whether his killer thought he was despatching Johnnie Stewart, Laurence Gregory, Gregory Lawrence or J Farthing. There could be different motives for all of them!'

Grant groaned. 'Just when I thought things were looking a bit clearer!' he said.

TWELVE

Blaircomrie

The two detectives were well into their train journey south by the time Beth and Moira met for lunch the following day. Though they'd spoken on the phone, they'd not seen each other since Jill Lawrence's surprise visit, and Moira was agog for details.

'It gave me quite a jolt, reading all those names in the paper,' Beth admitted after she'd reported their conversation. 'Who'd have thought that Johnnie, who seemed so laid-back and open, should have had so many secrets?' She gave a little shiver. 'I didn't know what I was getting myself into, that's for sure. Believe me, Moira, except for Mr Barnes I'll stick to women in future. Talking of which, I'm having Johnnie's room done over – repainted, new curtains and bed linen – and it should all be ready next week. Then I'll advertise for a new lodger.'

Moira said hesitantly, 'Don't you think it might be wise to wait for the dust to settle a bit?'

'What dust? What are you talking about?'

'Well, the house was shown on *Crimewatch* only ten days ago – the outside, anyway. People might feel a bit hesitant about living in a room whose previous occupant was murdered.'

'But he wasn't murdered in the house! If anyone's stupid enough to think that, I wouldn't want them as my lodger anyway!'

Moira bit her lip, and after a moment said peaceably, 'To get back to this Mrs Lawrence, what was she like?'

'Small, fair, nicely spoken. I liked her. You should have seen her face when I identified Johnnie as her husband, though. I thought for a moment she was going to pass out.'

'But she must have known!' Moira objected. 'She'd seen the sketch in the paper – that's why she'd come.'

'Yes, but to prove to herself that it *wasn't* him. Remember she'd been mourning him for over a year. It was too much for her even to contemplate, and then it bounced back and hit her in the face.'

She crumbled the bread roll on her plate, not looking at her friend. 'I can't believe I was such a fool, letting him seduce me so easily. He must have thought I was a pushover.'

'I'm sure he was fond of you in his way,' Moira said gently. She paused. 'Have you remembered anything else about that paper he got you to sign?'

'No – another example of being a fool, but we'd been laughing and joking and were just about to go out when he pulled it from his pocket and said casually, "Oh, by the way – be a love and sign this for me, would you?" And he put it on the breakfast table in front of me. There was some typing at the top of the page but I didn't get a chance to read it. I asked him what it was and he said, "Oh, just something I need for work, showing I have a permanent address." And the thought that he regarded my home as his "permanent address" sounded so wonderful I just . . . signed.'

'Oh, Beth!'
'No fool like an old fool,' she said bitterly.

Foxclere

Edward had spent every evening that week in the golf club bar in the hope of seeing Owen Jackson, but in vain. By Thursday he was beginning to think he'd have to phone to arrange a meeting, whereas he'd been hoping for a more casual approach.

Ever since Sunday, when Jill had poured out the incredible story of her husband's resurrection, Gregory Lawrence had been on his mind, the more so since the previous day's press appeal listing a string of what could only be other aliases – Jake Farthing, for one, which was almost beyond belief. What the hell had the man been playing at? His only means of learning more was through Owen.

That evening, however, his patience was rewarded; as he was ordering his second drink Owen joined him at the bar and was about to perch on one of the stools when Edward suggested they take their glasses to a vacant table. Slightly surprised, Owen followed him over.

'Last time we met,' Edward began as soon as they'd seated themselves, 'you were telling me about Gregory Lawrence; since then, various facts have emerged about him, one of them being that he wasn't killed by that bomb in Egypt after all.'

Owen paused, his glass halfway to his lips. 'Come again?'

'In fact,' Edward continued, 'he's on the point of being identified as a man who was stabbed in Scotland a few weeks ago.'

Owen stared at him. 'You're not serious?'

'I am. Heavens, man, have you been incommunicado this week? There've been appeals in the press and on TV for any information on him, along with a string of other names he seems to have been using.'

'He's been alive all this time? God!' Owen paused, trying to assimilate the news. 'As it happens,' he went on, 'I *haven't* seen any news this week; I was struck down with summer flu – the worst kind, believe me – and this is my first outing. I've spent the last few days in bed not wanting to do anything but sleep, least of all keep abreast of the news, which would only depress me more.' He paused again, shaking his head in disbelief. 'But if he wasn't killed, where the hell has he been for the last year and why didn't he re-join his family?'

'I was hoping you could explain at least some of that.'

'Me?' Owen stared at him.

'You said you saw him in Cairo shortly before he was "killed". How did he seem?'

Owen's expression of surprise gave way to one of dawning incredulity. 'My God!' he said softly. 'It just might have been true!' He took a long draught of beer. 'You ask how he seemed: the answer is, drunk – very drunk. I was surprised because he'd always been able to hold his liquor, but that night he cornered me as though I was the proverbial wedding guest and poured out a ludicrous story that simply beggared belief. Frankly, having tried unsuccessfully to shake him off, I stopped listening.'

Edward had gone still. 'What did he say?'

'Oh, some highly coloured story about having a fatwa on him, would you believe? He rambled on about how some Islamic sect was out to get him and was threatening his relatives. "I can't even go home," he said, "or I'd be leading them straight to my wife and family."'

He took another drink. 'But if, incredible though it seems, it was actually *true*, and he really *did* survive the bomb, it would have suited him very nicely to be presumed dead.'

Edward was having trouble following him. 'But why in the name of heaven were they after him? What could he possibly have done?'

Owen lifted his shoulders. 'He was a jack of all trades, as I told you, and at that point was into freelance photography, selling pictures of war zones to the press and so on. Possibly he snapped something he shouldn't have, or—'

He slammed his hand down on the table. 'God, yes! It's coming back to me now! A couple of weeks earlier there'd been the hell of a hoo-ha over an aborted peace plan: the head of an Arab state had been due to attend a conference in Baghdad with the aim of brokering a peace deal or something, but he pulled out at the last minute, causing quite a lot of offence – you must remember it. Anyway, it later transpired that he'd been warned an attempt was to have been made on his life. The gang behind the plot was rounded up and several members beheaded.'

'I don't see—' Edward began.

'Greg was actually claiming it was he who'd blown the whistle on them, for God's sake! Said he'd somehow got wind of the plot through his dubious contacts and tipped the sheik off. Is it any wonder I'd stopped listening to what I assumed was his drunken rambling?'

Edward stared at him in growing horror. 'You think it might have been true? Then could it have been the same mob that set off the hotel bomb – and it was Lawrence they were after?'

'God, no – an established group claimed responsibility for that; it was a pure fluke he was caught up in it – he wasn't even staying there. But it gave him a way out and if what he said *was* true, and I'm beginning to think it might have been, I for one don't blame him for taking it.'

'And this stabbing in Scotland,' Edward mused. 'Is it possible that, despite his precautions, they finally caught up with him?'

'That, my friend, we might never know.'

Edward related the story when he went for his piano lesson the next day.

'So it sounds as though he really wanted to come home,' he finished, 'but wouldn't risk putting you and the family in danger. A self-imposed exile, in fact.'

Jill's eyes filled with tears. 'I *knew* there must have been a good reason. Thank you so much for taking the trouble to find out, Edward; it helps a lot.' She paused. 'You'll have seen the press appeal and all those names he used?'

Edward nodded. 'It must have come as a shock.'

'Actually, we'd had prior warning; an old friend of Greg's phoned when I got back from your house on Sunday. He told me about the Jake Farthing connection, and also . . .' She straightened her shoulders and determinedly held his gaze. 'Also that he apparently had another family in Yorkshire. They knew him as Laurence Gregory.'

'God, Jill!'

'The police have taken their DNA, and when Richard phoned to tell them who he was, they said they'd like his and Georgia's as well, if they'd agree.'

Edward moistened his lips. 'And did they?'

'Most definitely; in fact, they're having it done today. It's the only way we can begin to sort out this mess.'

She put a hand to her head and he ached to comfort her but could think of nothing to say. 'I'd been wondering whether he spent some of these last months in Yorkshire, but apparently his sons were told he died years ago.' She gave a shaky laugh. 'He seems to have made a habit of "dying" when living became inconvenient. What I need to know is the time frame: were we the chicken or the egg? In other words, did they have him first, or did we? Or did we unknowingly share him?'

Edward said gently, 'He chose to live with you, didn't he?'

'Some of the time,' she said bleakly. 'But as Richard pointed out, he was away a great deal, supposedly to do with work. Who knows how many other families might come crawling out of the woodwork?'

Her voice had risen to the edge of hysteria and he caught hold of her hand. 'Jill, don't. I'm sure it wasn't like that.'

'Are you? I'm not. I don't even know how many there are in the Yorkshire group and I simply *can't* take in the fact that they're related to my children.' She gave a little shake of her head. 'And as if that isn't bad enough, how am I going to face my friends after all this publicity?'

Aware of her slipping control, she made an effort to pull herself together. 'But that's enough of that,' she said more calmly. 'You're supposed to be having a lesson, aren't you, so if you'd like to go and sit at the piano we can run through what you've been practising this week.'

And since he could think of nothing to add by way of comfort, Edward did as she asked.

Richard had also been suffering from unwanted publicity and his lunchtime appointment to have mouth swabs taken – with the implication that he mightn't be his father's son – had added considerably to the stress. He was convinced he was the subject of the whispering in corridors, either because of his father's colourful past or, even worse, Maria.

It was now five days since the anonymous note had been left on his desk, and it had been preying on his mind ever since. Who could have left it? And why? Were they intending to publicize the affair, report him to the Head? He'd deliberately not mentioned it when he'd met Maria the previous day, fearing that she might by some change in her demeanour incriminate both herself and him still further. Thank God it was almost the end of term, when he'd be free of her. By now he was bitterly resenting her hold over him – he who'd always prided himself on being in control. Even the act of love-making was no longer pleasurable but an unappeasable hunger, and added to this lethal mix of embarrassment, worry and sexual tension was the emergence of these unknown relatives who had suddenly and so unexpectedly come on the scene.

Learning his father had at least two other sons had been a body blow; the belief that he was the only son had been his sole comfort whenever Greg had snubbed or ignored him. Eventually, he'd told himself, his father would come to appreciate him and they'd become staunch allies, the men of the household. Even after his supposed death he'd clung to the belief that, had Greg lived, they would have come together. Now even that meagre consolation had evaporated, adding to the stress that was piling on him from all directions.

'Sir?'

Tearing himself away from his introspection, Richard looked down at the small boy in front of him.

'Very good, Harry. You can do the rest for homework,' he said.

'I still can't believe you actually did it!' Sue Little stared at her friend with a mixture of admiration and apprehension.

Pat Stevens, a fellow Reception teacher, was triumphant. 'I told you I would, and I did!'

'But suppose someone had seen you go into his study?'

'So what? I could have had a dozen reasons.' Pat gave a satisfied little smile. 'It should be giving old po-face something to mull over!'

'But suppose you're wrong and there's nothing in it?'

'Oh, there's something in it all right. Come on, it was you who put me on to it in the first place, telling me about him driving her and Toby to hospital.'

'Yes, but he was on the scene when it happened. I never meant—'

'All the same, no other kid has had the four-star treatment. So after that I paid them more attention, and, like I said, blow me down if they didn't drive off together after school. They didn't see me – I'd promised Jackie a lift and was waiting in my car at the far end of the car park – but I saw them all right. And if *further* proof was needed, as I told you, I came round the corner from the dining hall last week in time to see him bundling her into his study. For God's sake, what more do you want?'

'How about her? Has she given anything away?'

'No, but she always looks like the cat that got the cream.'

Sue sipped her coffee uneasily. 'So what did it actually say, the note?'

'Just a quote from *The Sound of Music*: "How do you solve a problem like Maria?"'

Sue gasped. 'Pat, you didn't!'

'Oh, but I did! And I'd give a month's salary to have been a fly on the wall when he opened it!'

At which point the bell for the end of break halted the conversation.

'Richard?'

He glanced at his watch, biting back an expletive. 'Good morning, Mother.'

'I'm glad I caught you; there's something else the Scottish detectives should know.'

'Can't it wait, Mother? I'm running late as it is.'

'No, dear, it can't wait, which is why I'm phoning. I'd have rung earlier but I've only just learned of it myself.'

He sighed audibly. 'I'm in the car; just a minute while I switch to hands-free. Right, fire away.'

For the next five minutes, as he negotiated the lunchtime traffic, he listened in growing amazement to the story of the supposed fatwa.

'But that's nonsense!' he burst out as she came to the end of her account. 'For one thing, that's not how fatwas work. All right, he might have received threats, but I very much doubt it was a fatwa.'

'Whatever it was,' Jill said curtly, 'it was the reason he didn't feel he could come home, and what's more it gives a possible motive for his murder.'

'I very much doubt—'

'I'm not interested in your doubts, Richard, I'm asking you to pass it on to the detectives. Can I rely on you to do that, or do I have to contact Georgia?'

'I'll tell them, of course, though—'

'That's all I wanted to hear,' said his mother, and ended the call.

Stonebridge

Will burst in as Sylvie was bathing their baby.

'I've found her!' he crowed. 'Dad's wife or widow or whatever she calls herself!'

'What do you mean, found her?' Sylvie bent over the rim of the bath, supporting her daughter with one hand and gently splashing her with the other, to the child's delight.

'Who she is, I mean.' Will seated himself on the lavatory lid. 'It seemed likely from the names in the press that Dad had simply switched his around and was actually Gregory Lawrence, so I googled that and found a listing for a Mrs Gregory Lawrence in Sussex. QED, or Quite Easily Done, as we used to say at school.'

'And what good will that do?' Sylvie asked, rinsing the shampoo off their daughter's curls.

'I'm going to write to her, suggesting a meeting.'

Startled, Sylvie turned to him. 'Will, you can't!'

'Why not? I'm not proposing we should become bosom pals, just that we meet on one solitary occasion to exchange what, if anything, we know about Dad and try to understand why he did what he did.'

'They'd never agree. It will have come as even more of a shock to them because they *knew* him. They're probably trying to convince themselves you don't exist.'

Will flushed. 'Well, like it or not we *do*, and since Dad and Mum met when he was at uni, she presumably got in first.'

'But he didn't stick with her,' Sylvie pointed out more gently. 'He moved on, married someone else and had another family.'

Will leant forward. 'I could have understood him dumping her when she was pregnant with David; a lot of men do a disappearing act at that stage. But he came back, Sylvie, *after he was married*

– and I was the result. I have to know if there was any reason for it, if he was going through a bad patch with his wife and perhaps thinking he'd made a mistake.'

'If so, he lived with that mistake for thirty-odd years.' She lifted the baby out of the bath and, wrapping her in a towel, sat down with her on the stool. 'Have you spoken to David?'

'No, and I'll only tell him if and when she replies. Come on, love, back me up here. How about giving me a hand in drafting the letter?'

Sylvie sighed. 'Let's get Amélie settled, then we can discuss it properly.'

'I knew I could count on you!' Will said.

Foxclere

Victoria had been reluctant to leave Richard that Saturday morning; the news about Greg's double life had hit him hard and the DNA appointment the previous day, together with a rambling story of Jill's about terrorists, had been the final straw. Personally she hadn't seen the point of the DNA; once Jill had identified that man as her husband it was obvious Richard and Georgia were his children, but the Scottish police didn't seem to see it that way.

And Richard had been under a strain even before these latest developments; he was always exhausted by the end of term, but this was something else, as though he were living on a knife-edge. She'd tried gently questioning him but he'd immediately closed up, assuring her he was only tired.

'Are you going to the golf club?' she'd asked brightly as she was leaving the house, but he'd shaken his head.

'There are enough people at school obliquely questioning me about Father without laying myself open to any more.'

'Darling, what Greg did is no reflection on you! Just hold your head up and meet them eye to eye.'

'Easy to say.'

'Well, what will you do then, till I get home?'

'I brought back a stack of reports I can look through and I've some to write myself. That'll keep me busy, and there's some cricket on the box this afternoon.'

She'd hesitated. 'Would you like me to phone Nigel and say I can't make it today?'

'Of course not. Go and flog your paintings; I'll be fine.'

Nigel had some news for Victoria on her arrival at The Gallery.

'I saw Jeff Parker in the pub last night – you know, the guy who has that art shop in Brook Street. He was talking to a pal of his who's also in the trade, and he happened to say there'd been a bloke in trying to track down pictures by local artists.'

'Really?' Victoria perched on the edge of the counter. 'Did he describe him?'

'Yes, and it was our friend Bernard, all right. What's more, the other guy said he'd had a woman in making the same enquiries, and her description fitted Tina.'

Victoria's eyes widened. 'Did you say they'd both been here?'

'You bet I did. It looks as though they've been doing the rounds of all the art shops in the area. We agreed they're hell-bent on tracing a particular painting but they don't seem to know which one, which is odd to say the least.'

Victoria glanced down the length of the shop. 'Well, we've still got the Lockhart seascape and market scene, but he didn't seem interested in them apart from asking how long we'd had them, of all things! I told him the seascape had been for sale for a month or two and the other much the same, though I remembered after it was one of a later batch.'

'Well, if we have another attempted break-in I'll give the police their names,' Nigel said. 'They seem a very dodgy pair.'

The doorbell chimed and a couple came in with a little boy of about seven. Victoria's heart sank; children could be a liability unless they were kept under close supervision, and sadly those who visited The Gallery seldom were.

'We've just moved house,' the woman said brightly, 'and as it's bigger than the last one, we haven't enough pictures to go round.'

'That's good news,' Nigel said smoothly, moving forward. 'Would you like to browse and see if there's anything that takes your fancy, or are you looking for a particular artist?'

'No, no one in particular. We'll just look round, if that's all right.'

'Please do,' Nigel answered, keeping a weather eye on the boy, who had taken a small rubber ball out of his pocket.

'Not indoors, Jeremy,' said his mother automatically, but predictably the child took no notice. Why the hell didn't she take it away from him? Nigel wondered irritably.

The family moved slowly down the room, pausing at each painting while their son began bouncing his ball, and, since it almost always eluded him, running up and down the shop in pursuit of it.

Catching Victoria's less-than-happy expression as vases teetered and decorative jars tinkled, his mother said apologetically, 'He'll be careful, but he gets bored if he's nothing to play with, and we don't want to be rushed into making a decision.'

And Victoria, wishing they *could* be rushed, smiled and murmured, 'Of course.' She turned away and busied herself dusting the pottery, hoping to disguise the fact that she was guarding it from an errant bounce.

'You said you wouldn't be long!' The child's whining voice drifted down the room.

'We won't, darling, I promise; just a few more minutes.'

'But I'm *bored*! You said we could go to the park!'

When his parents ignored this latest complaint, he threw the ball violently against the wall, where it hit the frame of the Lockhart market scene. Everyone held their breath as the picture skewed sideways, hung briefly from one hook, then, as it gave under the weight, crashed to the floor with a splintering of glass.

'Jeremy!' his mother gasped, horror-stricken.

Grim-faced, her husband grasped the child by one arm and marched him out of the shop, leaving his wife to face the music.

The woman seemed close to tears. 'I'm so terribly sorry – he didn't do it on purpose!' She dropped to her knees and began to pick up shards of glass but Nigel, swiftly arriving on the scene, raised her to her feet.

'Please, leave it, you'll cut yourself,' he warned.

'We'll pay for the reframing, of course,' she assured him breathlessly. 'At least the picture itself doesn't seem to be damaged.'

Victoria, helplessly surveying the carnage on the floor, suddenly bent closer. 'What's that?' she asked curiously, edging a piece of frame aside with the toe of her shoe.

Lying amid the broken glass was a small silver key.

THIRTEEN

Foxclere

Still apologizing profusely, the child's mother, a Mrs Sinclair, had left her card so they could contact her about the repair, but they'd no time to examine their find as a steady trickle of customers continued throughout the day, and it wasn't until they closed at four o'clock that they were free to give it their undivided attention.

'Where exactly did it come from?' Victoria puzzled. 'It's too bulky to have been inside the picture – the back wouldn't have gone on.'

Nigel picked up a broken piece of frame. 'This is fairly deep, isn't it? It could have been wedged under the overhang. It would have been visible if anyone had looked closely, but perhaps it was only a temporary hiding place and for some reason whoever put it there never got back to retrieve it.'

'Either that, or when he went back the painting had been moved,' Victoria hazarded.

'Then it must have been either in a shop or at a framer's. Who did we acquire this one from?'

'The artist herself, Alison Lockhart. Don't you remember, she brought it in to show us and gave us first option?'

'So she did; she could have come straight from the framer's. Hang on a minute.' Nigel bent to examine the backing that was now propped against the wall. 'Thought so! There's a label here giving the name and address of the picture-framer. Bernard was keen to look at the back, wasn't he? Suppose he wanted to check if it had been at the place where the key was hidden?'

'But why hide it in the first place? And, the million dollar question: what does it open? It doesn't look like a door key; I suppose it could belong to a safe but they're mostly combination these days.' She picked it up and turned it over in her fingers. 'There's a number on one side – two-five-six – and a stylized outline of some kind of bird on the other.'

'Well, whatever it opens, it must be what Bernard and Tina were after. If they'd only been honest about it instead of skulking around and trying to break into our premises we could have handed it in at the insurance brokers, but there must be some reason for all this subterfuge, so our best bet is to contact the police. We can give them his name and tell them about his suspicious behaviour.'

'And the address of the framer,' Victoria added. 'But before we do any of that, we'd better phone Ms Lockhart. It's remotely possible the key might belong to her, though it seems highly unlikely.'

A quick call confirmed that the artist knew nothing about any key and could not imagine how it had become lodged under the frame. 'When you find out, do tell me!' she said.

'So now for the police,' Victoria said. 'Have you got the number of the local nick?'

'I can find it.'

Minutes later he was through to the police switchboard. 'I'd like to speak to someone in CID, please,' he said. Then, in answer to a question, 'My name is Nigel Soames and I'm part-owner of an art shop. I want to report an attempted break-in.'

There was a pause, and Victoria listened while Nigel reported the failed break-in and the finding of the key. 'We've had some suspicious characters hanging around,' he added, 'and we're wondering if it's the key they were after . . . Yes.' He glanced at his watch. 'Yes, very well. Thank you; we'll come straight down.'

He switched off and turned to Victoria. 'The guy I spoke to would like us to go down, hand in the key and give him more details.'

She glanced at her watch. 'Damn, it's getting on for four thirty. Richard will be expecting me.'

'I'll deal with it if you like.'

'No, I don't want to miss anything. I'll phone and tell him I'll be late. With any luck he'll still be watching the cricket.'

At the police station they gave their names to the officer at the desk and asked to see DS Finch, to whom Nigel had been speaking. Minutes later they were approached by a fresh-faced young man who introduced himself, shook their hands and showed them into

an interview room, where they were joined by another officer, one
DC Jones.

Having confirmed their names, addresses and mobile numbers,
Nigel handed Finch the key, which he examined carefully.

'Now, tell me again where you found this,' he said. 'You own
an art shop, I believe?'

'That's right.' It was Victoria who answered. 'And finding the
key isn't the only odd thing that's happened recently. The first
thing we noticed was a man who hung around outside the shop
for a couple of weeks, looking in the window or sitting in the café
directly opposite. Then a woman came in, allegedly to look at
some paintings though she seemed more interested in where we'd
obtained them than the pictures themselves. After which the man
reappeared and this time he also came in, asking the same questions as she had. Then, to crown it all, Nigel saw them together
in town.' She hesitated. 'And in the middle of all this, we had the
attempted break-in.'

Finch glanced at Nigel. 'You mentioned that on the phone but
I couldn't find any record of it.'

'We didn't report it; they didn't get in, so there seemed no
point.'

Finch shook his head reprovingly. 'It should still have been
reported. These people you mentioned; I suppose it's too much to
hope that they left their names or contact details?'

Nigel flushed. 'They didn't, no, but as it happens I was in the
High Street one lunchtime and saw the man come out of Selby
and Frodsham the insurance brokers and go into the White Horse.
I . . . followed him and as I was pretty sure he wouldn't recognize
me I sat down at a nearby table. He was joined by the woman
who'd also been to the shop, and I was able to catch their names
– Bernard and Tina.'

'We'll have to recruit you into CID, Mr Soames,' Finch said
dryly.

'I'm also guilty of playing detective,' Victoria admitted. 'When
Nigel told me about this, I rang the firm and asked to speak to
"Bernard". The girl on the switchboard said, "Bernard Davies?"
I said yes and hung up.'

To forestall any further comment she hurried on to Bernard's
behaviour on entering the shop, his questions about who'd recently

bought paintings and his eagerness to examine the back of them. 'We wondered if he hoped to find out who'd framed them,' she finished.

Finch pursed his lips, looking down at the key.

'What kind of key would you say it is?' Nigel asked.

He shrugged. 'Probably some kind of safe deposit. The difficulty will be in tracking down which one; there's been a growth of private businesses opening up all over the country. Needle in a haystack.' He rose to his feet and they stood with him. 'Well, thank you for bringing it in and for all the other information.' He handed Victoria a card. 'If there are any further developments at your end – another break-in attempt, whether or not it's successful, or a further visit from this couple – please contact me immediately.'

'They'll probably just file it and forget all about it,' Victoria said dispiritedly as they walked down the steps of the police station.

Nigel shook his head. 'They might have a month ago, but now they'll be super-sensitive regarding anything to do with art or attempted break-ins. The press are giving them a hard time over the country-house burglaries, particularly after that man's death. There was a list of them in today's paper – three museums, two stately homes and four country houses in the last six months.'

'We've had this conversation before,' Victoria said impatiently. 'There can't possibly be any connection between us and this ghastly murder investigation.'

Nigel took her arm as they crossed the road. 'They'll be pulling out all the stops, that's all I'm saying, and for that reason our little key is likely to get more attention that it would otherwise have done.'

'Well, if it leads to a solution about Bernard and Tina, so be it,' Victoria said with feeling.

Blaircomrie

When Grant and Coombes returned to the police station on Monday, they were met with the news that the hit-and-run driver had been identified.

'And you'll never guess who he turned out to be!' a uniformed DS told them exultantly.

'Then you'd best tell us, hadn't you?' Grant, tired after the long train journey and his curtailed weekend, was in no mood for guessing games.

'Only a director of Parsons Makepeace, one Norman Patterson by name!'

Grant turned to stare at him. 'You're not serious!'

'Oh, but I am! The dead man was in his department! He's an arrogant bastard, though; he'll take a bit of cracking.'

'But he must have some kind of explanation? Does he live in that area himself?'

'No; says he was on his way to see Petrie, momentarily lost control of his car, mounted the pavement and hit someone. He'd had a couple of drinks after leaving the office and was afraid of losing his licence, so since people were already running to help the victim, he just accelerated away. Swears he didn't know either that it was a fatality or that the victim was Petrie till he heard it on the news.'

'You believe that?'

'Sure, and pigs can fly. If he'd wanted to speak to Petrie, he'd had all day at the office to do so.'

'And his reason for not coming forward?'

'That nothing he said or did could help Petrie and the firm was in enough trouble without any more bad publicity. In other words, he was watching his own back. The worrying thing is he damn near got away with it.'

'But assuming it was deliberate, what was the motive?'

'We've not dug that out of him yet but we've applied for extra time.'

'Well, the best of luck,' Grant said. 'Actually, we've a bit of news ourselves, concerning Johnnie under one of his pseudonyms. Are you ready for this? There's a theory that he might have been targeted by a gang of Arabs. Now, if you'll excuse me, I'm in need of a strong coffee.'

And leaving the sergeant staring after him, he left the room.

Foxclere

Georgia had just returned home at lunchtime when there was a knock on her door and she opened it to find her mother on the landing, pale-faced and holding a letter.

'Mum! Come in! Everything OK?'

'Not really,' Jill said. 'I received this this morning.'

They went into the sitting room, once Jill and Greg's bedroom, where Jill handed her the letter. 'Read it aloud,' she invited, seating herself on the sofa, her eyes fixed on her daughter's face. 'It might help me to take it in.'

Georgia sat down opposite her. '"Dear Mrs Lawrence,"' she began, then her eyes slipped to the signature at the foot of the page and she gave a little gasp.

'Go on,' Jill instructed.

'"I hope you will forgive me for approaching you at this sensitive time,"' she continued, '"but I'm sure you will appreciate that the sudden re-emergence of our father has been as big a shock for my family as it must have been for yours. My brother and I never knew him, having been told he was killed shortly before I was born, and we've always been conscious of an empty space in our lives. As we've grown older we've wondered more and more what kind of man he was, but our mother, who died recently, was always reluctant to speak of him.

'"The purpose of this letter is to ask if you would consider a one-off meeting"' – Georgia glanced fleetingly at her mother's set face – '"somewhere neutral such as a hotel, so that, if you were willing, you could share some of your memories with us. I appreciate you might well have misgivings at this proposal, but please let me assure you I have no hidden agenda, financial or otherwise; just the hope of filling in a long-felt gap in our lives.

'"It might be that you're as curious about us as we are about you, since I assume neither of us knew of the other's existence. I can't stress enough how grateful we would be if you could agree to meet us, and hope very much to hear from you.

'"Yours sincerely, William Gregory."'

As Georgia stopped speaking silence seeped into the room. Then she said quietly, 'Well, there's a bolt out of the blue. How do you feel about it?'

'How do I feel?' Jill repeated. 'How do you *think* I feel?'

'I don't know, Mum. I don't even know how *I* feel.'

'He's got a bloody nerve!' Jill said viciously. 'And how did he find out my name and address?'

'I don't know, but I can see his point.'

Jill frowned. 'You can?'

'Suppose it had been the other way round and Dad had abandoned *us* years ago and lived with his family in Yorkshire. I'm sure I'd have been just as curious to know about him as this . . . William is.'

'He probably wants to contest the will,' Jill said. 'Well, he hasn't a hope in hell.'

Georgia, unsure about legal rights, said quickly, 'I'm sure he doesn't – he says as much.' She paused. 'And if I'm honest, ever since we heard about this other family I've been curious about them.'

'You're not saying we should meet him?' Jill asked incredulously.

'What harm could it do? A one-off, he said, and I'm sure that's what it would be. It's not as though they live close by; we'd never come across them again.'

There was a short silence, then Jill said crisply, 'Well, you and Richard must do as you think fit, but I certainly have no intention of meeting him.'

'We wouldn't do anything to hurt you,' Georgia said softly. Then, 'Can you tell me why you're so against seeing him yourself?'

'Because,' Jill said in a low voice, 'it would make it all real.'

'Oh, Mum!' Georgia slipped to the floor and knelt beside her, taking hold of her hands. After a minute Jill gently freed them and patted her arm. 'I know I'm being silly,' she went on. 'They have far more reason to resent us than we do them, and this boy is holding out an olive branch. But until we know how and why Greg really died, I feel I can't move on.'

She met Georgia's eyes. 'I presume Richard told you about the fatwa?'

'No. What was that all about? I heard him saying something to the detective but he was in a rush to get back to school and I'd no chance to ask him afterwards. From his tone he wasn't taking it seriously, so I didn't either, and to be honest I forgot about it.'

Jill gave an exclamation of annoyance. 'He might not take it seriously, but I do. It would explain why Dad never let us know he was alive.'

Georgia looked startled. 'I'm sorry, Mum, I didn't realize it was important. So what's the story and where did it come from?'

'A friend of Edward's who met Greg in Cairo shortly before the bomb blast.' And she repeated the story of the aborted peace talks and subsequent threat.

'But he was still killed later,' Georgia said. 'Do you think they caught up with him?'

'I doubt it; if they had they'd have made some announcement "claiming" responsibility, as though it was something to be proud of.'

'So who else's secrets did he give away?' Georgia asked with a wan smile.

There was a moment's reflective silence, then Jill knotted her hands in her lap. 'To return to the letter, will you do something for me?'

'If I can.'

'Will you tell Richard about it? I'd . . . rather not have to go through it again.'

'Of course I will.'

'And assure him I've really no objection if you both want to go ahead with a meeting.'

'Truly?'

'Truly, and I'll be happy to babysit.' She smiled ironically. 'To be honest, I'd be interested to hear what they're like, but not to the extent of meeting them myself.' She held up a hand to forestall Georgia handing back the letter. 'You'd better take that with you.'

'Very well. Now, can I persuade you to stay for a bite of lunch?'

Jill shook her head, rising to her feet. 'Not today, I'm afraid; I've a full afternoon's tuition ahead of me.' She paused. 'Let me know what you both decide.'

'I will.' Georgia walked with her to the door, where she bent and kissed her cheek. 'Don't worry about this, we'll sort it out.'

She watched her mother start down the stairs before closing the door, deciding that she'd discuss it with Tim before broaching her abrasive brother. Tomorrow would be soon enough to put Richard in the picture.

*   *   *

Tuesday was one of Victoria's days at The Gallery, so Georgia left a message on their answerphone to say she'd something important to discuss with them, and unless she heard from them would call round that evening at about six.

She and Tim had talked over the matter exhaustively the previous evening, and had reached the decision that they would agree to meet William Gregory, whether or not Richard and Victoria joined them.

'It seems churlish to refuse,' Tim had said. 'He sounds a reasonable chap and you can't blame him for wanting to find out all he can about his father. As for the fatwa thing, that beggars belief, though if it could happen to anyone, it would be Greg it happened to!'

'As Mum said, it would explain his lying low. Who knows, when enough time had passed he might have risked coming back to us.'

Tim put an arm round her. 'Quite possibly,' he said.

Richard was about to go for lunch when there was a tap on his door and, before he could respond, it opened and Maria slipped into the room.

A wave of heat suffused him. 'Maria! What—?'

She moved swiftly over to him and laid a finger on his lips. 'I couldn't wait till Thursday,' she whispered.

'God, not here! You can't . . .'

But she could, and did. Then, as swiftly and silently as she had come, she was gone, leaving him leaning weakly against his desk. With an effort he moved slowly to his chair, slumped into it and, putting his head in his hands, stared down at the polished wooden surface. Why in God's name hadn't he taken her by the shoulders, turned her round and marched her straight out again?

It was, he thought numbly, the ultimate humiliation, that she should invade this room, the traditional sanctum of the deputy headmaster, and demonstrate her power over him with such careless ease, confident he'd neither the will nor the power to refuse her. Would he *never* be free of her, and if not, what would become of him?

*   *   *

Victoria opened the door to Georgia just after six.

'Come in, Georgia! That was a slightly worrying message you left!'

'It wasn't meant to be, but in the last couple of days various things have come up that you should know about.'

'How intriguing! Can I get you a drink? We've just opened the bar.'

'Just half a glass of wine, then, please.'

Richard stood up as she came into the room. 'So what's all this about?' he asked.

'Give her a chance to sit down!' Victoria remonstrated. 'And pour her a small glass of wine, would you.'

Georgia seated herself on the sofa, looking about her and admiring as always the quiet elegance of this converted seventeenth-century cottage – dark oak beams, a wide stone fireplace, now hidden behind a large vase of flowers, and graceful antique furniture that she had always coveted. It was very obviously a home without children.

She took the glass Richard handed her and drew a deep breath. 'Thanks. Well, the first thing to say is that Mum has received a letter from the Yorkshire family.'

Richard stiffened but Victoria leant forward interestedly. 'Really? What did they want?'

'In short, to meet us.'

'Over my dead body!' said Richard forcefully.

'Hush, darling! Go on, Georgia.'

'I think the best thing is to read you the letter.' She slid it out of its envelope and read it aloud for the third time. As on both previous occasions it was greeted by silence.

'Mum's refusing to consider it,' she said, 'but Tim and I are prepared to meet him.'

'God, Georgia, how can you even contemplate it? I'm definitely with Mother on this.'

'Aren't you the tiniest bit curious about your half-brothers?'

'*Don't* call them that!'

'Like it or not, that's what they are. And as William says, it was as much of a shock for them as it was for us to hear of Dad's resurrection, even if it was sadly temporary.' She paused. 'Did you tell Victoria about the fatwa theory?'

'No, I did not!' Richard declared. 'It was pure fabrication!'

'*Fatwa?*' Victoria looked from one to the other in bewilderment, and Georgia briefly outlined the details.

'He was probably planning not to come home even before the bomb blast,' Richard said, 'and this was a means of covering himself. We now know his whole life was composed of invention and deceit.' He turned to Georgia with a frown. 'Who is this Edward French, anyway, and why is he sticking his nose into our family business?'

'He's a student of Mum's,' Georgia said. 'I met him once, briefly.'

'And he thinks that gives him the right to burrow into what doesn't concern him?'

'He was only passing on what his friend told him,' Georgia said mildly. 'But to get back to William: what do you think?'

Victoria looked at Richard, and when he didn't speak, said tentatively, 'I think it would be good to meet him. If we didn't, we'd always regret missing the opportunity.'

'I shouldn't,' Richard said.

Victoria turned to Georgia. 'You and Tim go ahead and arrange a meeting, and let us know when and where it will be.' She smiled. 'In the meantime, I'll work on Richard!'

They talked of other matters for a few minutes, then Georgia rose to go and Victoria saw her out. 'You can count us in,' she said quietly at the door. 'I know my husband; when it comes to the crunch curiosity will get the better of him.'

'I'll write back, then, and let you know when it's arranged.'

As she got into her car, Georgia had a brief moment of doubt. What if, by agreeing to this meeting, they were opening Pandora's box and the Gregory family fastened on them like some bloodsucking incubus? Or was she mixing up her myths? Whatever, she was being ridiculous: they would meet their newly discovered relations and see what – if anything – transpired.

Determinedly she turned the key in the ignition and moved off slowly down the road.

Stonebridge

Will said, 'They've agreed to meet us!'

David frowned. 'Who have?'

'The Lawrences, of course. I've had a letter from Georgia Peel, née Lawrence, in answer to mine, saying that although her mother doesn't feel up to it, she, her husband and her brother and sister-in-law would be happy to meet us and answer any questions we might have to the best of their ability.'

'You bloody fool! I told you to leave well alone!'

'David, we know *nothing* about Dad except that he was amusing and witty and left Mum in the lurch when she needed him most. I need to know he wasn't a complete toe-rag.'

David stared at him, breathing heavily. 'Have you spoken to the grandparents?'

'Yes, I read them my letter over the phone before posting it.'

'What was their reaction?'

'Grandpa wasn't surprised – I'd said I wanted to find out more. I think Gran was a bit apprehensive.'

'Me too.'

'Come on, David! What harm can it do, one single meeting? And it might explain a lot of things.'

'Suppose I don't agree?'

'I'll go by myself.'

There was a pause. Then: 'And where exactly are you proposing it should take place?'

Will felt a small spurt of triumph. 'A hotel somewhere. London would probably be best; I should think they'd go up by train and we could fly down. Sylvie will stay home with Amélie – she doesn't trust anyone else to look after her – but I hope Julia will join us. Gran said they'd love to have the twins for the day.'

He waited for David to make a comment, but when he remained silent continued, 'I recommend not committing ourselves to a meal in case it doesn't go well. So let's suggest morning coffee, and if all progresses smoothly we could move seamlessly on to lunch.'

'I see you've given it some thought,' David said dryly. 'When do you propose this should take place?'

'As soon as possible, in case they go off the idea; this weekend, ideally.'

'This weekend! God, how can we arrange—'

'There's nothing *to* arrange, except booking our flights. That's what I'll suggest, anyway, and hope they're free.'

'But today's Thursday, for God's sake!'

'There was a phone number on the letterhead; that'll speed things up.'

'You haven't a hope in hell,' David said flatly.

Foxclere

'Jill? Is this a bad time to ring?'

'Hello, Edward. No, it's fine; I've an hour's break between pupils.'

'Look, I'm sorry at the short notice but I'll have to cancel this week's lesson; I've just heard a business colleague has died and it's his funeral tomorrow.'

Jill felt a stab of disappointment; at the moment Edward was one of the few fixed points in her firmament. 'I'm sorry; did you know him well?'

'We worked together years ago but latterly just kept in touch via Christmas cards. Still, I feel I have to go.'

'Of course.'

There was a brief pause, then he said, 'I was wondering how your family reacted when they heard about the fatwa?'

'Richard refused to countenance it, but to be honest it was rather superseded by my receiving a letter from Greg's other family suggesting we meet.'

'Good grief! And are you going to?'

'Richard and Georgia are – they're going up to London on Saturday – but I opted out. I didn't feel I could face it.'

'I'm not surprised.'

It would be good to talk things over with Edward, and eight days was too long to wait.

'Would you like to come over for lunch one day next week?' she asked impulsively. 'As a thank-you for driving me to and from Gatwick and looking after me on my return?'

'You've already thanked me enough, but I'd love to come to lunch!'

'Good, then I can tell you how the London meeting went. I have lessons on Monday and Tuesday, so let's make it Wednesday. Twelve thirty?'

Thank you. I look forward to it,' he said.

Blaircomrie

Thursday lunchtime, and Beth and Moira were at their usual table.

'I see Johnnie's been pushed out of the headlines,' Moira said.

'By the hit-and-run driver? Yes, bit of a shock, that, being someone from the same firm. He must have known his victim, which makes it sound deliberate.'

'One of them was probably sleeping with the other's wife,' Moira remarked cynically.

'No doubt; but on a more cheerful note, the renovation of my guest room is now complete! I hung the new curtains yesterday and it looks lovely, Moira; you must pop round and see it. *And*, even better news, I have a new lodger to occupy it and she's moving in over the weekend!'

'My goodness, that was quick!'

'I didn't even have to advertise – she did! I saw it in the personal column of the *Gazette* and got in touch with her straight away. She came round, saw the room and loved it, and Mr Barnes got back from work as she was leaving, so she met him too.' Beth threw her friend a triumphant glance. 'What's more, she even brought up Johnnie's name; she'd connected the address with that on *Crimewatch* and sympathized with us for having gone through such a traumatic experience.'

'Well, that's great, Beth,' Moira said sincerely. 'She'd have been bound to hear about it soon enough – it's good that you didn't even have to tell her. What does she do, by the way?'

'She'll be working at the local radio station – producer or something. She's unmarried, in her forties, and her name is Helen Phillips. Honestly, Moira, if I'd handpicked her I couldn't have done better!'

'Well, that's great!' Moira said again. 'Johnnie Stewart, RIP.'

'Amen to that,' Beth agreed.

Stonebridge

That same lunchtime Will phoned Georgia, and after a momentary hesitation she agreed it would be as well to meet sooner rather than later. They settled on the lounge of the Argyll Hotel in Mayfair at ten thirty on Saturday morning.

She'd sounded pleasant enough, Will thought as he clicked on his brother's number. He could only hope he wouldn't regret his precipitous machinations.

Blaircomrie

Jim Scott, crime reporter of the *Blaircomrie Gazette*, had embarked on a one-man mission to solve the murder of Johnnie Stewart. The man had been increasing in both interest and importance over the last few weeks as his different personas came to light, and Scott reckoned any hand he had in bringing his murderer to justice would do his career no harm at all; he'd always had his sights set on the nationals. And as 'Johnnie Stewart' was the man's local identity, and, in all conscience, the only one he had any hope of coming to grips with, that was the one on which he would concentrate.

The police, of course, had been slogging away at the case for weeks and had interviewed regulars at the pub where Stewart went every night, but, judging by the press conferences, who it was who'd stuck a knife into him in a dark alley last month remained a mystery that was baffling Blaircomrie's finest.

However, Scott reckoned the pub clientele were more likely to open up to him than to 'the polis' whom they treated with habitual caution, some of them with good reason, and with this in mind he had for the last ten days or so been frequenting the pub – no hardship, admittedly – and attempting to ingratiate himself with the regulars. It had taken a considerable number of rounds, but some of them were beginning to open up to him and he was starting to piece together odd snippets of conversation in the hope of being able to build up a complete narrative.

But this was by way of an ongoing operation, and as a change of scene he decided to have another go at winning over the land-lady, who'd not been very responsive at their last meeting. He felt sure she must hold some key to what had happened, though possibly without realizing it. He'd done her a good turn in telling her about the Yorkshire claimants; time to call in the favour. And since he doubted she'd agree to an interview if he phoned in advance, he called at the house on the Friday evening.

'Evening, Mrs Monroe!' he said breezily as she opened the door. 'I was wondering if you've time for a quick word?'

Her lips had tightened. 'Not really, no. I'm preparing my evening meal.'

'Give me a break, Mrs M,' he wheedled. 'I have to give my readers *something* to read over their cornflakes. I tipped you the wink about the Yorkshire family, now there's this other lot down in Sussex. How do you feel about your ex-lodger's multiple personalities?'

She still gave no sign of inviting him in. 'He was always Mr Stewart to me.'

'There must have been *some* hint, surely, that there was more to him? The odd thing he said or did that didn't quite fit in with the Johnnie Stewart character?'

'Since I was no authority on what you term the Johnnie Stewart character, I wouldn't have recognized it if there had been. Now' – she was beginning to close the door – 'you'll have to excuse me; I have something on the stove.'

And that, Scott thought ruefully, appeared to be that. Back to the pub, then.

FOURTEEN

London

Since he was in the position of host, Will was anxious to be at the venue before his relatives and had booked an early flight. Consequently he, David and Julia arrived at the hotel with about an hour in hand.

'We had a coffee on the plane,' Julia commented. 'If we have another we'll be awash with it by the time they arrive. It's a lovely morning so let's go out and explore the district for a while.'

Will glanced at her, aware of her restlessness; he'd been conscious for some time that things were not right between his brother and sister-in-law; there'd been occasions when Julia had seemed snappy and David too eager to please. He hoped sincerely that whatever it was would soon blow over, for the twins' sakes as well as their own.

It was considerably warmer in London than it had been in Yorkshire and they walked in the sunshine for the next half hour, admiring the handsome buildings and strolling in Green Park before wending their way back to the Argyll Hotel.

By this time there were several groups in the lounge partaking of morning coffee and David wondered how the newcomers would know who to approach. But when, soon after they'd seated themselves, four people came in together, he experienced a jolt of déjà vu, for the taller of the men bore an uncanny resemblance to himself – more so, in fact, than did Will, who took after their mother.

'Well, at least there's not much doubt who you are!' Georgia Peel said with a half-laugh as she introduced herself and her companions. They all shook hands, but David was uncomfortably aware of the veiled hostility in Richard Lawrence's eyes.

While chairs were pulled up and coffee was being served they chatted lightly about their respective journeys and the current heatwave, but as the waiter moved away Will, as the instigator of the meeting, took it upon himself to open proceedings.

'First, I'd like to say how grateful we are to your agreeing to meet us,' he began, 'especially at such short notice. My wife sends her apologies – she's at home with our year-old daughter.' He paused.

'To sketch in our position, until a few weeks ago we believed that our parents had been married, that our father's name was Laurence, or Larry, Gregory, and that he'd been killed in a train crash in France a few weeks before I was born.'

'When did you begin to have doubts?' asked Victoria.

'Well, we were taken aback when we saw the e-fit in the paper – it was so like the only photo we had of Dad – but Mum had sworn our grandparents to secrecy, so it never entered our heads it could actually be him. They were on holiday at the time, and when they phoned we mentioned having seen it. Obviously alarm bells started to ring, they checked for them- selves online, were convinced it was Dad and realized we'd have to be told the truth immediately, before his real identity was revealed. Though as it turned out they didn't know the whole story.'

'You said your mother died recently?' Georgia asked.

'Yes, someone crashed into her car, killing her instantly.'

'I'm so sorry.'

David leant forward. 'We don't want you to get the wrong impression of her,' he said. '"Larry", as she always called him, was the love of her life. They'd met while he was at Durham University and she was doing nursing training. My grandfather said they were very close for a year or so, then he graduated and moved back down south. Mum was heartbroken for a while but life went on, they lost touch and she qualified as a nurse.'

Will took up the story. 'But then he came back up north for a few months on a job assignment and took up with Mum again, moving into her flat. And soon after he returned home she discovered she was pregnant. Our grandparents wanted her to tell Larry but she wouldn't, not wanting, as she saw it, to force his hand, and again they briefly lost touch.'

Georgia, looking puzzled, turned to David. 'Would you mind telling us when you were born?'

'On the twenty-fourth of May nineteen seventy-eight.'

Georgia gasped, exchanging an incredulous look with her brother.

'That's significant?' David asked, an edge to his voice.

'It is rather. It was our parents' wedding day.'   .

They looked at each other, stunned.

'So you, not Richard, were his first child,' Tim said slowly. Victoria reached for Richard's hand but he shrugged her away.

'But . . . William?' Georgia enquired hesitantly.

'Another job assignment a few months later.' Will's voice was dry.

'And again he stayed with . . . your mother? I'm sorry, I don't know her name.'

'Sally. Yes, that's right.'

Richard spoke for the first time, his voice strained. 'So he knew about . . . David?'

'When he came back, obviously; he seemed delighted to find he had a son.' Will drew a deep breath. 'Mum became pregnant again soon after, and suggested they got married. Which was when he told her he was married already.'

'God!' Georgia said softly. 'So what happened?'

'She threw him out!' Will said with spirit. 'She never saw him again, but to give him his due he made a very generous settlement on us, so he must have had *some* conscience.'

'And your surname?' Victoria queried. 'How did that come about?'

'At uni Dad had been known as "Larry" Lawrence, which is what Mum called him, but she must have known his real name. So when the family decided to make a clean break and move to an area where no one knew them, she simply inverted it and changed her own name to Gregory, which is how we were registered. Everyone thought she was a widow – including us!' he added with a wry smile.

'You said your grandparents didn't know the whole story,' Tim prompted.

Will bit his lip. 'They thought, of course, she'd changed her name to Dad's surname. They'd never heard of Gregory Lawrence and hadn't realized we were called after someone who'd never existed.' Will straightened his shoulders and looked challengingly at Georgia. 'So, that's our story. Now, over to you.'

She glanced at her brother, but he was studiously avoiding her eye. 'Well, obviously we knew nothing of all this and it's come as a complete shock, especially to our mother. For our part, at least, it was all over before we were born.'

'Not quite all,' Will said. He turned to Richard. 'As a matter of interest, what's your date of birth?'

Richard hesitated, reluctant to reveal that Jill had been pregnant on her wedding day. 'Fifteenth of December nineteen seventy-eight.'

'Well, I arrived eight months later,' Will said, 'so we do overlap slightly.'

There was an embarrassed silence, which David broke by asking, 'Did he always spend long periods away from home?'

Georgia rallied. 'Yes, all his life he kept switching from one job to another, but they all involved a considerable amount of time away.'

'So he wasn't what you'd call a family man?'

'I suppose not, though we all loved him and he seemed to love us.'

Richard made a movement but his sister quelled it with a glance.

'So what kind of work did he do?' Will pursued. 'Was it writing-based? We were staggered to hear about Jake Farthing.'

'So were we!' Victoria said.

Will stared at her. 'You didn't know?'

They all shook their heads. Richard said curtly, 'The different sections of his life were never allowed to overlap. And no, his other work wasn't writing-related. He was in IT for a while, then had a spell organizing trips for travel companies. There were other jobs over the years, but the last was freelance photography, particularly of trouble spots.'

'But you also believed he was dead?'

Georgia nodded. 'Yes, for the last year or so. We heard he'd been killed in a suicide bombing in Egypt.'

'No body,' Richard said succinctly.

'But why—?'

'Didn't he come home? That's what we couldn't understand, until this last week.' And she related the fatwa story.

Will let out his breath in a low whistle. 'Well, he was certainly a colourful character. I suppose that's why he became Johnnie Stewart.'

'They were his middle names,' Georgia said.

'Even so, it looks as though they might have caught up with him.'

'My mother thinks not; she believes if they had his killers would have opted for publicity.'

'Considering the life he led,' Richard remarked tightly, 'people were probably queuing up to do away with him.'

It seemed advisable to step back a little, so Will embarked on the questions he'd originally wanted to ask, about Greg's tastes in books, music, films and so on, and the tension gradually eased. Georgia produced a few photographs, one of them showing Greg and Jill in the garden at Woodlands, his arm round her shoulders. Somehow this domestic scene confirmed that it was to this family he'd belonged, and he and David really had no claim on him. It was a bitter, if not unexpected, pill to swallow.

'We've touched on Greg's many occupations,' Tim said as the photos were put away. 'What do you two do?'

'I'm a partner in a firm of solicitors,' David said, 'and Will's in IT.' He glanced at his brother, seeming to sense his deflation. 'Like Dad,' he added. 'How about you?'

'I, for my sins, run a commercial flower-arranging business,' Georgia said, 'dealing with offices, hotels, restaurants and the like. Tim's a bank manager, Victoria part-owns an art shop and Richard is a deputy headmaster.'

'That sounds impressive.' Julia turned to Richard. 'State school or private?'

'Private. We encompass the full span from age three to eighteen, so we're kept on our toes.'

'He's always exhausted by the end of term,' Victoria put in, 'but we're nearly there, thank goodness. It's the final sports day next Wednesday – we've had several for different age-groups – and they break up on Friday. Then come the long summer holidays.'

'You must already be close to the seaside, living where you do,' Julia said with a smile.

'Close enough, but we try to avoid it in the season. What's it like where you live? I know it's Yorkshire, but I'm not sure which part.'

'Stonebridge, North Yorks. It's on the edge of the moors – very pretty, actually.'

Richard had straightened. 'Stonebridge? A member of my staff comes from there; I wonder if you knew her – Maria Chiltern?'

To everyone's surprise David flushed a deep, painful red. Julia had stiffened, her eyes widening. 'Oh, we knew her all right,' she said, her voice trembling. 'She taught at our daughters' school and my husband met her one parents' evening when I wasn't able to go. He knew her *much* better than I did, didn't you, David?'

'Darling, I really don't think—'

'Could we possibly order some more coffee?' Tim interrupted. 'I've had two cups but I'm still thirsty.'

Richard stumbled to his feet. 'I'll go and find someone.'

He hurried from the room, grateful for the chance to compose himself. *David* had known Maria – more than just known her, from Julia's inference. It seemed he'd not only pre-empted the position of first-born son but also been the first recipient of Maria's favours. Suppose – his breath clogged in his throat – suppose she'd only come to him because he reminded her of David? That at the height of passion she'd been imagining she was with him?

'Yes, sir. Can I help you?'

Richard forced himself to refocus. 'Yes, please. We'd like some more coffee – the table by the window.'

'Of course, sir. I'll see to it at once.'

Reluctant to return immediately to the group, Richard was still hesitating when David came out of the lounge and turned in the direction of the men's room. Instinctively he went after him.

He was splashing his face with cold water and looked up as Richard came in. 'Sorry about that,' he said abruptly, reaching for a paper towel.

'I gather you blotted your copybook with Mrs Chiltern?'

'I was a fool,' David said bitterly.

'How long did it last?'

'A couple of terms or so. She just . . . went to my head. We thought we were discreet but inevitably someone saw us together. She left unexpectedly at the end of that term and I thought I'd got away with it; then, as luck would have it, Julia found out just recently.'

He screwed up the paper towel and tossed it in the bin. 'I heard later through the grapevine that her husband had got wind of some affair and whisked her away down south.' He glanced at Richard. 'Anyone succumbed at your school?'

A pulse was beating in Richard's temple and he fervently hoped the other man wouldn't see it. 'Not that I've heard,' he said.

'Well, I should keep your eyes and ears open if I were you. You don't want any rumours starting, particularly at a private school.'

'Definitely not,' said Richard aridly.

They walked in silence back to their families, each wrapped in his own thoughts.

'Coffee's on the way,' Richard said. Julia was still flushed, he noted, and the embarrassment that had been rampant when he'd made his exit obviously hadn't dissipated. Tim was in the middle of some story about his daughter, but no one seemed to be listening.

The coffee that no one wanted arrived and was poured out. Thank God we're not committed to stay for lunch! David thought. Julia was refusing to meet his eye. It was the sheerest bad luck that Maria's name should have come up just when things were teetering back to normal. He could only hope that Will's presence on the flight home would help to defuse the tension.

The party broke up shortly afterwards. It was almost lunchtime but the fact was studiously ignored. The purpose of the meeting had been achieved; they had exchanged information about themselves and their shared father and, barring the possibility of attending his funeral, they need never meet again.

Hands were shaken, good wishes expressed and it was the Gregorys who left first. Richard waited until they'd gone through the swing doors before saying fervently, 'Thank God for that! I need a drink!'

'Let's move into the bar,' Tim suggested. 'We could have some lunch while we're there.'

'What did you think of them?' Victoria asked minutes later as they studied the bar menu.

'I rather liked them,' Georgia replied. 'It did strike me, though, that Sally was somewhat careless to become "accidentally" pregnant twice. Hadn't she heard of the pill?'

'You mean you think it was deliberate?' asked Victoria.

'Probably not the first time, but when Dad came back and seemed so proud of his little son, she might have thought a second baby would anchor him. It was uncanny how alike you and David are, Rich.'

In more ways than one, Richard thought grimly.

It was as though Tim had read his mind. 'Pity you mentioned your schoolmistress,' he said. 'That really put the cat among the pigeons! What's she like?'

'A Pre-Raphaelite painting,' Richard replied, remembering his first impression of her. 'Pale face and a cloud of auburn hair.'

The memory of a barely glimpsed woman in a doorway flashed across Georgia's mind and was instantly dismissed as untenable; Richard would never play away in his own backyard.

'Sounds as though she should come with a health warning!' she said.

Foxclere

Richard and Tim had both left their cars at the station.

'I presume you'll be reporting to Mother?' Richard said as they were about to separate.

Georgia nodded. 'She's been looking after the kids anyway.'

'Not,' he continued, 'that's there's much to report. A waste of time all round, in my opinion. If you remember, I was against our going in the first place.'

'It was for their benefit rather than ours,' Georgia pointed out. 'All the same, it was quite an eye-opener to learn how Dad operated in his youth. I have to say I think he treated Sally disgracefully.'

'And your mother too,' Victoria reminded her. 'William was conceived after she and Greg were married. Will you tell her that?'

'I'm not sure.'

Tim took her arm. 'Come on, love, let's get home.'

'We owe you a meal,' Victoria said. 'I'll give you a ring once term's over; perhaps by then someone will have been arrested for Greg's murder.'

It was just after four when they turned into Woodlands driveway and the children, who were playing in the garden, came running to greet them, followed by Jill.

'How did it go?' she asked.

'I'll tell you over a cup of tea,' Georgia replied.

Tim patted her arm. 'You two go on in; I'll stay and do swing duty.'

Jill led the way into her kitchen and filled the kettle. 'Well, what are they like? Did you get on with them?'

'Yes, I think so. David, the elder son, was the image of Richard – it was quite spooky.'

Jill bit her lip. That was not what she wanted to hear.

'He and his wife seem to be going through a bad patch,' Georgia added. 'It was rather embarrassing.'

Jill brushed that aside. 'And what were they able to tell you?'

As tactfully as she could, Georgia repeated the Gregory brothers' story, managing to omit the exact date of William's birth.

Jill set two mugs on the table. 'So he did know this Sally first. I wondered about that.'

'Yes, by some years. He was apparently the love of her life.'

'And he didn't tell her when we got married?' Her voice was carefully level.

'Not at first. As soon as she found out, she sent him packing.'

'Quite right too.' Jill sipped her tea thoughtfully. 'Poor woman,' she said.

Stonebridge

It had been an uncomfortable flight home. Though David addressed Julia several times she continued to ignore him and eventually, tiring of acting as go-between, Will had opted out and put on his headphones. Unfortunately, though, as David had driven them all to the airport he had to suffer an equally tense car journey back to Stonebridge.

As he thankfully got out of the car at his gate, Will said, 'The grandparents are coming for a meal on Monday to hear about the meeting. You're very welcome to join us – seven thirty for eight.'

David glanced at his wife's closed face. 'Thanks, Will. Could we come back to you on that?'

'Of course.'

It was a relief to open his own front door and hear the homely sound of his daughter's contented crowing. Smiling to himself, he followed it to the kitchen, where, seated in her playpen, she was engaged in chewing a teddy bear while her mother heated her milk.

Sylvie turned from the stove at his approach and he bent to kiss her. 'Welcome home, wanderer!' she said. 'So, was it worthwhile? Are you glad you contacted them?'

'Yes, I am. They seemed very pleasant and we learned quite a lot about Dad which, after all, was the object of the exercise.' He paused, ruffling his daughter's curls. 'Richard's an odd bird – looks the spitting image of Dave. There were some awkward moments, which was only to be expected. The most noticeable, though, was when it emerged that Dave seemed to have been playing away with a member of staff at the twins' school.'

Sylvie widened her eyes. 'Really?'

'You know I've been thinking for some time that he and Julia were having problems? This must have been the reason.'

She frowned. 'But I don't understand; how could it come out when you were meeting your relatives?'

'Well, they say it's a small world. It transpires the woman now teaches at the school where Richard is deputy head. Pure bad luck as far as Dave was concerned and on the way home you could have cut the atmosphere with a knife.'

'Then let's hope they can now get it sorted once and for all,' Sylvie remarked, and lifted her daughter into her high chair.

*   *   *

It wasn't until they were in their bedroom and Julia couldn't just walk out of the room that David was able to corner her.

'Look,' he said desperately, 'let's not go back to square one over this. I behaved badly and God knows you've punished me for it, but it's all in the past and we were starting to put it behind us. It's a damn shame Richard had to bring up Maria's name but you needn't have reacted as you did. It put the kibosh on the whole meeting.'

'Oh, so it's my fault now, is it?'

He sighed, regretting his last comment. 'That's not what I meant and you know it. But you're behaving as though I'm still seeing her. Just because he mentioned her doesn't bring it back into the present.'

She didn't reply but he saw tears on her cheek and felt more hopeful. 'Come on, darling,' he coaxed, 'let's put it behind us. And thanks again for coming with me; it meant a lot to have you there.'

'Even though I put the kibosh on the meeting?' she asked tremulously.

'You can put the kibosh anywhere you like!' he said, and was rewarded by a reluctant smile. He moved forward and put his arms round her. She didn't resist and he breathed a heartfelt sigh of relief.

'I love you, Julia Gregory,' he said.

FIFTEEN

Blaircomrie

At nine thirty on Monday morning, DI Mackay's phone rang.

'The manager of the Scottish National Bank is on the line, sir; he wants to speak to "someone in authority" but won't say what it's in connection with.'

'Well, I dare say I fit the description,' Mackay said. 'Put him on, Jen.'

'To whom am I speaking?' The voice was crisp and business-like.

'DI Mackay, Blaircomrie CID. And you, sir?'

'Robert Stevenson, manager of the Blaircomrie branch of the SNB. Something most unusual has come up, Mr Mackay, and we're uncertain how to deal with it. Some weeks ago one of our clients rented a safe deposit box with instructions that if he did not reclaim the contents within a certain time frame, we were to open the box and hand its contents to the police.'

Mackay raised an eyebrow. 'Which, as I presume you've not heard from him, you're about to do?'

'It's not quite that simple. The bank has a legal duty of confidentiality and would need clear and irrefutable proof that these were indeed the instructions of the client before we could release any documents to a third party, including yourselves. We have a letter from him on file in which a witness to his signature confirms his identity, but unfortunately since this wasn't notarized it's not a legal document. Furthermore, we've unfortunately been unable to contact our client.'

Mackay sighed. 'Can you disclose his name?'

'Again, this is slightly unusual. The account is in the name of GJS Lawrence for J Farthing.'

Thank you, God! 'Then I think we may be in a position to help you; the Mr Lawrence in question was presumed dead in July last year. However, it is our belief that he was living in this town under the name of Johnnie Stewart for at least two months prior to his murder some six weeks ago.'

That shocked Stevenson out of his formality. 'Good God, the man who's been in all the papers?'

'The same. In which case, though he wasn't dead in July last year, he very definitely is now, and therefore unable to confirm anything, so I presume there's nothing to prevent your bringing the contents of the box straight round? They could be crucial evidence in a murder enquiry.'

'I appreciate your impatience, Mr Mackay, but the box can only be opened by our own guard key in conjunction with the key assigned to the client. Was this by any chance found in Mr, er, Farthing's possession?'

'I can check, but surely that needn't—'

'Furthermore,' Stevenson continued smoothly, 'in the event of the owner of the box being deceased, it would have to be opened in the presence of the executor of the estate in accordance with probate and bank regulations. The contents would then form part of the estate.'

Mackay slammed his hand on his desk. 'Is that really necessary? The family live in Sussex and—'

'You have a contact number for them?'

'Well, yes,' Mackay admitted reluctantly.

'Then might I suggest you telephone them, explain the position and request that either the executor of the estate or a representative of the legal firm handling it should visit us at the earliest opportunity. And once the procedure has been carried out here at the bank, I shall personally deliver the contents of the box into your hands. Perhaps you'd be good enough to let me know in due course when we might expect this representative.'

He ended the call and Mackay swore fluently before calling Grant's extension. 'A potential development, Sandy, but first can you go through Johnnie's effects in the crime property store and see if there's a bank key among them? Also, I urgently need Richard Lawrence's contact number.'

'OK, boss, I'll get right on to it. What's happened?'

'I'll fill you in when you've found them.'

Foxclere

Richard had spent a miserable Sunday as all the nuances and ramifications of what he'd learned the previous day circled in his head, shifting and taking on new interpretations each time he thought of them, so that first one and then another assumed significance. But however much they alternated, one irrefutable fact always took precedence: his father had known David before he himself had been born – had, in William's words, been 'delighted by' his first born, though unacknowledged, son. So what hope had Richard ever had of achieving that premier place in their father's affections?

And close on that bitter realization came the acceptance that David had also pre-empted him in Maria's affections, to the extent that her husband had had to remove the entire family from his reach. Looking back, it struck Richard that the unravelling of his whole life dated from his meeting with her. Though he'd undeniably been attracted to her, it would have been a passing fancy had she not instigated their affair by that first kiss. It now seemed to him that she'd been playing him all along for her own gratification and amusement, possibly because he reminded her of David. What was it Georgia had said about a health warning?

Having resolved to block all such introspection and concentrate on his daily schedule, he was considerably annoyed when, during the first lesson on Monday, the mobile in his pocket began to vibrate. He extracted it with the intention of switching it off, but the ID window was showing Number Withheld, which, in this new life, equated with the police, and his heart turned over. In the name of heaven, what now?

'I'm sorry, class,' he said, striving to sound calm, 'I have to take this important call. Please read through what we've been discussing and I'll ask you questions on it shortly.'

He left the room, positioning himself in the corridor where he could keep an eye on his class through the glass panel in the door.

'Richard Lawrence,' he said into the phone.

'Good morning, sir,' came the Scottish voice. 'DI Mackay, Blaircomrie CID. I'm sorry to trouble you but there has been a development in the investigation into Mr Gregory Lawrence's death and we need to contact the executor of his estate.' He paused. 'Am I right in supposing that would be you, sir?'

Richard briefly closed his eyes. Fresh humiliation and from an unexpected source. 'No, no, the family solicitors handled it. May I ask what the development is?'

'I'm not in a position to disclose it at the moment, sir. If you could give me the solicitors' name and contact number?'

'I don't know their number offhand but the firm is Lansdowne, Forbes and Hunter and I believe it was Mr Jeremy Tyson, the senior partner, who dealt with it.'

'Thank you, sir – we'll be able to trace him from that. I'm grateful for your assistance.'

There was a click and the dialling tone sounded. Richard stood listening to it for several minutes before switching the phone off and returning to the classroom.

Blaircomrie

'Mr Farthing's' assignment key, having been located among Johnnie's possessions at the police station, was duly couriered across to the bank to await the arrival of the Lawrences' solicitor who was taking the midday flight. It was just after two thirty that, the procedure at the bank having been followed, he and Stevenson arrived at the police station. The pair were shown into Mackay's office where he and Grant awaited them.

Hands were shaken all round, after which the bank manager solemnly laid a bulky jiffy bag on Mackay's desk.

Mackay, who wasn't sure what he'd been expecting, looked at it blankly. 'That's all?'

'That's all that was in the box, Mr Mackay.' It was Stevenson who replied. 'But as I explained on the telephone there was also a letter that had been filed separately. Please feel free to read it.'

He passed over a standard-sized envelope. It was addressed to the manager of the bank, with printed instructions to the effect that if unclaimed it should be opened on 21 July 2014 immediately prior to unlocking the deposit box.

Mackay flicked a glance at the impassive faces of his visitors before drawing out a single sheet of paper. It was dated Friday, 30 May.

I solemnly swear, he read, *that the contents of my safe deposit box are genuine and were handed to me personally by Martin Petrie on the day before he was killed in a hit-and-run incident.*

Petrie? Mackay exchanged a startled look with Grant, who was reading it with him.

In view of this unlikely 'coincidence,' the letter continued, *I am lodging these papers to await developments, and intend to reclaim them by 21 July at the latest; if I fail to do so, I request that the box be opened under appropriate conditions and its contents handed to the police.*

His signature was appended and, beneath it, *As witnessed by Elizabeth M Monroe* was written, along with the date.

'Bingo!' said Grant softly. He turned to his visitors, briefly explaining who Petrie had been and that there was an ongoing investigation into his death.

The two men nodded, but, discretion being ingrained in both of them, neither made a comment. After a minute, Stevenson turned to the solicitor. 'Would you care to do the honours, Mr Tyson?'

'Certainly.'

The flap of the jiffy bag had been reinforced with sticky tape and Mackay passed him a paper knife with which to slit it. Having done so, he withdrew a thick wad of paper, some of it held together with an elastic band, and a digital voice recorder. All four men watched with varying degrees of incredulity as Tyson spread them out on the desk.

Among the papers were photocopies of letters and invoices addressed to Parsons Makepeace, causing a further intake of breath by the two policemen, and several badly typed pages with crossings out and alterations in ballpoint, in which Petrie listed his growing unease about the means employed in trying to obtain the shopping mall contract. Other documents proved to be receipts for the supply of building materials across which he had scrawled SUB-STANDARD in large capitals.

Tyson picked up the voice recorder and turned it over in his hands. 'This will be protected by a pin number,' he said.

'There's a number circled in red scrawled on the front page of that typescript,' Grant pointed out. 'Worth a try, sir.'

As indeed it proved to be. They listened in silence as Petrie recounted conversations between directors of the firm about its parlous financial position and their decision, against his advice, to purchase what were cheap but obviously sub-standard materials; of how, as a safeguard, he had systematically photocopied incriminating documents, and his sense of horror and guilt at the collapse of the mall. He maintained he'd been awaiting the results of the investigation, and resolved that if his suspicions proved correct he would produce his evidence.

'These last few months,' he went on, 'I have had to live with the knowledge that if I'd come forward earlier the disaster might have been averted, but I'd no proof the materials would prove dangerous and it was pointless to make accusations that not only could not be substantiated but would have brought condemnation on myself. I trust these documents I'm belatedly supplying will bring about some kind of justice.'

'Well,' Mackay said flatly as the recording came to an end, 'a credible motive has been the one thing we were lacking for the hit-and-run, and, like Johnnie, I don't believe in coincidence. It seems someone got wind of what Petrie had been up to, giving Patterson a strong reason to despatch him to his maker.'

'And quite likely,' Grant added, 'Johnnie Stewart as well.'

'What do you think, boss?' Grant asked when their visitors had left. 'Are we about to clear up two murders for the price of one?'

Mackay pursed his lips. 'Seems fairly likely, wouldn't you say?' He flicked a glance at the other man. 'More likely than that fatwa story, anyway.'

Grant snorted. 'Pure moonshine, that was.'

'He *was* in Cairo at the time of the bombing. That much has been established.'

'Och, I'm not disputing he was there, it's the rest I can't swallow. As good an excuse for not going home to the wife as I've heard in a long time.'

Mackay sighed. 'You could be right, Sandy, you could be right. In the meantime, there's work to do. Get Patterson in for further questioning, will you. We'll see how he reacts to the latest evidence.'

Norman Patterson looked to be what he presumably was: a prosperous, well-established businessman. His suit was of good quality and even in the confines of the interview room, Grant noted, he was wearing a tie. Iron grey hair swept back from his temples, his face was lean, his eyes deep-set and penetrating, his voice low and cultured. But his previous confidence appeared to have been dented and he was twisting the gold ring on his little finger.

His lawyer, sitting beside him, also looked less confident than when he'd arrived at the police station fifteen minutes earlier.

'Mr Birch will have advised you, Mr Patterson,' Mackay began once the tape was operating, 'that we have obtained further information concerning the business dealings of Parsons Makepeace, which we believe has a bearing on Mr Petrie's death.'

As Grant opened the folder on the desk and extracted a plastic envelope containing a selection of documents from the safe deposit, the colour drained from Patterson's face.

'Where the hell did you get those?' he demanded sharply.

Mackay raised a hand. 'I'm asking the questions, Mr Patterson.'

'God,' he murmured under his breath, 'he must have been planning this all along.'

'Mr Patterson, I advise you to say nothing,' the solicitor broke in urgently.

But Patterson was shaking his head. 'No, Birch, this is it; there's no going back from here.'

'I request time alone with my client,' Birch broke in. 'Really, I must insist—'

Patterson began talking over him. 'All I can say is that it was a moment of madness – totally unpremeditated – and one I shall regret for the rest of my life.'

He took a deep breath, looking from one of his interrogators to the other. 'I've worked for Parsons Makepeace since I left university,' he began. 'It was like an extended family and our relationships were social as well as business – godparents to each other's children and so on. For years the firm did exceptionally well but the recession hit us badly; fewer houses were being built, building permits harder to come by. People were pulling their belts in all round. We began to feel the pinch and after a year or two things became really serious.'

He broke off to ask for a glass of water, which was swiftly provided.

'Then we heard about the prospect of a new shopping centre here in Blaircomrie and it was like the answer to a prayer. We tendered for it, keeping prices as low as possible, but were underbid by a competitor to the tune of several thousand pounds. We cut back as far as we could and put in another bid, but again it was rejected. Then, as defeat stared us in the face, we were approached by a foreign company offering to supply materials at what, frankly, was a ludicrously low figure. And here I accept full responsibility: I made no attempt to look into the firm – on the contrary, I preferred to know nothing about them. We had an urgent discussion and I persuaded my colleagues to accept the offer without delay. It enabled us to reduce our price significantly and we pipped our competitors to the post.'

He took another sip of water. 'It was a turning point for us. As work began more orders started to come in and our prospects improved dramatically. The mall, as you may remember, opened with a fanfare of publicity, all the major retailers fighting for a site.'

He stopped speaking, then went on heavily, 'Then, just before Christmas when trading was at fever-pitch—' He broke off.

'I went into denial,' he continued after a moment. 'We all did. We couldn't accept that the materials we'd used had any bearing on the collapse. Yes, we'd taken a calculated risk, but damn it, do you imagine we'd have even considered it if we'd had the slightest inkling of what might follow? Nonetheless, as a precaution we'd systematically shredded all our files, emails and faxes relating to the purchase more or less as they came in.'

He made a hopeless gesture towards the papers on the table. 'Martin had obviously pre-empted us. He'd been against the deal from the beginning and was becoming a liability; he'd started to drink heavily, he looked drawn and admitted he wasn't sleeping at night. We continued to stress that nothing had been proved, but that last evening, just as we were leaving the office, he suddenly said, "I can't go along with this any longer, Norman; over a hundred people died, and we killed them!"

'I took his arm and steered him into the nearest pub where I tried to reason with him, but he was beyond listening. He muttered something about having discussed it with someone and taken his advice – which put the fear of God into me – after which he pushed back his chair and walked out of the pub. I was left sitting there wondering what the hell to do and drinking my second double whisky, faced with the bleak fact that my whole life was about to disintegrate, not only my career but my home, which is heavily mortgaged, my children's education and probably my marriage once the truth was known. And I knew that somehow he had to be stopped.

'I knew he travelled home by bus – I'd often heard him say, "If I hurry, I can catch the 402" – and without pausing to consider any plan of action I collected my car and drove out to his stop A couple of buses arrived and the passengers spilled out, but he wasn't among them. I was beginning to think I'd missed him when he appeared and turned in the direction of his house, a ten-minute walk.'

Patterson took a handkerchief out of his pocket and wiped his face. 'I sat there for a while,' he went on, 'trying to sort things in my mind, but the whisky had numbed it and everything was a blur. I decided to go after him – but I swear at that point it was only to try further reasoning. So I set off, and as I rounded a corner he came into sight walking ahead of me. And . . . that's when madness took over. Without any prior intention, I swear, I put my foot down and aimed straight at him.'

Patterson shuddered. The other three men sat unmoving, waiting for him to continue. His hand trembled as he reached for the water and drank what remained in the glass.

'But again you were too late, weren't you, Mr Patterson?' said Mackay. 'You knew he'd already passed on the information, so killing him was no longer enough – you had to go after Johnnie Stewart too. Or Gregory Lawrence, to give him his proper name.'

Birch emerged abruptly from his paralysed silence. 'Are you bringing another charge, Inspector? I understood my client was being questioned concerning Parsons Makepeace and the death of Mr Petrie—'

Patterson brushed him aside, looking at Mackay with an expression he could have sworn was genuine bewilderment. 'Who?' he asked blankly.

'Come, now, Mr Patterson. Mr Petrie was overheard arranging to meet him, wasn't he? Perhaps he was followed and seen to hand over these very papers?'

'I haven't the slightest idea what you're talking about,' Patterson declared.

'You're not trying to tell us you haven't heard of Johnnie Stewart? If so, you must have been in outer space for the last month or so.'

'Of course I've heard of him; he was the man who was stabbed in the street and turned out to have several aliases. But where does he enter the equation?'

Mackay indicated the papers on the desk in front of him. 'It was he, or rather his bank manager, who handed these in.'

Patterson wrinkled his forehead. 'Are you saying Martin knew him?'

Mackay's heart was sinking fast. Either Patterson was an extremely good actor or, damn it to hell, he was innocent. Nonetheless, he doggedly continued. 'He did indeed; and I suggest that when Mr Petrie told you he'd confided in someone, he went so far as to name that individual as Johnnie Stewart. So he had to be dealt with too.' He paused. 'As you say, he was stabbed in the street. Nine days after Mr Petrie's murder.'

'I insist on having a private conversation with my client,' Birch said firmly, but again Patterson brushed him aside.

'Nine days after Martin's death,' Patterson repeated. 'What date would that be?'

'Thursday, fifth of June.'

'Ah.' Patterson sat back in his chair and released his breath in a sigh. 'On Saturday the thirty-first of May my wife and I left the country for a holiday that had been booked months in advance. My passport will confirm that. I'm sorry, Detective Inspector, but though I appreciate it would be convenient, you can't pin that one on me.'

Stonebridge

'So you didn't meet his wife?' Nina said.

'No; she didn't feel up to coming.'

'A pity; I'd like to have known what she looks like.'

'We did see a photo,' Will offered. 'She's small and fair – quite pretty.'

'As pretty as your mother?'

Will looked down, embarrassed, and Nina said contritely, 'I'm sorry, darling, that was unfair. I'm just wondering what she had that Sally didn't that made him want to marry her.'

They were sitting over pre-dinner drinks. To Will's relief David and Julia had elected to join them and the atmosphere between them seemed less tense. Perhaps, as Sylvie had hoped, Saturday's embarrassment had instigated the first tentative steps towards a rapprochement.

Will glanced at his wife, who was handing round a dish of the bite-sized canapés she'd prepared in lieu of a first course. He couldn't imagine either of them looking at anyone else, but David must once have felt the same. Perhaps their mother too; the course of true love had had a bumpy ride in their family.

'What of the offspring?' Henry asked.

'The son, Richard, looks very like David,' Julia said. 'It was a bit disorientating.'

'He was a surly individual,' David added. 'I had the impression he resented us, which I suppose is understandable.'

'More understandable for you to resent them,' Nina said sharply.

'And the daughter?' Henry pursued.

'She really made an effort to be friendly, as did the two partners. Under other circumstances I think we could have been friends.'

'Was their DNA also taken?' Henry asked gruffly.

'Yes, but they haven't had the results yet. Not that there's much doubt, when you look at Richard and me.'

Nina said in a low voice, 'If Sally had lived just a few months longer she'd have learned about all this. I don't know whether to be glad or sorry that she didn't.'

Blaircomrie

A hundred and twenty miles to the north, Jim Scott was continuing his personal mission at the Stag and Thistle. By now he was on first-name terms with several of the regulars and that evening, for the first time, he dared to introduce Johnnie Stewart into the conversation.

'That guy who was stabbed a while back,' he began casually, 'did they ever find out who did it?'

His companions sobered, avoiding each other's eyes. 'No,' one answered after a moment. 'Bad business aw roond. The polis hae been here more than once but nothin's come of it. Seemingly someone lay in wait fur him, thinkin' he'd had one ay his wins at poker.'

'And had he?' Scott enquired, sipping his beer.

'Och aye,' came the laconic reply. 'He aye won, that 'un. Lucky in cards – horses and dugs tae, frae aw accoonts.'

'And unhappy in love?' queried Scott with a lop-sided smile.

'Only he could tell ye that.'

Scott turned and leant against the bar, surveying the room and nodding at those who caught his eye. 'Who's that fella at the corner table? I've never seen him speak to anyone.'

'Och, you'll nae get any sense outta auld Jock. Lives in a world ay his ain these days. Get within a yard o' him and he'll nab ye and start spinnin' his tall stories. A guid poker player, though, till the drink addled his brain. If he's nae too far gone he comes up the stair tae watch us play.'

Could be just the man he needed, Scott reflected. He straightened. 'Then I'll go and do my Christian duty by having a word with the old soak.'

'On yer ain heed,' rejoined the man at the bar, 'but I warn ye – dinna believe a word he says!'

Arming himself with a tankard of what his quarry was drinking, Scott made his way to the corner table.

'Mind if I join you?' he asked cheerfully, setting down the tankard in front of its other occupant. At closer quarters the man wasn't as old as he'd thought, though he was unquestionably very drunk. His bloodshot, rheumy eyes moved from Scott to the tankard in some surprise; it seemed he wasn't used to anyone approaching voluntarily, let alone being supplied with a free drink.

'Guid oan ye,' he muttered, pulling it towards him.

'I hear you were quite a poker player in your time,' Scott ventured and received a surprisingly sharp look.

'Better'n yon mob plain the noo,' Jock responded, reaching for his glass. 'An' nae cause fur cheatin' an' aw.'

Scott's ears pricked. 'Surely no one here cheats?'

Jock snorted. 'I'd no' say that. Nae man keeps winnin' a' the time wit'oot cheatin'.'

The hairs on the back of Scott's neck began to stir. He said carefully, 'Anyone specific in mind?'

Jock flashed him a look and merely grunted in reply. Careful, Scott warned himself; don't want him clamming up.

'I suppose, being a good player yourself, you'd soon spot it if someone *did* cheat?'

Jock emptied his original glass and reached for the tankard. 'Could dae wi' a wee chaser,' he muttered.

Scott went back to the bar and ordered one.

'He's sized ye up fur a sucker!' warned the man he'd been speaking to.

Scott merely smiled, paid the barman and returned to the table. In his absence Jock appeared to have sunk lower into the mists of drunkenness and he doubted the wisdom of the chaser which, nevertheless, he put down on the table. Too bad if plying the man with drink made him totally incomprehensible.

'So what are the signs of cheating?' he began.

At first it seemed Jock was not going to reply, but then he mumbled something that Scott couldn't catch. 'Come again?'

'Winnin' every bluidy game.'

Scott took a gamble. 'Like Johnnie Stewart?'

Jock's face darkened. 'Aye. I warned him often enough but he paid nae heed. Robbin' 'em blind he was, week efter week. Warned him that wan day he'd get some o' his ain medicine.'

Scott was holding his breath. 'And he did, didn't he? Someone robbed *him*?'

Jock nodded with satisfaction and wiped his mouth with the back of his hand. 'Said I'd teach him a lesson, but he paid nae mind. "Puir auld Jock", he called me, like I waur beneath his notice. But I showed him, reet enough.'

Scott swallowed convulsively. Could this conceivably be a confession of murder? Even if it were, who would believe him? The man seemed barely capable of standing.

'Someone did, certainly,' he agreed, and jumped as Jock thumped his fist on the table.

'Said *I* showed him, laddie!' The rheumy eyes were flashing. 'Think I'm no' able? Weel then, wha's this?'

He fumbled in the depths of his jacket pocket, struggling to free what was inside it, and withdrew an old wallet, shabby and dirty but made of good quality leather. Barely breathing, Scott watched as his companion opened it, pulled out a crumpled snapshot and tossed it on the table in front of him. It showed a couple sitting on a park bench in the sunshine. And the man, beyond any shadow of doubt, was Johnnie Stewart.

Tentatively he reached for it, but Jock snatched it up and tucked it firmly back inside the wallet. 'Believe me now, do ye?' he challenged, but Scott was incapable of replying.

SIXTEEN

'So how was the family get-together?' Nigel enquired on the Tuesday morning.

Victoria raised her shoulders. 'I suppose, not having a benchmark for such events, the answer is as good as can be expected.'

He laughed. 'Which means what?'

'There was understandable caution on both sides but we all behaved fairly well till almost the end, when Richard inadvertently opened a bag and a cat jumped out.'

Nigel raised an eyebrow. 'Care to elucidate?'

'It appears that a member of staff at his school comes from the same neck of the woods as the Gregorys, and when he asked if they knew her it became painfully obvious that David had had an affair with her.'

'Oh dear!'

'Yes, it was all very embarrassing.'

'How did Richard and Georgia feel, meeting new half-brothers?'

Victoria bit her lip. 'It seemed water off a duck's back as far as Georgia was concerned,' she said after a moment. 'But I suspect Richard was more upset than he let on. No one would think it, but beneath that controlled exterior he has his insecurities and this is proving a big one.'

Bloody Greg! she thought privately; Richard had always been unsure of his father's affections and the sudden appearance of an older half-brother seemed to have trebled his doubts. 'No doubt he wished it was David living with him rather than me,' he'd said bitterly on their return home. 'Father was delighted with him, William said; more than he ever was with me.'

'Darling, that was when he was a baby!' Victoria had comforted him from an aching heart. 'And he wasn't delighted enough to stay with him, was he?'

'Will you see them again?' Nigel enquired, breaking into her thoughts.

'No need,' she said crisply, and after a glance at her face he did not pursue it.

They were kept busy for the next hour or so but as the shop temporarily emptied Victoria was hoping for a quick coffee before another influx. The chance was denied her, though, as the doorbell chimed and a tall young man came in. He looked vaguely familiar, but it wasn't until he approached her that the elusive memory clicked into focus.

'DS Finch!' she exclaimed and Nigel, who was checking the ledger, looked up.

'Good morning,' he said, looking around him. 'No customers?'

'Mid-morning lull.'

'Just as well, because I was hoping for a private word. I've some excellent news for you; it'll become public later today but I felt you deserved to be the first to hear it.'

They looked at him expectantly and he continued, 'Largely thanks to you, we've managed to track down the gang who've been robbing country houses and were responsible for the death of Mr Lancing.'

Nigel looked bewildered. 'I'm delighted to hear it, but . . . thanks to us?'

Finch nodded. 'You provided two clues which proved vital: the names of the couple who'd been behaving suspiciously and the key you found in the picture frame.'

Victoria gasped. 'They were connected to the *murder*?'

'Indirectly, yes. We apprehended them along with several of their associates, and – the icing on the cake – the key you handed in led to a cache of miniatures, snuff boxes and other artefacts from the raids.'

There was a moment's stunned silence. Then, 'How did you identify it?' Victoria asked.

'We'd a stroke of luck there; someone at the station recognized it as coming from Swan Securities; he'd moved house recently and used the same facilities.'

'But why was it hidden in the frame?'

Finch held up a hand. 'Look, I'm giving you this ahead of the press release because you were a valuable part of the investigation, but there's a limit to what I can tell you.'

'Please!' Victoria wheedled. 'It would have taken you longer to find them without us!'

He hesitated.

'Please!' she said again, and he capitulated.

'All we've established so far is that the key was supposed to change hands in the framing shop – who incidentally had no part in it – but the man who should have met the key-holder wasn't there. He was at a loss what to do, and when someone came into the shop behind him he panicked, thinking he'd been followed, and, not wanting to be found with the key on him, wedged it into the frame of the nearest picture and fled.'

'*Was* he being followed?' Nigel interrupted.

'I doubt it – certainly not by us. Anyway, he waited half an hour or so, then went back to retrieve it; but by then the picture had gone, and all the assistant would tell him was that it had been collected. He'd been in too much of a panic to register any details of the painting, just its approximate size and that there'd been a sticker above it reading Local Artist.'

'So our theory was right!' Nigel said with satisfaction.

'What about the earlier thefts?' Victoria asked. 'Might this lead to more being recovered?'

'A lot will have been passed on by now but we're hopeful of retrieving some items.' Finch glanced at his watch. 'I must be on my way. Thanks again for your help; it gave us just the lead we needed.'

Richard was finding it difficult to concentrate that morning. Added to all his other concerns, he was now worrying about why the family solicitor – in the guise of his father's executor – should have been summoned to Scotland. Would Tyson have returned home by now, or still be north of the border? He resolved to phone him at the end of school and find out what was behind it.

He took a quick look round his study to check there was nothing he needed to take with him, then opened the door at the precise moment that Maria was hurrying past with an armful of exercise books. Instinctively he reached out, seized her arm and pulled her into the study, closing the door behind her.

She gave a little half-laugh. 'Is this wise, Richard? Someone might see us.'

'Someone already has,' he said tightly.

She looked alarmed. 'How do you know?'

'Because a note was left on my desk reading, *How do you solve a problem like Maria?*'

She gasped, her hand going to her mouth. 'Do you know who wrote it?'

'It could be anyone, couldn't it?'

'But – that's awful! Does Mr Hill knows?' Hill was the headmaster.

'I doubt it; he'd have called me in before now.' He passed a hand over his face. 'Thank God it's almost the end of term; it'll have died down by September. We must just be extra careful for the next few days.'

'Then why risk bringing me in here?'

He straightened. 'Because I've something to tell you.'

She glanced towards the door, anxious about the time. 'What?'

'I met someone you know at the weekend. Someone from Stonebridge.'

'Really? Down here? Who was it?'

'We were in London actually. And it was my half-brother.'

'Your half-brother lives in Stonebridge? Why didn't you say, when I first told you where I came from?'

'Because I didn't know.'

'That he lived there? Surely—'

'I didn't know I had a half-brother.'

She considered that for a moment, then shook her head. 'Sorry, you've lost me. Anyway, I didn't know anyone called Lawrence in Stonebridge.'

Richard said deliberately, 'His name is David Gregory.'

She froze, those wide eyes that had so captivated him widening still further. 'David Gregory is your *brother*?'

'Half-brother,' he corrected. 'Small world, isn't it?'

She moistened her lips. 'What did he . . . say?'

'Enough.' He paused. 'Didn't it strike you that we look alike?'

'I . . . just a little, I suppose.'

'We're obviously a type you find attractive.'

She flushed. 'That's unfair, Richard.'

'Is it? Isn't that why you kissed me that first time?'

'*No!* Please don't think that!'

'It doesn't matter what I think; we've come to the end of our Thursdays.'

'Not quite; it's sports day tomorrow – I'm helping out with the teas, making sandwiches for my sins – but there's another day before we break up. At least we'll have that.'

He stared at her, despising himself for his longing, even now, to hold her. Yet could he make love to her, knowing that David of all people had preceded him? 'I think not,' he said.

Victoria was full of the news about the robberies when she returned home that evening.

'Remember me telling you about the key we found and that odd man who came into The Gallery?'

Richard nodded without removing his gaze from the television.

'Well, guess what! The key was to a safe deposit box containing loot from the stately homes robberies!'

She waited expectantly and when he made no comment, said impatiently, 'Well, what do you think of that?'

'Well done,' he said.

'"Well done"? Is that all you can say?'

'What do you want me to say?'

She stared at him for a moment. 'You really are impossible sometimes, Richard,' she said, and went to the kitchen to prepare their meal.

The weather had been getting steadily warmer over the past week, and by the following day the heatwave was fully established.

'I shall be stewing all day,' Victoria said resignedly at breakfast; on Wednesdays she helped out at a local charity shop. 'It's stuffy at the best of times and by this afternoon it'll be unbearable. But what about sports day? Will the children be able to run in this heat?'

Richard raised his shoulders. 'It's now or never; there are only two days of term left. At least we have air con in the classrooms, thank God.'

'But you'll have to put in an appearance, surely?'

He nodded. 'Though with luck from the shade of the pavilion balcony.'

'Well, never mind; this time next week we'll be preparing for Malta, and won't mind how hot it gets!'

London

Paul Devonshire was meeting Vivien for lunch, and, having arrived early, was filling in the time by checking emails on his tablet. There was nothing of interest so, hopeful for news about Greg, he clicked on the website of the *Blaircomrie Gazette* and struck gold.

'My God!' he exclaimed under his breath, just as his daughter joined him and pulled up a chair.

'No, only me,' she said. 'No obeisance needed.'

He looked up absently. 'Sorry, darling, but the *Gazette* is excelling itself today! Fresh evidence has come to light about the collapse of that shopping mall and the firm that built it is coming under further scrutiny. Police have named the hit-and-run driver who killed one of the firm's employees as – wait for it! – one of its directors, and finally – and this is what I was looking for – there's breaking news about Greg's murder. It says here "A source close to the inquiry confirmed that a suspect is being questioned and a charge is believed to be imminent".'

'And I thought Blaircomrie was a quiet little town,' Vivien observed.

'Well, it's certainly put itself on the map now.' He closed his tablet. 'Unless Jill watches the lunchtime news she won't have heard of it; I wonder if I should phone to warn her?'

'Not before lunch,' Vivien said firmly. 'I only have an hour, remember, and I'm starving. Let's have a look at that menu.'

Blaircomrie

Jock Drummond was being dried out, which promised to be a lengthy process, but his responsibility for the murder of 'Johnnie Stewart' was in little doubt.

'So,' Mackay remarked to Grant, 'despite the wild theories put forward, our Johnnie wasn't stabbed because of any fatwa or because he knew why the mall collapsed, but for the most mundane of reasons – he was just too lucky at cards. It's a funny old world.'

Foxclere

It was set to be the hottest day of the year and Jill and Edward were enjoying their pre-lunch drinks under a garden umbrella.

'So what was the report on the family meeting?' he enquired, gazing over the sunlit lawns.

'Georgia said they were very pleasant, but I'm glad I didn't go,' Jill confessed. 'Greg treated their mother extremely badly and I don't think I could have faced them; I'd have felt guilty, somehow, for snatching him away from her.'

Edward said gently, 'I'm sure you don't need telling how ridiculous that is.'

She turned to him, her eyes worried. 'He and Sally had been lovers when he was at university and he made use of her afterwards by staying with her when he was working up there. He'd already returned home by the time she found she was pregnant and she refused to tell him. Georgia said she'd told her parents she didn't want to force his hand.'

'But I understood there were two sons?'

Jill bit her lip. 'He went back a few months later, didn't he, and enjoyed home comforts again. Georgia was vague about timings but it was after we were married, and though Sally was pregnant again she sent him packing as soon as he told her.'

Jill paused, looking into her glass. 'She never married and brought those boys up by herself. I feel so sorry for her.'

'He was quite the Lothario, wasn't he?' Edward reflected, remembering Owen's comments.

Jill set down her glass and stood up. 'Excuse me for a moment while I put the finishing touches to lunch,' she said, and though Edward cursed himself for his tactlessness, she had recovered her equilibrium when she reappeared at the French windows a few minutes later.

'I suggest we eat inside; it's too hot out here now the sun's more or less overhead.

'Not very elegant surroundings,' she apologized as he took his place at the kitchen table. 'I had to forfeit the dining room when we divided the house and it's now my bedroom. At least we're having a cold lunch so there are no cooking smells to contend with!'

'It's a charming room,' Edward assured her. 'You've seen my barn of a kitchen – I envy you this!'

She served watercress soup with a swirl of cream, followed by salmon salad.

'As a matter of fact, I've some news myself,' he began as he helped himself to new potatoes. 'I've heard from my daughter for the first time since she went to Canada.'

Jill looked surprised. 'That was quite recently, then? I'd thought . . .'

'Two years ago, actually.'

'Oh? I'm sorry, I'd no idea—'

'Why should you? We had a falling out, I'm afraid, with the result that she took off saying she never wanted to see or hear from me again. She changed her mobile number and though I made numerous efforts to find her, I wasn't able to.'

'How upsetting for you,' Jill said quietly.

'She had a point; I was a selfish bastard in those days. I hope I've learned my lesson.'

She half-smiled. 'Is that my cue to reassure you?'

He returned her smile, shaking his head. 'Not at all, but the point of her writing is to let me know she's about to marry and, much to my amazement and delight, she wants me to give her away. Perhaps she's mellowed as well!'

'Well, that's great news! Will it mean your going to Canada?'

'For the wedding, yes, but in the meantime she's bringing her fiancé over to meet me; they're arriving at the beginning of next month.'

'Goodness – short notice after such a gap. Will they be staying with you?'

'I think she's hoping to, but with our recent history she's waiting to be invited. Of course they must come, but I'll have to get the house habitable again; you saw the state it's in.'

'There's nothing at all wrong with it,' Jill declared stoutly. 'What's more it's her home – it's what she'll be expecting.'

'I hadn't thought of that, but you're right. That's a relief.' He paused, flicking her a glance. 'I'd very much like you to meet her.'

Jill, about to lift her fork, paused. She started to say something, changed her mind and asked simply, 'What's her name? I don't think you've ever mentioned it.'

'Lucy, and her intended is Nick Swanson. I thought it might help to break the ice if we all, including you if you would, go out for a meal their first evening.'

'She might get the wrong idea,' Jill said awkwardly.

'And what would that be?'

Startled, she met his eyes then looked away. The conversation had taken a unexpected turn and she wasn't sure how to deal with it.

He leaned towards her. 'Jill, I might as well tell you that the break-up was over how Lucy thought I treated her mother.'

'Please, Edward, I—'

'Let me finish; it's important to me that you know the truth. Business always came first in our married life; I was seldom home and Cicely was too sweet to complain. Consequently when she became ill I failed to notice and she didn't tell me because she didn't want to worry me when I was "so busy". By the time I realized there was a problem things had progressed too far and the tumour was inoperable. That's something I shall have to live with for the rest of my life.'

'I'm so sorry,' Jill said softly.

'I like to think my values have changed, and if Lucy's prepared to forgive me it will ease the burden considerably.'

'She must have, or she wouldn't want you at her wedding. Now that she's so happy, she probably wants you to be as well.'

'So will you meet her?'

'She'll still be grieving for her mother, Edward; perhaps—'

'She'll resent you? I don't think so; my daughter is a much nicer character than I am.'

She smiled. 'Then I'll be very happy to meet her. Now, would you like coffee? The sun's moved off the terrace so we can take it back outside.'

'Let me help you clear the table first.'

'There's really no—' She broke off as the phone sounded in the hall. 'Excuse me a moment.'

'Jill? It's Paul Devonshire.'

'Hello, Paul.'

'I hope I'm doing the right thing phoning you, but I thought you'd want to know as soon as possible. It seems the Scottish police are about to charge someone with Greg's murder.'

Jill caught her breath, and in the kitchen Edward paused, a plate in his hand. 'Who is it, do you know?' she asked after a moment.

'No, they haven't released a name.'

'Did the terrorists catch up with him?'

There was a pause. 'Terrorists?'

She made a dismissive gesture, realized he couldn't see it, and said, 'It was just one theory, that's all.'

'Definitely one I never heard of. It was breaking news on the local paper's website just now. It'll be on the box this evening, hopefully with more details, but I thought it might . . . put your mind at rest to know the end's at last in sight.'

'Thanks, Paul. It's very good of you to phone.'

'Perhaps, when this is all done and dusted, we might meet for a drink, for old times' sake? It would be good to see you again.'

Jill hesitated, unsure whether she wanted to resurrect links with the past but conscious that he had twice supplied her with news of Greg. She owed him a meeting.

'I should like that,' she said. 'In the meantime, thanks again, Paul. We'll see what they say on the news.'

When she did not immediately return to the kitchen Edward went to the doorway and found her standing motionless by the phone.

'Good news or bad?' he asked.

'A friend of Greg's called to say they've arrested someone for his murder. It'll be on the news this evening.'

She looked helplessly at Edward, unspoken appeal in her eyes. He went to her, put his arms round her and felt her lean against him.

'It'll be all right,' he said.

'Phew, what a scorcher!' Sue Little murmured, running a finger under the collar of her dress. She and the school nurse, Joan Pendley, were at the pavilion end of the field, watching the eight-year-olds line up for their relay race.

'They're a hardy bunch,' Joan replied approvingly. 'I was expecting them to go down like flies in this heat, but not a bit of it. It was one of the mothers who passed out half an hour ago.'

'Is she all right?'

'Yes, I sat her down in the shade with a glass of water. Several members of staff are in the pavilion preparing tea; they'll keep an eye on her.'

'I wonder how long this heatwave will last,' Sue mused. 'We're off to Spain next week but it hardly seems worth going when it's like this here. We could have a paella in the back garden and save ourselves a fortune!'

Richard was operating on autopilot. The blazing heat, combined with the noise of cheering and shouting as team-mates and parents spurred on the runners, had given him a raging headache that wasn't helped by the music blaring from the loudspeaker, inter-rupted periodically by equally ear-splitting announcements of the next race.

But the heat and noise were only partly responsible for his malaise; that morning he'd received a text from Maria, again pleading with him to meet her one last time before school broke up. *Though surely this isn't the end?* she'd added. *Any gossip will be forgotten by next term, so as long as we're careful there's no reason why we shouldn't resume our Thursdays.*

A feeling of hopelessness engulfed him; having proved himself incapable of ending their weekly assignments, he'd been counting on the end of term for deliverance from his bondage. During the eight weeks of the summer holidays, he'd promised himself, he would systematically airbrush her out of his life until their close-ness was totally obliterated, so that by September she'd have reverted to being a junior member of staff whom he occasionally glimpsed in assembly.

But now that text promised ongoing torment. Because if he couldn't somehow expunge her from his life, he would be destroyed.

A smile plastered to his face, he continued to return greetings from parents and members of staff, but was scarcely aware of what he said to them. How much longer was this hellish afternoon going to last? If he wasn't careful he'd pass out, and that would do little for his reputation. He'd had virtually nothing to eat today; perhaps a sandwich and a cold drink would help his headache. He began to make his way towards the pavilion.

*   *   *

It was ten minutes later, as the younger ones were being marshalled together for a three-legged race, that the festive atmosphere was shattered by a high-pitched scream that rang out above the military march blaring from the loudspeakers. Heads turned in its direction and those closest to the pavilion could see one of the younger teachers standing at the rear corner of the building, her hands to her mouth as she gazed behind it.

Joan and Sue, exchanging a startled glance, started to run towards her, joined by those nearest them, and as they rounded the corner a horrific sight met their eyes. Spread-eagled on the grass lay the limp figure of Maria Chiltern, her red hair in a cloud about her head, her green eyes staring sightlessly at the sky as a dark stain slowly spread across the front of her blouse. And standing over her, a bread knife in his hand, stood the deputy headmaster, Richard Lawrence.